LOVE IS GRAND

ANNALISA DAUGHETY

LOVE IS GRAND

A WALK IN THE PARK – BOOK 3

BARBOUR
PUBLISHING

Scripture quotations are taken from the *Holy Bible*, New Living Translation, copyright © 1996, 2004. Used by permission of Tyndale House Publishers, Inc. Wheaton, Illinois 60189, U.S.A. All rights reserved.

Scripture quotations are taken from the HOLY BIBLE, NEW INTERNATIONAL VERSION®. NIV®. Copyright © 1973, 1978, 1984 by International Bible Society. Used by permission of Zondervan. All rights reserved.

This book is a work of fiction. Names, characters, places, and incidents are either products of the author's imagination or used fictitiously. Any similarity to actual people, organizations, and/or events is purely coincidental.

Cover design: Faceout Studio, www.faceoutstudio.com
Cover photography: Steve Gardener, Pixelworks Studios

Published by Barbour Publishing, Inc., P.O. Box 719, Uhrichsville, OH 44683, www.barbourbooks.com

Our mission is to publish and distribute inspirational products offering exceptional value and biblical encouragement to the masses.

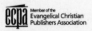 Member of the
Evangelical Christian
Publishers Association

Printed in the United States of America.

DEDICATION

This book is dedicated with love to Megan Reynolds—my cousin, my friend, and one of the funniest people I know. Thank you for checking on me during the madness of deadlines and edits—and for insisting that I go out and have fun every now and then. You rock!

SPECIAL THANKS

I'm constantly amazed at the people in my life who encourage me, pray for me, and walk with me through the publication process. Thanks to the entire team at Barbour Publishing. Becky Fish, thanks for helping me whip this book into shape—I appreciate your input so much! Vicky Daughety, Christine Lynxwiler, and Jan Reynolds—thanks for reading along as I wrote and offering invaluable feedback. Kristy Coleman, Vickie Fry, and Kelly Shifflett—thank you for answering a million questions about motherhood. Dax Torrey, thanks for the encouragement and wise words—and for being such a good sport about the fictional Professor Torrey. Dustin McGee, thanks for lending the use of your first name—and by the way, I'm so proud of you! Ivo Pletka, thanks for keeping me laughing, even through the stress of a deadline. Our family gatherings are much quieter now that you're across an ocean. There are countless others who've encouraged me along the way—and though it would be impossible to list all the names here, I am so thankful.

So do not fear, for I am with you;
do not be dismayed, for I am your God.
I will strengthen you and help you;
I will uphold you with my righteous right hand.

ISAIAH 41:10 NIV

PROLOGUE

At least a full minute had passed since either of them had said a word. Ever since her husband's untimely death, Ainsley Davis's life had been filled with uncomfortable silences. It was like people didn't know what to say to her. But today, she was the one without words. Ainsley shifted uncomfortably in her seat, avoiding eye contact with Dr. Sinclair. Not that she was counting on anything, but the ticking of the wall clock was hard to ignore.

"It's okay. Take your time." He finally broke through the silence and peered at her through wire-rimmed glasses. "I know it's difficult."

She wondered if his cardigan sweater was supposed to make her have a warm and fuzzy *Mr. Rogers* flashback. Even Fred Rogers and his theater of puppets couldn't make discussing her husband's death any easier. "I'm not sure what 'moving on' means to me." She used her fingers to make quotation marks in the air. "Besides, how do I know if I'm even ready?"

Dr. Sinclair rubbed his chin thoughtfully. "The first step was realizing that you needed help. I know coming in to speak to me hasn't been easy. But you've made lots of progress here." He rose from his seat and pulled a book from his crowded bookshelf. "I'd like to give you an assignment."

Ainsley wrinkled her nose. With a fourteen-month-old at home, she barely had time to change clothes, much less do homework. "What's that?"

"Do you keep a journal of any kind?"

"I used to. In college." She managed a smile. "But not since." She sighed. "I meant to keep a pregnancy journal, but I couldn't bring myself to do so. And I wish I would've written things down this past year. You know, to document Faith's first year." Just another of her failings as a mother.

He nodded. "I want you to take this and feel free to write in it whatever you want."

"Whatever I want?" She took the blue journal from him and flipped through the book. The blank pages filled her with dread, a reminder of the many unknowns in her future.

Dr. Sinclair sat back down and crossed his legs. "You might start out with things about yourself. Your life. Things that scare you or make you happy. If you like, you might journal about the transition you're making back to the workplace and how it makes you feel." He pressed his fingertips together. "Of course, returning to the Grand Canyon will likely flood you with memories. Feel free to jot those down, too."

She bit her lip. "Will you read it?"

He smiled. "No," he said, shaking his head. "No one ever has to read it. It's for your eyes only. I suspect this will be very therapeutic for you. Especially since you won't be able to come here on a regular basis any longer."

"I guess I can try it." Even to her own ears, the words sounded hollow and uncertain. But she'd promised her friends and family that she'd give grief counseling her best shot. And she didn't want two months of weekly sessions with Dr. Sinclair to be for naught. So she'd try and stick to his assignment. For a little while at least.

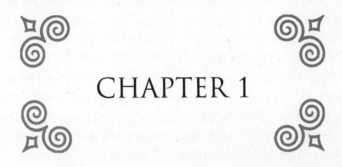

CHAPTER 1

I have no idea what to write in this journal. I am sitting here in the basement of my parents' house—the house I grew up in—and I have no idea what to say. I think I'll have to ease in to these "dear diary" moments. So here goes. Today is my niece's high school graduation. She's my favorite niece. Okay, she's my only niece, but I love her a lot. And I'm not going to the ceremony. I told my sister that Faith was getting a cold, but really I just don't want to go. Family events make me too sad.

Julie Wilson, still clad in her graduation gown, ran toward Heath Bowden's shiny red extended-cab truck. "Please don't be mad," she called to his retreating figure. "It was only a hug. Dave and I have been friends forever. Since preschool." Her breath came in ragged waves as she finally caught up with her boyfriend.

"You made me look like a fool," Heath growled, his handsome features twisted by anger. "Everyone in this two-bit town knows that he's crazy about you."

Julie reached a trembling hand out and touched Heath's muscular forearm. "And they also know that I'm crazy about you," she said softly. It was true. Even the cafeteria ladies in her high school knew how much she loved Heath. The cheerleader and the dropout had made waves since their first date more than a year ago.

In one swift motion, Heath flung her hand from his arm. He grabbed her upper arms, nearly lifting her from the ground, his thumbs digging into her tender flesh. "If I ever see you so much as speak to him again. . .you'll be sorry." With that, he tossed her to the ground, limp as a rag doll.

She caught herself with her hands, wincing as the gravel from the parking lot came in contact with her palms.

"Julie, are you okay?" Claire Petty rushed to her friend's side and knelt down beside her. She glared up at Heath. "What is wrong with you?"

"Claire to the rescue, huh?" Heath pulled the last cigarette from the package and tossed the empty wrapper on the ground. "I guess you'll be telling her daddy." He lit the cigarette and took a long drag. "But you should really keep your nose out of our business."

Claire ignored him and helped Julie to her feet. "Why don't you ride with me? There's a graduation party at Remy's, and everyone would love for you to be there."

Julie shook her head. "We're going to dinner." She forced her mouth into a shaky smile. "I'm fine. Tell everyone I'm sorry to have missed it."

Claire bit her lip. "Jules." She put an arm around Julie, shielding her from Heath's sight. Claire lowered her voice to a whisper. "Please come with me. He still looks angry."

"I know how to handle him. Don't worry." Julie pulled away from her lifelong friend. "Don't tell, okay? Promise me?" The last time Claire had observed Heath's temper, she'd warned Julie that if it happened again, she'd tell Julie's parents.

Claire shook her head. "Hate me if you want to. I don't care.

But you need help."

Julie watched her friend walk toward the west side of the parking lot. *I'm going to be in a heap of trouble when I get home.*

"You comin' with me or what?" Heath asked, climbing into the cab of the truck.

Julie walked around to the passenger side and hesitated for a moment before she opened the door. Heath wasn't a bad guy. She just needed to try harder not to make him mad.

Heath pulled the truck out of the parking lot and toward his favorite Mexican restaurant.

Julie leaned her head against the seat and tried to ignore the tight feeling in her throat. It would've been nice if she could've chosen the restaurant tonight, since it was her celebration. For a moment, she thought about all her friends at Remy's. Graduation night, and she was missing the final high school party. The buzzing of her phone pushed the thought away.

She glanced down at the incoming text message: CALL US IMMEDIATELY. LOVE, DADDY. Usually her daddy's habit of signing his name to his text messages made her laugh, but this time, she didn't even crack a smile.

"Problem?" Heath glanced over at her.

"Nope." Julie turned her phone off and stuffed it into her bag. "Everything is just fine."

◎ِ◎

As soon as Heath turned the truck onto Julie's street, they saw the glow. Every light in her house burned bright, a not-so-subtle message from her parents. There was no point in trying to sneak in unnoticed, as she'd hoped. "Ugh," Julie grimaced.

Heath put the truck in PARK and pulled her closer to him. "They'll get over it. It's barely after midnight. You're not even half an hour late." He leaned down and planted a kiss on her forehead, no sign of his earlier anger. Just as she'd expected, he'd calmed down as soon as they were alone, and they'd had a nice time together.

Except for one thing.

If it had been up to Heath, she'd have found a way to spend the night at his place. It was the one thing they fought over every time. "I'm tired of hearing about your *virtue*," Heath said through gritted teeth. "You're not daddy's little girl anymore. It's time for you to grow up and be a woman." And by *grow up*, she knew he meant stay the night with him. Julie wasn't ready for that step. She'd always believed in waiting until marriage. "Why rush into it?" she pleaded with him. "We have the rest of our lives together." The argument ended as it usually did, with him telling her to get in the truck because he was taking her home. Tonight, though, he added an ultimatum. "I waited for you this past year because you're underage, and I know your old man would like nothing better than an excuse to throw me in jail for taking advantage of his little girl." His words dripped with sarcasm. "But as soon as you turn eighteen, you can do whatever you want. And you'd better be ready to turn this into an adult relationship. Otherwise, I'm through."

The last sentence echoed in Julie's head as she tried to lose herself in his embrace. She didn't want to lose him, but her beliefs held her back from spending the night with him. Why couldn't he understand that she wasn't ready yet? So far he'd taken her no with only a little griping, only sometimes calling her *baby* and *immature*. After she turned eighteen, that would change.

She pulled out of his grasp and looked up at him. Ruggedly handsome, he'd shaved his normal stubble for her graduation and traded in his standard jeans and T-shirt for dress pants and a button-down. No tie, but that was okay. "I'd better go in. I'll talk to you tomorrow."

"I love you, Jules." He opened his door and helped her out of the truck.

She leaned against his broad chest. Hearing him say those words made her heart melt. "I love you, too." Julie liked the way she was the only one who really understood him. Even his parents had written him off. But not her. She saw past his bad-boy image. Someday he would become the man she knew he could be. He just needed time.

The porch light flicked off, then on again, and Julie jumped back. "Get out of here before Daddy comes out." She gave Heath one last kiss and scurried up the sidewalk. Time to face the music.

"Well, well. Look who finally decided to come home." Her dad sat on the stairs in the entryway, a cell phone in his hand. "I was getting ready to call the police."

Julie glared at him. "Daddy, don't be ridiculous. I'm not even half an hour late."

"I'm aware of your curfew. After all, I'm the one who set it." He rose from the stairs and motioned for her to follow him into the living room.

Mama sat on the couch, aimlessly flipping through a *People* magazine. "Did you have a good night?"

Julie nodded, wondering if she'd walked into some kind of trap. "Yep." She leaned down and kissed her mother on the cheek. "Okay, good night." She started toward the stairs, hoping against hope that they'd just let her go.

"Not so fast, young lady." Daddy's stern voice stopped her in her tracks. "We need to talk to you."

Julie exhaled loudly and flounced down on the couch. "What?"

Her parents exchanged a glance. Finally, Mama put the magazine on the coffee table and met Julie's gaze. "Honey, we're worried. Claire called us on her way to Remy's. She told us what happened in the parking lot."

Daddy paced the floor like a caged lion but didn't speak. His frown, though, spoke volumes.

"It wasn't nearly as bad as it looked. Really." Julie was used to defending Heath to her parents.

Mama reached over and pulled up the cap sleeve on Julie's purple top. The bruises stood in stark contrast to her creamy skin. "It looks pretty bad to me," Mama said softly.

Unexpected tears sprang into Julie's eyes, and she quickly blinked them back. "It was just a misunderstanding. And you know I bruise easily."

Daddy stopped pacing and pulled the footstool in front of where Julie sat. He sank onto it and looked her square in the eye. "I know that you think you're an adult. But you aren't. Not yet. You still live under my roof. And I will not allow you to see that boy again."

Julie's heart pounded. She clenched her fists and stood. "What are you going to do, ground me for the whole summer? My birthday will be here in August, and then I'll be free to do whatever I want to."

"Actually, we aren't going to ground you." Mama raked a hand through her shoulder-length red hair. "As it turns out, we've found you a job."

"A job?" Julie asked, confused. She'd been looking for a job for the past few weeks but hadn't found one yet. She wanted to save some money before college started in the fall. "Where?" And what did a job have to do with her and Heath?

Her parents exchanged a look.

"It's time to start packing," Daddy said. "Because you're going on a trip."

CHAPTER 2

*The anniversary of my best and worst day is coming up
soon. That's right. They happened on the same day. I
wonder how many other people in the world can say that?
On a random Tuesday morning, your dad and I found
out for sure we were going to be parents. Best. Day. Ever.
Hands down. We both agreed on that. Then later that same
afternoon, he was killed in an accident. While I was at
home deciding what color to paint the nursery. As you well
know, I still haven't recovered. I couldn't reconcile my best
and worst day then, and I can't now, close to two years later.*

The words swam before Ainsley Davis's eyes. Her curly cursive
handwriting looked just like it had in junior high. She reread the
sentences and wondered how old her daughter would be when
she read them. Of course, Dr. Sinclair said no one ever had to
read the journal. But writing her story seemed pointless if no one
ever read it. Where was the therapy in that? After a couple of days
of aimless journaling, she'd decided to write each entry with Faith
in mind.

Maybe this whole thing had been a bad idea. Anger and sadness warred inside her. She slammed the notebook shut and hurled it against the yellow wall. Her mom's idea of cheery.

Faith's startled cry sounded from the next room.

I am the worst mother ever.

Ainsley wiped the tears off her face and picked up the notebook. She tiptoed across the hall and peeked into her daughter's room. Faith's eyes were closed, and her gentle breathing caused her chest to rise and fall. It looked like she had lulled herself back to sleep. Thank goodness she hadn't inherited Ainsley's insomnia. Which had only worsened since Brad's death.

"What's the ruckus?" Patricia Garrett asked, stepping into the basement apartment Ainsley had lived in for the better part of two years.

Ainsley met her mother's inquisitive gaze. "Nothing. I'm nearly finished packing." She motioned toward the boxes stacked against the wall, each of them labeled clearly. "Brad's parents are coming tomorrow to go through the things that are in storage."

"Are you sure there's nothing there you want to keep?" Mom furrowed her brow. "Faith might want some of her father's things once she gets a little bit older."

Ainsley shook her head. "I've already talked to Sandra about it. Anything sentimental can be Faith's if she ever wants it." She shrugged. "They'll keep his things at their house in the meantime. You know they have that huge attic that's nearly empty."

Mom nodded and sank onto the lumpy, striped sofa. "Speaking of empty, this house is going to seem empty without you and Faith here." She patted the sofa cushion and motioned for Ainsley to sit down.

Ainsley perched on the couch next to her mother. If only she could curl up in a ball and let Mom play with her hair, like when she was a little girl. But instead, she had her own little girl. And it was time to start making their own life together. Past time, really.

"It's going to be an adjustment for all of us. This is the only home Faith has ever known. She's going to miss you and Dad so much." She grabbed Mom's hand. "And so am I."

Mom reached over and smoothed Ainsley's long, dark red hair. "Are you sure about this, honey? No one is forcing you to go yet. You have all the time in the world."

If there was one thing that her husband's untimely death had taught Ainsley, it was that she didn't have all the time in the world. And no matter how unprepared she felt, the time had come to get out of the hiding place her parents' basement had turned into. "I'm sure."

"Your father is going to pick the moving van up in the morning." Mom rose from her spot on the couch. "He wants to be loaded and on the road by noon. It's going to be a long day. You should get some sleep."

Ainsley's mouth twisted into a tiny smile. "I wish it were that easy." When sleep did come, usually in random fits, her dreams were plagued with memories of Brad. Images of their wedding, life together, and his funeral flashed through her subconscious each night.

Mom paused at the steps that led up to the main floor. "Your dad says some of the pills on the market today have very little side effects. And they could help you a lot."

Ainsley rolled her eyes. "I've told you before that I don't like taking pharmaceuticals. I'll just stick to natural remedies. Maybe valerian root or some nice chamomile tea."

Mom snorted. "The fact that the daughter of a physician is so anti-doctor, anti–prescription drug is a mystery to me." She shook her head. "Not to mention how much it hurts his feelings. Good night, dear."

"Night." Ainsley's preference for natural remedies proved to be a constant source of conflict between herself and her parents. As soon as she'd been able to make her own decisions about her health, she'd opted for homeopathic care rather than traditional. But that was about the only thing she and her parents didn't see eye-to-eye on, and since Brad's accident, she'd been happy in their house. At least, she'd been as happy as her grief would allow. And tomorrow? Her friend Vickie had called it the first day of the rest of her life. But there was something no one knew. Not her friends, her family, or her therapist. Something that so far, she'd only confessed to God. Ainsley was pretty sure the biggest part of her had died along with Brad in that awful fire. And a change in location wasn't going to change the void she felt inside.

◎◎

Ainsley couldn't shake the nerves in her stomach as she watched her dad and brother load her belongings into the moving van. With each box that went in, she realized there was no turning back. Today, she returned to her job as a park ranger at the Grand Canyon, ready or not.

"Here's Rachel and Julie," Mom said as Ainsley's sister and niece pulled into the driveway. "I hope having Julie stay with you for the summer is a good idea."

Ainsley hoped the same thing. But it meant Faith didn't have to go to day care right away. What a huge relief. "Hi, sis." Ainsley hugged her older sister Rachel. "Thanks for loaning me your kid for the summer." She grinned and watched as Julie dramatically lugged a suitcase from the backseat. With her long legs and strawberry blond hair, she was a dead ringer for a teenage Rachel.

Rachel raised an eyebrow. "I should be the one thanking you. Just wait until Faith is nearly eighteen, and you'll understand. If Julie and Dave had to stay under the same roof this summer, I'm pretty sure I'd have to be committed."

"Is she still upset?" Mom asked.

"She's fighting both of us tooth and nail. Julie's always been a good girl. That boy is no good for her, though. And she knows it, deep down. But she's too stubborn to admit it." Rachel sighed. "I don't know what we'd do if you weren't looking for a babysitter this summer. Julie needs to be as far away from Heath as possible. I think she'll have a good time once she's actually there."

"Don't talk about me like I'm not here." Julie dragged her stuffed pink suitcase over to where the older women stood. "I can totally hear you."

Rachel reached out and tousled her daughter's hair. "Lighten up, Jules. You're about to spend the summer at one of the most beautiful spots in the world."

Julie snorted. "Miles away from my friends and without any stores. Or my car. Sounds super fun." She directed her green-eyed gaze at Ainsley. "Please tell me we at least will have Internet."

"It's nice to see you, too." Ainsley grinned at her only niece.

A flush crept up Julie's face. "Sorry." She hugged Ainsley, then her grandmother.

"And yes, we'll be connected to the outside world. I might even spring for cable TV if you're good."

Julie grinned. "At least I can shop online, right?"

Ainsley laughed. "Right." Even though she'd been surprised at Rachel's plea that she let Julie live with her for the summer, she had to admit having a teenager in the house would liven things up. And provide conversation. Faith's vocabulary was still limited to one-syllable words.

"Look who's up." Brook Garrett, Ainsley's sister-in-law, stepped outside, a toddling Faith at her side. Faith's face lit up when she saw Ainsley. She scrunched up her nose and smiled a mostly gummy grin that revealed six teeth—four on top and two on the bottom.

"There's my girl," Ainsley exclaimed.

Faith took off in her mother's direction, running as fast as her chubby legs could go.

Ainsley watched as her daughter ran over the uneven ground. "Wait," she called out, hurrying toward Faith. She snatched the little girl up before she could fall.

Startled, Faith began to cry. Her loud wails filled the yard.

"What happened?" Dad called from where he stood at the moving van.

"She's fine. I just didn't want her to fall down." Ainsley cradled Faith to her as the child's cries subsided.

Julie trotted over and held her hands out to Faith. "Come here, little one. Let's go see if Grandma has anything yummy in the kitchen."

Faith was all smiles again as she jumped into her cousin's arms.

"I'm sorry," Brook said. "Should I not have let her walk to you?"

Ainsley shook her head. "She's still not the steadiest walker. I don't like to let her walk out in the yard because I don't want her to get hurt."

Rachel laughed. "All babies fall as they're learning to walk. Don't be so overprotective."

The sting of her sister's words hit her like a whip. "Says the woman who's shipping her daughter miles away to keep her from some boy? Maybe it runs in our family."

Rachel drew back like she'd been slapped.

Ainsley knew she'd gone too far. "Sorry," she said softly.

"Me, too." Rachel gave a tiny smile. "Let's blame Mom for passing the overprotective gene on to us."

Mom looked from one daughter to the other. "You both turned out just fine. And I happen to think my grandchildren are perfect, so we must be doing something right." She grinned. "How about we go help your father load the rest of those boxes?" she asked, ushering her daughters and daughter-in-law toward the moving van.

CHAPTER 3

*My friend Dustin is actually the person who introduced
me to your dad. Dustin and I had these biweekly dinners
where I'd tell him about my week and then I'd pretend to be
shocked when he'd tell me outrageous stories about the crazy
things he'd done. One night a week, I was in charge—and
I'd actually make a home-cooked meal. On his night to be in
charge, we'd always have the same thing—something from
the grill. Usually burgers. Dustin is a notorious playboy. I
mean, I can't even count the number of women he's dated.
And honestly, living in a community as small as ours, I don't
understand where he even finds them. So one night when he
told me there was going to be a guest at his house, I totally
expected it to be some bimbo. Instead it was your dad. Turned
out, he was an old friend of Dustin's and had just been hired
on with the forest service as a firefighter. We started dating
soon afterward, and I guess the rest is pretty much history.*

Dustin Cooper sat on a bench and watched a group of Japanese
tourists pose for photos. Their laughter filled the air outside the

historic El Tovar Hotel. He hadn't slept at all last night, despite his exhaustion. Old memories and lost opportunities had flitted through his mind, a nocturnal film reel of his worst hits. He'd finally given up and gone for a run just before daylight, thankful it was his day off.

"Howdy, stranger." Lindsey Jane plopped down next to him. "Haven't seen you in ages." Once upon a time, Lindsey had been his on-again, off-again girlfriend. Mostly off. But in times of distress, she could always be counted on to lend an ear or share a meal.

He grinned. "I've been busy."

"So I've heard. Busy reinventing yourself, according to some." She leveled her blue eyes at him. There was a time one look from her would've made his heart race. But no more. Maybe they had finally moved into the friend zone for good.

"People change." He shrugged and stretched his legs out in front of him, noting the worn insoles on his Nikes. Next time he was in Flagstaff, he should pick up some new running shoes.

"I hear your girl is coming back." She raised an eyebrow in his direction. "How is she?"

Dustin shifted uncomfortably. Leave it to Lindsey to dredge up the past. And to try and get a reaction out of him. "She isn't 'my girl' and never was. You know that." He narrowed his eyes at her. "In fact, you made sure of it." He wiped a trickle of sweat from his forehead. "As for how she's doing, I have no idea. I haven't seen her in a while."

"That's likely to change soon." Lindsey tossed her blond hair. "I have no doubt that you'll be part of the welcome wagon for Ms. Ainsley." She put a manicured hand on his bicep and squeezed. "A grieving widow like her probably needs a strong man in her life." She winked.

He bristled. He remembered all too well the days he and Lindsey had double-dated with Ainsley and Brad. After every date, Lindsey would complain that Ainsley and Brad were the most boring couple she'd ever met. And the next day at work, Ainsley would question his taste in women. "Not cool, Linds. I know you've never been a fan, but after what she's been through, you'd think you could cut her a little slack."

She jerked her hand from his arm. "Oh, lighten up. My little jokes used to make you laugh." Her full lips formed a pout. "Besides, it isn't that I wasn't a fan. I just didn't go for her whole holier-than-thou routine. Guess even all that religion couldn't save her husband."

She'd gone too far this time. Brad had been his friend since childhood. Dustin jumped up from the bench, glaring. "I'm outta here. You're just as toxic as you always were." After he'd introduced Ainsley and Brad and they'd immediately coupled up, he'd been crushed. It felt like he'd lost his two best friends. Lindsey had served as a distraction, despite her claims that he was jealous. He hadn't been jealous. Not really.

Lindsey rose and stretched her long, shapely limbs. "Oh, get over yourself." She patted her mouth in an exaggerated yawn. "You're no fun anymore, Dustin."

He turned to go. "I could say the same about you."

"You could. But you won't." She let out a tinkling laugh. "Call me though. When things with Ainsley blow up in your face." She paused. "Again."

Her mocking laughter seemed to follow him the entire two miles to the residential area, where his house stood. His stomach churned.

His old friend Ainsley would be back any day now. Back in his neighborhood. Back in his life.

❧

Jake McGuire tried to catch the waitress's eye, but she was busy laughing at something the guy at the next table had said. He glanced around to see if there was another waitress in sight. No such luck. He sighed. In his thirty-five years on this earth, he'd never been accused of being patient. Not once that he could remember. Even on fishing trips with his dad, if the fish weren't biting, Jake was ready to go. He drummed his fingers on the table a little louder than necessary, but the waitress wasn't fazed.

"Oh, honey. I wish I could help. But I'm sure not the outdoorsy type." Her laugh rang through the hole-in-the-wall diner. She stepped toward Jake's table, her eyes still on the other customer. "If I think of anyone who might be interested, I'll let you know."

Still laughing, she filled Jake's coffee cup with water. "Is there anything else I can get you?" He looked down at the clear liquid, swirling with the remnants of his black coffee.

"Actually, I was hoping to have more coffee. Minus the water." He grinned and reminded himself he was on a mission to relax. This wasn't a stakeout. Lives didn't depend on whether or not he left the diner by a certain time. So while the old Jake might've been irritated by her faux pas, the new Jake was going to learn to go with the flow.

"I'm so sorry." Her face flushed with embarrassment as she stared into his cup. She motioned at the man seated at the next table. "He had me flustered. I'll go get you a fresh cup." She snatched the stained ceramic mug from the table and hurried off.

"Stacy's something else," the other customer said, laughing. "I come in here at least once a week just to tease her." He gave Jake a quick once-over. "I'm Shane. Shane Farmer."

"Jake McGuire."

"You on vacation, Jake?" Shane asked.

Was he on vacation? Not exactly. The situation was a little complicated. What do you call it when you're just running from your real life? "Guess you could say I'm temporarily relocating."

"To Williams, Arizona? Why?" Shane wasn't buying it.

"Nah. I'm hoping to be closer to the canyon. Maybe Tusayan." Jake cleared his throat. It wasn't like him to share his plans with a stranger, but his life had been filled with silence since he'd set out on his journey. "I used to hike there a lot with my dad. I'm planning to spend a few weeks camping." Jake's camper was old but sturdy. When his sister's friend had offered to sublet his apartment in Phoenix for the summer, he'd made the impulsive decision to hit the road. His decision had surprised his close friends and family. Jake wasn't exactly known for his spontaneity.

Shane sat up with interest. "You don't say. My family runs a guide service for hikers." He took a sip of coffee. "We're short a guide, and the high season starts soon." He squinted his eyes in Jake's direction. "You're not lookin' for a job, are you?"

Jake pondered his words. He hadn't planned to get a real job, but maybe it would be nice to have something concrete to do. Something to keep his mind off his problems. "Maybe. If the hours are flexible enough." He didn't want to work full-time. After five years of double shifts and overtime, he needed a break. Especially after these past few weeks.

Stacy set a steaming cup of coffee in front of Jake. "Here you go, sugar." She turned to grin at Shane. "You need anything?"

Shane shook his head. "Actually, I might've just found a new employee."

Stacy giggled. "Great. That'll show that brother of yours, huh?" She slapped a ticket onto the Formica table. "Pay when you're ready."

"My baby brother up and left the business. Right before our busiest season. We don't expect him back."

Jake nodded. "I haven't hiked the canyon in a few years. But I'm in good shape. It shouldn't take long to get acclimated." Even on days he worked long hours, Jake always managed to fit in some gym time. Sometimes he thought it might be the only thing that kept him from being eaten alive by stress.

"I'm taking our team on a hike day after tomorrow. We're meeting at Bright Angel Trail at 6:00 a.m. sharp. If you decide you're interested, meet me there. We'll consider the hike your interview." Shane stood and fished a card from his wallet. "Here's my card in case you have any questions."

Jake sat in silence and sipped his coffee. Maybe this was just what he needed. Besides, if it didn't work out, he could always quit. After all, running away seemed to be the only thing he was good at lately.

CHAPTER 4

I hope you love the Grand Canyon as much as I do. Working there as a park ranger was my first job out of college. And I loved it. I never got tired of gazing out at the canyon. When I think of the years your dad and I spent living and working there, I'm always surprised to remember how happy I was. As tough as leaving Mom and Dad's is going to be, I can't wait to move back and start working again.

As soon as Ainsley drove her Honda Accord Hybrid through the entrance of Grand Canyon National Park, her heart begin to pound. It seemed like a lifetime ago that she'd left the park on the day of Brad's accident. She'd never returned. Dad and Tommy had packed her things and brought them back to Flagstaff.

"You okay?" Rachel asked from the passenger seat.

Ainsley didn't respond. She checked the rearview mirror and saw the van that carried her parents and Julie. Tommy and Brook were behind them, their truck bed full of furniture. She put her blinker on and pulled the car into a small parking lot. The big sign bearing the park's name was a favorite stopping point for first-time visitors, and a family was posed in front of it, laughing and smiling for the camera.

"Seriously, sis. What's going on? Do you want to take a picture?" Rachel wrinkled her forehead, puzzled at Ainsley's behavior.

"I. . .yes. A picture. Of Faith. It's her first time here, you know." That would buy her some time. Ainsley frantically tried to remember where her camera was. And willed her heart to stop pounding.

Rachel drew her eyebrows together. "Are you sure? This might not be the best time." She motioned to the backseat. "She's sound asleep."

Ainsley's chest got tighter and tighter. Another minute and she'd be gasping for air.

"You don't look so good." Rachel pulled a bottle of water from her bag. "Here, drink some of this." She unscrewed the cap and pushed the bottle to Ainsley's lips. "Hold the bottle. I'm going to go tell them we thought they might want to take a picture." She shot another worried glance at Ainsley and climbed from the car.

Ainsley appreciated Rachel not alerting their parents to her odd behavior. She needed to get it together. All she could think of was the deep canyon up ahead. What if something went wrong with her brakes? What if she couldn't stop and drove the car right over the edge, just like Thelma and Louise? She wiped away a tiny trickle of sweat from her forehead and leaned her head against the seat.

The passenger door opened, and Rachel peeked her head inside. "They decline the photo op. Dad says he wants to get everything unloaded and you settled so we can return the van to the rental place on time."

"Can you drive?" Ainsley asked, surprised at how shaky her voice sounded.

Rachel nodded. "Sure." She walked around the car to the driver's side and waited.

Ainsley climbed slowly from the car, not meeting her sister's eyes.

Once they were settled, Rachel reached over and patted Ainsley on the leg. "It's okay. You're going to be fine." She pulled the car onto the road. "Just breathe."

"I didn't expect to react this way. What if I'm not ready to be here?"

Rachel pursed her lips. "Then you'll transfer to a different park," she said matter-of-factly. "It was time for you to move out of Mom and Dad's basement. I'm surprised you haven't gone stir crazy being there for so long. And I think you do need to come back here, at least for a little while."

"Turn left here," Ainsley directed.

"Is your rental house near where you used to live?" Rachel asked.

Ainsley shook her head. "Not on the same street or anything, thank goodness. But it's in the same general area." She glanced down at the tattered piece of paper her new address was written on.

Rachel let out a loud sigh. "I know you don't want my advice." She grinned. "But I'm going to give it to you anyway."

"Okay." Ainsley peered out the window as they passed many sights familiar to her. There was the resident doctor's office for simple things like allergies and sinus infections. The school was on the left. If she stayed here, Faith would attend there someday. The thought of sending her baby to school made her heart pound even harder.

"I know this is going to be difficult for you. But try and find some kind of fun for yourself. Something that doesn't have to do with Faith or with work." Rachel paused. "Something that is just for you."

Ainsley managed a laugh. "Oh, come on. Don't you remember what it was like to have a toddler? And to work? There won't be time for anything else."

"You need to make time." Rachel shook her head. "Time for yourself will energize you. It will make you a better mother. A better employee. Trust me. Even if you just take up running again. Or biking." She bit her lip. "Or maybe you'll meet a nice guy to have dinner with every now and then."

Ainsley glared at her sister. Biking or running she could handle. But dinner? No way. "Don't be stupid. I'm not going to just go out to dinner with some man." Had Rachel completely lost her mind? "Besides, no man is going to want to go out with a widow who has a toddler." She'd never referred to herself as a widow before.

"You never know what God has in store for you." Rachel was silent for a minute. "At least promise me that you'll go into this new chapter of your life with an open mind."

"I have an open mind," Ainsley muttered.

Rachel slowed the car down as they entered the residential area of the park. "You *used* to have an open mind." She sighed. "I get it. Life hasn't turned out the way you expected it to." She reached over and gripped Ainsley's hand. "But your life is not over. You're young. You're smart. You have a lot of love to give and an amazing daughter." She brought the car to a stop to let a pedestrian cross. "I don't want you to give up on living your dream life."

"My dreams died in that fire. And you know it." Ainsley's eyes filled with tears.

Faith stirred in the backseat. "Ma–ma," she said, followed by a stream of gibberish.

"I think one of your dreams just called you from the backseat." Rachel touched her sister on the shoulder. "And maybe it's time you mustered up the strength to find some new dreams. You know that's what Brad would've wanted."

"Turn left at the next street," Ainsley directed. She wanted to get out of the car and be through with this conversation. Because she had a sinking suspicion that her sister was exactly right.

Julie pulled her strawberry blond hair into a ponytail. Man, it was hot. Of course, unloading a million boxes hadn't helped.

"Last one," Grandpa said, handing her a box.

Julie went carefully up the steps that led to the porch and through the propped open door. She set the box in the dining room with the others.

"Thanks for helping," Ainsley said, looking up from the box of dishes she was unpacking. "Why don't you take a break?"

Julie shook her head. "I think I'll unpack my things. Which room is going to be mine?" She'd only had one room her entire life. This was going to be weird. For a second, she thought about pleading with her mother to let her return home. No. She couldn't do that. If she were at home, Dad would keep her underneath his thumb all summer. At least here, she'd have some freedom. Ainsley was her mom's youngest sibling and had always treated Julie more like a friend than a niece.

"Do you mind if your room has a desk and bookshelves in it?" Ainsley asked.

Julie smiled. "Nope. As long as there's a bed, I'm cool."

Ainsley pointed down the narrow hallway. "Great. The last room on the left will be yours. You can arrange it however you like."

"Thanks." Julie trotted down the hallway and into the room that would be hers until August. Until she turned eighteen and could make her own decisions. She took stock of the room. The twin bed was small, but at least she'd be used to the size before she went off to college in the fall. Her grandparents had given her new twin-sized bedding for graduation, and her mother had let her bring it to use for the summer.

"Let me help," Mama said from the doorway. "It'll go faster. Besides, I want to get you all settled before we have to leave."

They worked together to unfold the new bedding. The sheets were white with pink polka dots that matched the pink comforter and pillow shams. Julie loved the color pink, even though she didn't wear much of it. Claire always said it clashed with her hair.

Once they were through, Mama sat down on the bed and patted the space next to her. "Come here, honey."

Julie sat down next to her mother and leaned against her. "Are you having second thoughts about leaving me here?" she asked in what she hoped was a pitiful voice.

Mama burst out laughing. "Trying to send me on a guilt trip, huh?" She put an arm around her only child. "I'm not having second thoughts. I think this is the very best place for you to spend the summer."

Julie sat upright and regarded her mother. "I'm not totally stupid, you know. My mama didn't raise no fool." She grinned. "I would've been fine at home."

"I have no doubt you'd have managed. But don't you think it would've been way too tempting to sneak out and see Heath? I was young once, you know. I know all the tricks."

Julie gave her a thin smile. "He isn't a bad guy." She sighed. "He really isn't." Saying good-bye to Heath had been so hard. She'd cried for two days and refused to speak to her daddy.

"He has an awful lot of maturing to do. And he needs to learn to get that temper of his under control. Don't pretend it doesn't bother you." She reached over and took Julie's hand. "Someday, you'll meet someone who treats you like a princess. Who respects you and adores you and would never do anything to hurt you." She let go of Julie's hand. "And when you do, you'll wonder why you ever gave Heath so many second chances. Mark my words."

A loud sigh escaped Julie's mouth. "Mama. Please. Heath cares so much about me. He's sick about what happened graduation night. And he's going to miss me so much this summer." She chose to leave out the promise Heath had made to come and visit her at the canyon. No one needed to know that.

"Just try and spend this summer concentrating on your job here. Ainsley needs you. She's going to have a hard time of it, I'm afraid. She spent so much time isolating herself at Mom and Dad's, I think this transition is going to be really difficult for her."

Julie nodded. "I've noticed. She's on edge a lot. I just hope I do okay with Faith." She swallowed hard.

"You'll do fine." Mama reached over and smoothed a stray lock of hair that had fallen into Julie's face. "Remember, I'm only a phone call away if you ever need any advice." She smiled. "And I know a thing or two about taking care of a precocious little girl."

Julie grinned. "Thanks." She stood and began to pull clothes from her suitcase. She hated to admit it, but she was going to miss her parents this summer. If only there were a way for them to accept Heath, her life would be perfect.

CHAPTER 5

*I think a lot about what your future holds. Will you be
a doctor? An artist? Will you open your own business?
Honestly, I don't care what profession you choose as long as
you're happy. Although if you decide to be a lion tamer or
something crazy, you may have to remind me of that.*

Dustin watched the moving van drive away from the
residential area of the park. He was pretty sure Mr. Garrett had
been behind the wheel. He'd fought the urge to stop by to see
if they needed help unloading. He wasn't positive his presence
would be welcome. Uncertainty was a foreign feeling to him. His
job as a law enforcement ranger required him to be decisive.

On a whim, he caught the shuttle to the park general store.
Flowers. He'd take Ainsley some flowers. He already had a "welcome
back" gift for her, but he remembered how she always liked to
have fresh flowers in the house.

Twenty minutes later, he climbed back on the shuttle, clutching
a bouquet of tulips and feeling like a fool. At least Lindsey wasn't
around to see him.

He exited the park shuttle at the stop nearest his house so he could pick up Ainsley's gift. It had been sitting in his living room for a few weeks, ever since he'd heard she'd decided to come back to her old job.

After a short walk, Dustin stood outside her door. He paused for a long moment then lifted his hand to knock.

Before his fist made contact with the door, it swung open and he was face-to-face with a teenage girl. Her green eyes took him in for a moment. "Can I help you?" she finally asked.

"Oh. Hi. I'm, um, looking for Ainsley Davis." Had he misunderstood Edie when she'd told him which house Ainsley would be living in? "Do I have the wrong place?"

"It can't be." Ainsley said, walking up behind the girl. "Dustin," she whispered. "I wasn't sure if you still worked here."

"If you'd answered any of my calls or e-mails, you'd have known." At her crestfallen face, he immediately wished he could take the words back. Or at least say them in a softer voice.

"I'll let you two catch up." The girl backed away from the door.

"Sorry. Julie, this is my friend Dustin Cooper." Ainsley motioned toward him. "He's a law enforcement ranger here. And this is my niece, Julie." She put her arm around the girl's shoulder. "She's staying here for the summer and helping to take care of Faith."

Dustin smiled in Julie's direction. "Nice to meet you. Hope you enjoy your stay."

"Thanks." Julie nodded at him and walked out of the room.

Suddenly, he was face-to-face with Ainsley. "Here. These are for you." He thrust the flowers at her, embarrassed by his impulsive gesture.

"They're beautiful." Her mouth broke into a smile. "I can't believe you remembered that tulips are my favorite." She motioned inside. "Come on in. The place isn't unpacked at all, but we tried to at least get the living room in order before my family left."

Dustin picked up the package that sat at his feet and stepped inside. "This is a nice place." There were no guarantees about park housing. But Ainsley had definitely lucked out. The house wasn't too old, and it had fresh paint and floors that looked to have been redone recently.

"I'm happy with it. It will take me a little while to get everything unpacked and settled, but I'm kind of excited about it. Most of my things have been in storage for so long."

Sadness washed over him. Her things had been in storage since the day he'd had to come to her house and share with her the worst news imaginable. He'd often wondered if his being the bearer of that news was the reason she'd avoided him for so long. "It will be like they're new to you again, then. Like Christmas all over." He grinned.

Thankfully, she smiled back. "I guess so. I hadn't looked at it like that." She noticed the large package he'd placed on the floor next to the couch. "What's that?"

"A little housewarming gift."

She lifted the flowers. "You really know how to spoil a girl, don't you?" She grinned. "I'll have to find a vase for these later. I'm sure there's one packed away somewhere." She laid the bouquet carefully on the coffee table and turned her attention to the big box on the floor.

"Here's my pocket knife." Dustin reached into his pocket and pulled out his battered Swiss Army knife. "It should do the trick."

Ainsley eagerly ripped into the box and pulled out a red backpack. She set it on the leather couch. "Thanks," she said, her voice tinged with uncertainty.

He picked up the pack. "Don't you see? It's a backpack you can put your little girl in," he explained. "I know how much you love to hike the trails, and this way, she can go along with you and have a bird's-eye view." He pulled out a canopy. "It even has a little shade that goes over her head to keep the sun off her." Dustin had been so sure she'd love it. He, Ainsley, and Brad had spent hours hiking the canyon trails. After he'd noticed several tourists carrying toddlers in the baby backpacks, he'd inquired about them at the local sporting goods store. He'd gotten the top-of-the-line model for Ainsley to use with Faith.

She took the pack from him and sat it in the corner next to an end table. "It's perfect. Thanks."

Dustin couldn't shake the feeling that he'd upset her but didn't want to pry. "You're welcome."

Ainsley sat down in the brown leather chair that matched the couch. It was the same set that had been in the old house. Dustin remembered helping Brad move the furniture inside. Ainsley had them move the couch three times before she finally decided it was in the perfect spot.

"So, how have you been?" she asked.

"Okay. I got a promotion last year." He smiled. "But other than that, things are pretty much the same as they always were."

She grinned. "Remember my first summer here? You were already the big man around the park."

"And of all the shuttles in all of the park, you had to get on mine." He smiled at the memory. "If it hadn't been for me having an umbrella and rain coming down like a monsoon, you never would've spoken to me." He could still remember how she looked that day, fresh-faced with her wavy red hair flowing. The rain had started just as the shuttle reached their stop. He and Ainsley had been the only two passengers to get off, and it had only seemed polite to offer to walk her to her house.

"That's right. I'd forgotten." She smiled at the memory. "Of course, what you didn't know was that I'd already heard all about you."

He groaned.

"What? It's the truth." She laughed. "Mrs. Whittaker pointed you out one day when you jogged past the library. 'Stay away from that one, honey. He might be handsome, but he sure is trouble,' " Ainsley said in an old-lady voice.

"For your information, Mrs. Whittaker now says I'm like the son she never had." It was true. The ancient librarian doted on him now, his past transgressions forgiven.

"Whatever. You're probably part of the orientation film these days for all the unsuspecting twenty-something seasonal rangers. There's probably an entire section in there called 'Dustin Cooper, serial ladies man.' " She laughed.

Dustin wanted to explain to her how much his life had changed in the two years she'd been gone. But he knew how unbelievable it would sound. No. He'd have to show her. Let her figure it out for herself. "I don't think I've made it into any training videos." He looked around the living room, and his eyes settled on a framed photo of a little girl in a high chair, cake all over her face. "Wow." He picked the picture up from the end table. "She's adorable."

Ainsley smiled broadly. "That's Faith a couple of months ago at her first birthday party. She was so excited when she got her very own little cake."

"Clearly it was quite tasty." He carefully set the picture back in its place. "Can I meet her?" He remembered the day Ainsley's pregnancy suspicions had been confirmed. She and Brad had called him on their way home from the doctor. They'd put him on speaker to tell him the news and make sure he was free to go out to the El Tovar that night to celebrate. But that celebration had never happened.

"She's napping right now. But yes. I'd love for you to meet her sometime."

He leaned his head back against the couch. "I'm having a hard time wrapping my head around you as someone's mother."

"We all have to grow up sometime, Dustin." Her voice was

somber. "Except for maybe you."

Dustin scratched his head. This was harder than he'd expected it to be. "How are you doing?"

"I'm fine." Her hazel-eyed gaze dared him to question her further.

If she didn't want to talk about things, he wasn't going to force her. But he hoped that someday soon she'd open up and tell him the truth. He could see that she wasn't fine. "Great. I'm glad to hear it." He rose. "I guess I should be going. I've got errands to run." He crossed the living room to the front door. "But listen, let's get together again soon."

"Absolutely."

"In fact, how about I put together a little party? Just a few of your old friends. You can bring Julie and Faith."

"Are you still the master of the grill?" she asked, smiling.

"You know it. Let's say Friday night at six? It'll be fun."

She nodded. "We'll be there. Julie will be thrilled to meet some people."

He gave her one last glance before starting toward home.

CHAPTER 6

My family and friends accuse me of being an overprotective mother. And I suppose that's a fair assessment. But I'll be honest with you. I've gone through so much pain since your dad's accident. And I know there was nothing anyone could do to protect me from it. So for the short amount of time I can keep you from hurt—any hurt—I'm going to.

Julie read over the list incredulously. Her aunt was off her rocker. There was no way any sane person could remember these rules. "I've been babysitting for a long time. I'm even certified in CPR. There's no need for you to worry."

"I can't help it. Someday, you'll understand." Ainsley paced the length of the living room in her ranger uniform.

Julie was so tired of hearing people say that. Someday, she'd understand what love was. Someday, she'd understand what parenthood was. Someday, someday, someday. It was enough to make her scream. Instead, she smiled. "Really. I'll follow your schedule. If we go out, I'll put sunglasses and sunblock on her. I won't answer the door to strangers. I'll puree fresh bananas for a snack. I won't let her put her hands in the dirt and then put them in her mouth." Julie stopped, not even halfway through the list. She grinned at her aunt.

"I know it seems over the top." Ainsley looked at herself in the mirror that hung above the couch. She placed her Smokey Bear hat on top of her head. "Do I look okay?"

"You look great. I like your hair that way."

Ainsley touched the braids that hung down on either side of her head. "Thanks."

"Now, go. You don't want to be late on your first day back."

"I'll call and check in soon."

Julie followed her to the door. "Hope you have a good day."

"You, too. Make sure she goes down for a nap after lunch."

"I will." Julie waved at her aunt's retreating figure. She had no doubt she'd hear from Ainsley multiple times today.

She closed and locked the door, thankful for the silence. It had been a long night. Julie had tossed and turned in the little twin bed, and it had seemed like she'd looked at the clock every hour.

Julie peeked into Faith's room. The little girl was sitting in her crib, banging her favorite stuffed dog against the rails. "Hey, you." Julie plucked Faith from the crib. "How's my sweet girl?"

Faith wriggled in Julie's arms, still clutching the tattered dog. "You want to walk?" She set the toddler on the hardwood floor and watched as the little girl took off full speed ahead toward the kitchen.

"Are you hungry?" Julie asked, kneeling down beside Faith.

"Ba–ba–ba–ba." Faith grinned, showing her tiny teeth. She began pulling Tupperware lids from a box that sat on the floor and throwing them across the room.

Julie sank into a chair and watched as Faith emptied the entire box. Plastic bowls and lids were everywhere.

"Geen," Faith said, looking at Julie with wide eyes.

"Geen?" Julie repeated. Ainsley always understood Faith's fourteen-month-old vocabulary, but Julie hadn't mastered it yet.

Faith nodded. "Geen." She toddled over to a lid and threw it.

"Oh. I get it. You want to do it again?" Julie laughed and began collecting the lids and bowls. As soon as the box was full, Faith began to pull and throw them.

"Whatever makes you happy, makes me happy." Julie grinned.

"Oh my." Julie sighed into the phone. "I can't even begin to tell you how tired I am." She'd put Faith down for a nap and for the first time in many years, felt like she needed one herself.

"What do you think of the place?" Heath asked. She'd promised her parents she wouldn't call him but hadn't said she wouldn't answer if he called her.

"I haven't seen all that much of it. The house is okay, I guess. But I miss you. And Claire." Julie sighed again. "I can't believe I'll be here for so long. I mean, we are seriously out in the middle of nowhere."

"At least when you come back, you'll be eighteen. And not jail bait anymore." He chuckled.

"True." She thought for a moment. "So do you have any big plans this summer?" Heath had mentioned once that he might go back and finish up his GED, but he hadn't talked about it lately.

"Nah. Working. Partying. You know the drill."

She did. And she'd never admit it to anyone, but the fact that he seemed to be completely without ambition frightened her a little bit. "Have you checked into taking those adult education classes at night? I left a brochure at your apartment a couple of weeks ago. If you'd finish up, maybe we could be college freshmen together."

Heath swore under his breath. "Who are you, my mama? Don't try and make me into someone I'm not. If you don't think

I'm good enough for you now that you're gonna be a college girl, just tell me."

At his harsh words, Julie's heart pounded against her chest. "That's not what I mean at all, and you know it. I just know that you've mentioned going back and getting your diploma. I thought that since I'm out of town, you might be looking for something to fill your time with. That's all."

"Don't you worry about me, babe. I can find ways to fill my time."

That was what worried her.

CHAPTER 7

*I hope that someday, you understand how much I love you.
Motherhood makes me look at the world in a whole new
way. I see things through your eyes, and all of a sudden,
normal becomes magic. When you laugh, I laugh, and when
you cry, I cry. I didn't expect to be so consumed. I think
having you in my life makes me a better person. Not that I
was a bad person before. But motherhood certainly changed
me. It's hard to be selfish when there's someone depending
on you. A full-time job was an adventure. Marriage was an
adjustment. But motherhood changed me deep in my soul.
I think aside from the love God has for us, a mother's love is
the purest love there is.*

Ainsley couldn't concentrate on what her supervisor, Edie
Barrett, was saying. Edie had kept in touch with Ainsley since the
accident and had always made it clear that she'd love for her to
return. When Edie called a couple of months ago to let her know
a position was about to come open, Ainsley had been torn. But
she'd been praying a lot for guidance, and with Edie's phone call,

Ainsley couldn't help but think her prayer had been answered.

"I'm sorry. Can you repeat that?"

Edie laughed. "Are you worrying about that sweet baby at home?"

Ainsley flushed. "Is it that obvious?"

"Honey, we've all been there. When you're at work, you're worrying about your babies. When you're at home, you're worrying about work. Welcome to motherhood." Edie had three grown kids of her own, and Ainsley knew she'd raised them alone.

"Sorry. I just keep thinking of things I didn't tell Julie." Ainsley shook her head. "Please tell me this gets easier."

Edie grinned. "I wish it did. But there's always something to worry about, no matter how grown up your kids get."

"That's what I'm learning. Suddenly, all those warnings my mother gave me over the years have taken on new meaning." She tugged absently on the end of her braid. "But I'm glad to be back."

❧

"Is she okay?" Ainsley asked, as she made her way to Verkamp's Visitor Center. She knew it went against policy for her to be on her cell phone while working, but she couldn't stand it another minute.

"She's fine. She woke up from her nap, and we're about to have a snack," Julie said as Faith's sweet voice sounded in the background.

Ainsley's eyes filled with unexpected tears at the sound of her daughter. "Great. Just thought I'd check."

"Do you want to talk to her? I can hold the phone up to her ear."

"Yes, please." She listened as Julie told Faith who was on the phone. "Okay, go," Julie said, her voice far from the phone.

"Hi, Faith. It's Mommy." Ainsley nearly choked on the words.

"How's my baby girl?"

"Ma—ma—ma," Faith cooed.

"That's right." Ainsley laughed. "I love you and will see you soon."

"Hey." Julie's voice again. "She loved talking to you. You should've seen her smile."

Ainsley blinked back the tears. "Okay, I have to go. See you guys soon. Call me if you need me."

"Will do. Don't worry."

Ainsley disconnected the call and sank onto a bench. She felt like she'd been punched in the stomach. She'd never been away from Faith for more than a few hours. She'd worked for a few months at a park near Flagstaff, but it was only part-time. She took a breath and closed her eyes, thankful she didn't have to present any ranger programs today. Edie wanted her to ease back into the job.

"Excuse me," a deep voice said.

Ainsley jerked her head up to see a tall dark-haired man standing in front of her. Was her 'leave me alone' vibe not strong enough? Visitors thought they owned her while she wore a uniform, one of the major irritations of her job. "What do you want?"

An uncertain expression flashed across his face, but he plunged ahead. "I was wondering if you could tell me how far the walk is to the Yavapai Observation Station." He held up a park map. "I'm trying to decide if I should walk or just take a shuttle." He grinned, showing even, white teeth and a dimple in his right cheek. "I figured, who better to give me advice than a park ranger?"

Ainsley tried to pull herself together, but it was no use. As soon as she tried to open her mouth to form a sentence, the tears she'd been holding back spilled over. Embarrassed, she quickly wiped them away. She cleared her throat. "It isn't a bad walk to Yavapai," she said quietly, not meeting his eyes.

"I don't mean to pry, but is everything okay?" He sat down next to her. "I'm Jake, by the way. Jake McGuire."

She sniffed. "Nice to meet you. I'm Ainsley Davis."

"Ainsley. That's a unique name." He grinned again. "I like it."

She managed a smile. "Thanks."

"But tell me what a cute park ranger like you is doing crying on a bench? You can't even see the canyon from here. Seems like if you're going to sit and reflect on things, you should at least do it with one of the most beautiful sights in the world in your line of view."

Ainsley grimaced. At least she'd been caught crying by a tourist passing through and not a coworker or something. She could think of at least a couple of people who'd like nothing better than to see her falling apart on her first day back. "When you work here, I guess you don't always think about positioning yourself with the canyon in view." Especially when the depth of the canyon caused her heart to race. She couldn't even bring herself to walk along the rim.

"Sorry. I didn't mean anything by that. Just making conversation." His brown eyes crinkled at the corners as he smiled, once again flashing that dimple at her. "Trying to get your mind off of whatever it is that has you so upset."

"Thanks. I just got off the phone with my little girl. I miss her so much." She shrugged. "Guess I'll have to get used to it."

"Is she somewhere far away?" He looked puzzled.

She managed a smile. "That would make more sense, wouldn't it?" Ainsley motioned in the direction of the residential area of the park where her rental house stood. "Actually, she's only a mile or so away. I'm just not used to being apart from her." She met his gaze. "It's my first day back."

"I see." He raked his fingers through his shaggy brown hair. "My sister had the same problem when she went back to work after her maternity leave." Jake shook his head. "Said it was like going off and leaving her heart at home every day."

"Did it ever get easier for her?"

"I wish I could say it did. She stuck it out for a while, but once she had her second baby, she gave up. She works from home now. Guess she has the best of both worlds."

"Must be nice." Ainsley fell silent. She felt Jake's eyes on her and slowly turned her head to meet his gaze. "Can I help you with something else?"

He shrugged. "Just wondering if you could tell me the best place to get a bite to eat around here. I'm new to the area."

"New to the area?" Ainsley drew her brows together. "So you're not just passing through?" Had she mistaken him for a tourist?

Jake smiled. "I just moved here. From Phoenix. I'm working as a hiking guide for the summer."

"That sounds fun." Hiking used to be one of Ainsley's favorite activities. She loved the outdoors and could be found outside every chance she got. At least, until Brad's accident.

"I hope so. I just started. I kind of stumbled onto the job. I'm basically camping for the summer until I decide if I want to actually relocate."

"Where are you staying?"

"I'll be moving to different sites through the summer. Right now, I'm in Trailer Village." Trailer Village and Bright Angel Campground were the only two campsites located on park property at the South Rim of the canyon.

Ainsley nodded. "Cool. Several park employees live there."

"There's a campground in Tusayan I might try at some point. I figure I can try all the area campgrounds and see which one I like best."

She smiled. "That sounds like a good idea. But I think you'll really enjoy living here. There's a lot to be said about living so close to such a beautiful sight."

"That's what I'm learning. Now if I can just meet some

people, life will be even better." His brown eyes grew wistful. "I can already tell that's what I'm going to miss the most about Phoenix. My friends and family."

If there was one thing Ainsley could identify with, it was feeling isolated. "One of the law enforcement rangers is having a cookout at his house tomorrow night. Why don't you come? It would be a great chance for you to meet some locals." As soon as the words left her mouth, she wished she could take them back. What had come over her, inviting a stranger to Dustin's cookout?

Not that Dustin would mind. His mantra for cookouts had always been the more, the merrier. But what would other people think? Would she be judged for bringing a strange man to her welcome-back party? One more glance at Jake's handsome face, and she knew she didn't care. They could judge her all they wanted to. Jake was a newcomer to the community. And she kind of liked the idea of having a friend who hadn't been around to see her whole life fall apart.

CHAPTER 8

*I didn't date much before I met your dad. I had a couple of
boyfriends in college, but nothing serious. When I first started
working at the Grand Canyon, I got hit on a lot. I think it
was my hair. I've never really known how to act when a man
comes on to me. I don't see myself as a flirt or anything. My
friends have always given me a hard time because usually
even when a man is being flirtatious, it doesn't occur to me
until after the fact. The thought of being back in the dating
game at this point in my life terrifies me.*

Jake widened his eyes. "A cookout? That sounds great." He
flashed her a grin. "Are you sure your husband won't mind me
tagging along?"

A shadow crossed her face. "I'm not married. Anymore." She
absently clutched at her bare ring finger. "My husband died a
couple of years ago."

"I'm sorry for your loss." Jake had been trained to deal with
grief. It had been an almost daily part of his job. Until his own grief
had become too much to bear and he'd chosen to walk away.

She sighed and tugged on a dark red braid. "Thank you."

He wanted to ask more questions but knew better. Her hazel eyes were sad again. His earlier efforts to cheer her up had been dashed. "How old is your daughter?"

"She turned a year old a couple of months ago." Ainsley's lips turned upward. Not a complete smile, but at least it was close.

"I'll bet that was fun. I have a nephew who turned one earlier this year. He had an Elmo party." He grinned. "I don't remember having theme parties when I was a kid."

Ainsley's tentative grin turned into a full-blown smile. "We had a Dora the Explorer party for Faith. She loves all things Dora."

"My niece does, too. She's three. It's funny. I guess most single guys aren't well versed in children's TV shows, but that's what makes me the favorite uncle." He grinned. "Of course, my sister would say it's because I'm the only uncle. But still. I'll take points wherever I can get them." Had he been too obvious in letting her know he was single? He tried to gauge her reaction, but it wasn't clear.

"It's only going to get harder, let me tell you. My seventeen-year-old niece is staying with me for the summer. She used to think I was cool. But nowadays, I'm pretty sure she thinks I'm as lame as can be."

"No way. You're a park ranger, for crying out loud. I don't know if it gets any cooler than that."

Ainsley threw back her head and laughed.

He was proud of himself. From tears to laughter in one conversation.

"Seventeen-year-old girls do not think wearing green pants and sturdy brown shoes make one cool. In fact, last night she was going through my closet, shrieking in terror at some of the relics in there." She grinned then glanced down at her watch. "Oh my. I need to get going."

"Of course. Um. . ." He hesitated. "About the cookout. Where should I meet you?"

She looked startled. Panicked.

"Do you want me to just meet you there?" he asked. Of course she wouldn't feel comfortable telling him her address. They'd only just met.

"Tell you what. Take the blue shuttle line to the Backcountry Information Center. We'll meet you there around quarter to six. Dustin's house isn't too far from there."

"Sounds perfect." He rose. "Hope the rest of your day flies by and you get home to your little one soon."

Ainsley nodded. "Thanks."

Jake took off toward the Yavapai Observation Station. He wanted to look back, just to see if she was still there, but decided against it. He'd see her tomorrow night. The summer had just gotten much more interesting.

〄

Dustin Cooper stood in line at the park's only grocery store, his cart full of all the fixings for a cookout. He wished he'd had more time to prepare. A party like this one should've constituted a trip to the Sam's Club in Flagstaff. He sighed. But it was more than two hours one way, and he knew it would've been pushing it to get back to his house before the guests began to arrive.

Word of Ainsley's arrival had spread like wildfire through the tight-knit community. Lindsey used to call Ainsley and Brad the resident homecoming queen and king, and even though she meant it as an insult, Dustin had to admit she wasn't far off. Everyone was eager to welcome Ainsley back and meet her daughter and niece. So even though he'd only invited a handful of people, he expected many others to show up.

"Fancy meetin' you here," Lindsey purred from behind him. "You look like you could use some help."

"Twice in one week? I must be cursed." He couldn't help but return her smile. As much as Lindsey got under his skin, he'd never been able to ignore her.

"Blessed is more like it." She flashed brilliant white teeth. "And it happens to be your lucky day. I'm off work tonight, so I can offer my services as your sous-chef." Cooking happened to be her specialty. She worked as a chef at the El Tovar's upscale restaurant.

"Oh, I couldn't ask you to do that." Dustin began placing his groceries on the conveyer belt at the cash register. "I'm sure you can find more interesting things to do with a night off."

Lindsey reached into the cart for a soda, and her hand lightly grazed the length of his bare arm. She widened her eyes innocently. "Oops. Sorry."

He knew better. "Come on, Linds. We're not going down this road again."

"Let me help. Seriously." She continued putting his groceries onto the belt. "I heard you were throwing a party tonight. You're going to need someone to help you set up."

Dustin sighed. "The party is for Ainsley. Why would you want to help me throw a party for someone you've never been friends with?"

"Maybe I want to be like you and turn over a new leaf?" She raised perfectly arched eyebrows at him. "Did you ever think of that? You aren't the only person who can change."

He didn't feel like arguing. There was too much to do at home. Now that he didn't have a roommate, cleaning duties were all his. And he intended for his home to be spotless by the time the first guest arrived. Just one more way he was going to show Ainsley he wasn't the same sloppy guy he used to be. "Fine. Why don't you come over around five? You can help me get things set up outside."

Lindsey's blue eyes sparkled. "Yay!" She clapped twice. "I

knew you'd cave." She leaned close to his ear. "You're not as over me as you think you are," she whispered.

She was wrong. He was completely over her. But that didn't stop him from watching her walk away.

CHAPTER 9

My friends have been wonderful these past couple of years. After your dad's accident, it seems like a lot of people didn't know how to treat me. But Vickie and Kristy never made me feel like a freak because I became a widow before my thirtieth birthday. They were so supportive. They let me be sad when I need to be sad, and they remind me that Brad loved to hear me laugh. Even though the three of us are separated by many miles, a quick phone call makes it seem like they're right across the street.

A cookout in your honor?" Vickie Harris asked. "That sounds like a wonderful way to start the summer." Vickie was one of Ainsley's best friends from college. She worked as a park ranger at the National Mall in Washington DC. The two of them, along with another college friend Kristy Kennedy, had gotten their start with the National Park Service at Shiloh National Military Park in Tennessee, where Kristy still worked.

Ainsley laughed into the phone receiver. "I don't know about that. Being the center of attention isn't exactly my favorite thing."

"Don't worry. Now that you have a baby, your days of being the center of attention are over." Vickie giggled. "You'll just be more like her accessory."

"You know, you're exactly right. I hadn't thought about that. I could probably show up in a paper bag, and no one would notice. And that's fine by me." Ever since she'd become a mother, keeping up with the latest styles was a thing of the past. Not that Ainsley had ever been accused of being on the cutting edge of fashion.

"Why don't you have Julie help you find something to wear?" Vickie asked. Ever the fashionista, Vickie probably couldn't bear to think of her fashion-challenged friend attending a party in an out-of-date outfit.

"Right. Because a seventeen-year-old is going to have the same taste as me. Plus, I'm still carrying extra baby weight. Ugh. It's been more than a year."

Vickie groaned. "Okay, the last time I saw you, I thought you looked better than I've ever seen you look. So let's not start with the self-doubt."

"Maybe I will at least run a couple of outfits by Julie. She might not have the same taste as me, but it is nice to have someone here to make sure I don't go out in mismatched clothes."

Vickie laughed. "Sounds like a plan. Hey, have you talked to Kristy lately?"

"It's been a few days. Why? Is everything okay?" The last time the three of them had been together, it was for Kristy's wedding. Ainsley and Vickie were both bridesmaids at the very emotional ceremony.

"Everything is fine. You know me, though. I'm just trying to keep everyone on track. Now that we've settled on a date and location for our vacation, I want to make sure everyone books their tickets." Vickie had a reputation for being the planner in their circle of friends. Every trip, every event, she could always be counted on to make lists and print maps and make sure everyone was on the same page.

"Right." Ainsley sighed. Their summer vacation had been her idea. What could be better than three best friends renting a beach house together? But after seeing how hard these last couple of days away from Faith had been, she didn't know if she could stand to be away from her daughter for several days.

"Uh-oh. Why do I get the feeling you're having second thoughts?"

"Mainly because I am." Ainsley pulled a light blue sundress from the closet. It might pass Julie's inspection. "I don't know if I can stand to be away from Faith for that long."

Vickie was silent for a long moment. "I know I'm not the best one to give advice in this situation, since the only thing I'm responsible for at this point in my life is two ornery cats who probably celebrate when I leave them home alone." Although Vickie was single, she'd recently gotten engaged to Thatcher Torrey, a history professor. They planned to be married sometime over the holidays. "But didn't your sister tell you that time away from your child would make you a better parent?"

"I knew I shouldn't have told you that." Ainsley grinned. "Yes. I think Rachel said time away would reenergize me or something along those lines."

"And I think she's right." Vickie's voice grew somber. "You've been through a lot these past couple of years. And I know that being a single mother has to be tough. I think you deserve to reward yourself." Vickie paused. "I'll support whatever decision you make, though. You know that."

"I know. And I appreciate it. Mom said they would love to have Faith stay with them for a few days. And I know by midsummer, Julie will need a break." She sighed. "Okay. Count me in. Although, are you sure you can stand to be away from your betrothed for that long?"

Vickie laughed. "We'll manage. Although I'll tell you the truth: If I hadn't waited my whole life to be a bride, we'd just run to city hall tomorrow and tie the knot."

"And miss wearing your princess dress? I don't think so." Ainsley joined in her laughter.

"I know, I know. I could still wear it for pictures though, right?" Vickie asked hopefully.

Ainsley fished a pair of brown sandals from a box. "Like you said to me, I'll support whatever decision you make. But I know you, and I know how much you want a wedding with all the bells and whistles." Vickie had always been a hopeless romantic and had spent years dreaming of a fairy-tale wedding.

Vickie heaved a great sigh. "I knew I should've mentioned it to Kristy first. She's still so caught up in newly wedded bliss, she'd probably encourage a city-hall wedding." Kristy had married Ace Kennedy in October, and according to her most recent e-mail message, she found it hard to believe she'd been able to live without him for so long.

"I'm thinking she'll be on the same page as me about it. But if you want to give it a shot, go ahead." Ainsley caught sight of the clock beside her bed. "Oh wow. I'm running so late. And I haven't even started getting Faith ready. Jake is going to think I forgot about meeting him."

"Jake? Who is Jake?" Vickie demanded.

"He's this guy I met yesterday. A hiking guide. It's a long story. He doesn't know where Dustin lives, so I said we'd meet him and walk over together."

"The cookout is at Dustin's? Why have we been talking about mundane things like clothes and vacations when you could have been telling me what is really going on there?" Vickie wailed. "Were you in touch with Dustin while you were in Flagstaff?"

"Nope. He showed up at my door the other day with flowers and a welcome-back gift." Ainsley couldn't help herself. She knew this news would send Vickie spinning out of control. She also knew that as soon as they hung up, Vickie would speed-dial Kristy to see if she knew any details. After almost two years of living in her parents' basement and listening to her friends' play-by-play of their lives, it gave Ainsley a certain amount of satisfaction to have news of her own. Even though the news meant nothing, it still made her feel like an interesting person again.

"Flowers and a gift?" Vickie parroted. "I am so mad at you."

Ainsley laughed. "And now, I really have to go. I love you," she said sweetly.

"You, too. But you are *so* not off the hook."

"I know. Tell Kristy I said hello."

"Smarty pants." Vickie laughed. "You know me too well. I'll tell her."

◐◑

"Are you sure I look okay?" Julie asked as they walked toward the Backcountry Information Center. "Will I be the only person there who doesn't work here?"

Ainsley smiled at her niece. "You look like a supermodel." It was true. Julie's khaki shorts showed off her long, tanned legs, and the emerald green tank top just matched her eyes. "And there should be some people your age at the party. Lots of families live here, so I'm guessing there'll be people of all ages."

Julie took a deep breath. "You know that feeling when you're the new kid at a new school? That's kind of how I feel."

Ainsley nodded. "I know that feeling, and believe it or not, I'm right there with you." She sighed. "I haven't seen any of my old coworkers since Brad's funeral." The panicky feeling in her stomach hadn't eased up since they'd left the house. "If it's any consolation, Jake won't know anyone, either."

Julie raised an eyebrow. "Yeah. That makes me feel better."

Ainsley laughed. "I'm just saying."

Faith banged on the stroller tray. "Wawk," she said.

Julie smiled. "I must be getting better at Faith-speak, because I think she wants to walk."

"I think you're right." Ainsley carefully set Faith down on the ground. Faith's yellow sundress with a matching bow had been a gift from Vickie. "You have to hold Julie's hand." Faith squealed with delight as she stomped her feet on the pavement.

Ainsley pushed the empty stroller behind her niece and daughter for the short walk to the shuttle stop.

Jake stood in front of the stop, a nervous expression on his handsome face. "There you are. I was starting to think I'd imagined the invitation." He laughed.

Ainsley introduced him to Julie, then Faith.

"Nice to meet you," he said to Julie. "And Faith, too."

"Thanks." Ainsley scooped Faith up in her arms. "Let Mommy carry you the rest of the way," she said to her daughter. "Julie, do you mind pushing the stroller?"

"I can get it," Jake said, taking hold of the stroller. "I really appreciate you letting me tag along."

"Oh, it isn't a problem. These things are always really casual. People will probably come and go all night." Ainsley motioned to a street on their right, lined with houses. "This way."

As Jake and Julie made small talk, Ainsley clutched Faith a little tighter. The last time she'd seen everyone from work, her whole world had just exploded. And now, close to two years later, the last thing she wanted was their pity. She took a deep breath as they neared Dustin's house. It was showtime.

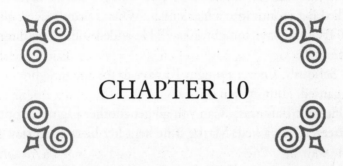

CHAPTER 10

When Dustin came to my door to tell me about your dad's accident, I slapped him. I told him he was making it up and asked him why he would do something so cruel. But he just stood there, tears streaming down his face. It was the only time I ever saw him cry in all the years we'd known each other. That was how I knew it was true. Seeing his reaction. I guess, in some ways, that might be part of the reason I didn't take his calls or answer his e-mails these past months. Because I knew that besides me, Dustin was the other person most affected. And honestly, I couldn't deal with anyone else's grief. I could barely deal with my own.

Dustin expertly flipped a burger onto the platter. Each time someone new arrived, his body tensed. He wanted Ainsley to have a good time tonight and to see just how much everyone at the park had missed her. Especially him.

"Hey, you." Lindsey trotted over, camera in hand. "Smile." She giggled.

He held up a hamburger and grinned as she snapped a picture. "Did someone designate you the photographer?"

She shrugged. "I just thought it would be nice."

Dustin grimaced.

"What?" she asked, her blue eyes wide. "I can be nice." She quirked her mouth into a half smile. "When I want to."

"Try to behave tonight, okay?" He added some new burgers to the grill.

"Seriously. I never thought I'd have to tell *you* to lighten up." She paused. "But lighten up."

He rolled his eyes. "Can you go get another bag of ice out of the freezer?" he asked. Maybe if he kept her busy, she'd stay out of the way.

"Consider it done." With a toss of her blond locks, she was gone.

Twenty minutes later, his yard was full of laughing people. And still there was no sign of Ainsley.

"Where's our guest of honor?" Edie asked, plopping a burger on her plate. "Thanks for doing this, by the way."

He shrugged. "You're welcome. I thought it would be a nice way to welcome her back."

"I know these past several months haven't been easy for you." Edie peered at him over her wire-rimmed glasses.

Before he could formulate a response, Lindsey stepped to his side. "Well, well. Look who finally decided to show up."

Dustin jerked his head toward the fence gate. He spotted Ainsley's red hair for a moment, just as a sea of people descended on her. He could hear the crowd oohing and ahhing over what he could only guess was Faith.

Finally, she made her way over to where he stood, a stream of people still trailing behind her. "Hi," she said, smiling broadly. "Dustin, I'd like you to meet Faith." The little girl on Ainsley's hip regarded him with eyes he recognized. "Wow. In so many ways she looks like you, but her eyes. . ."

"They're all Brad," Ainsley said softly.

Dustin grinned at Faith. "Hi there, little one. Welcome to the Grand Canyon."

Edie stepped in. "I'm dying to get my hands on her." She held out her hands to Faith. "Will you come see your Aunt Edie?" she cooed.

Faith considered it for a minute. Finally, she smiled and went to Edie's open arms with only a little hesitation.

"She gets passed around at church a lot," explained Ainsley. "So she's pretty good with strangers."

"Well, we won't be strangers for long." Edie bounced the little girl around. "Can I go show her off?"

Ainsley nodded. "Sure. Just don't let her down on the ground." She turned her attention back to Dustin. "You remember my niece, Julie."

He nodded. "Hi, Julie. Glad you could make it. What do you think of the park so far?"

Julie shrugged. "Honestly, I haven't had time to explore yet."

Dustin drew his brows together. Ainsley loved showing people around the canyon. He eyed his old friend. "You haven't given her the grand tour yet?"

"We've been busy," she explained. A strand of red hair had escaped her ponytail, and she tucked it behind her ear.

He nodded. "Well, I hope you get to see the place soon. I hate to think of you living at the most beautiful place in the world and only seeing the residential area." He smiled at Julie and motioned toward the table spread with food. "Help yourself to some food."

Julie grinned. "Thanks. I'm starving."

A tall, dark-haired guy lingered near Ainsley. Dustin didn't recognize him, but he could be a new seasonal ranger. "I'm Dustin." He held out a hand in the guy's direction.

Ainsley looked startled. "Oh. This is Jake McGuire."

Jake grasped Dustin's hand and gave it a firm shake. "Nice to meet you, man."

63

Dustin furrowed his brow. Had they come here together? Before he could inquire, Jake continued.

"I ran into Ainsley yesterday. She invited me to come crash the party. Hope that's okay."

Dustin glanced at Ainsley and noticed a blush creeping up her face. "Sure. The more, the merrier."

"Jake is working this summer as a hiking guide. He's staying at Trailer Village right now," Ainsley said, as if that explained everything.

Dustin nodded. "Glad to have you." He felt a hand grasp his forearm. Lindsey. He'd almost forgotten she was standing there until just now.

"We're so glad to have you back," Lindsey said to Ainsley, her hand firmly on Dustin's arm. "The park just hasn't been the same without you," she said sweetly.

Ainsley's gaze lingered on Lindsey's grasp. Finally, she met Dustin's eyes. "Thanks. It's nice to be back among friends."

"And Jake, I'm Lindsey." She gave him a sparkling smile.

"Good to meet you." Jake returned her greeting. "I think I'll go fill a plate," he said. He placed a hand on the small of Ainsley's back. "Would you like me to get you a burger?"

Ainsley turned toward him. "That would be great. Thanks," she said.

"And I'll just leave you two to talk," Lindsey piped up. "I need to go check on the ice, anyway." She gave Dustin's arm one last squeeze before she walked off.

An awkward silence filled the space between them.

"So. I see things haven't changed much since I've been gone," Ainsley motioned her head toward Lindsey's retreating figure.

Dustin shook his head. "It isn't what you think. She's actually just helping out."

Ainsley nodded slowly. "I'm sure she's a big help."

"What's with this Jake guy? Is he. . ." His voice trailed off.

Inquiring about Jake would be overstepping his boundaries. They weren't as close as they used to be. He had to keep reminding himself of that fact. "Is he from around here?" he finally asked.

She shook her head. "He's from Phoenix. He's here for the summer, and I think he plans to relocate if he decides he likes it."

"I see." Dustin couldn't help but notice the subtle changes in her appearance. She wasn't as skinny as she used to be, and he had to admit, the extra curves suited her. "Motherhood looks good on you," he said finally.

She blushed. "Thanks."

"And Faith is. . .well, she's incredible. I'd love to spend some time with her." He took a step closer to Ainsley. "I miss him, too, you know," he said softly. "He was my best friend."

Her eyes locked on his. "Dustin—"

"Did someone order a burger?" Jake held out a plate to Ainsley. "I wasn't sure what you wanted on it, so I put everything on the side."

She gave him a feeble smile. "Thanks," she said, taking the plate. "It looks delicious."

Dustin cleared his throat. "I should go check to see if we need more burgers." He hurried off, an unsettled feeling in the pit of his stomach.

๑୬๑

Julie fished around in the cooler for a Dr Pepper. Surely there was one in there somewhere. Finally, she dug one out from the very bottom.

"At least if it's way down there, you know it's good and cold," a deep voice said from behind her.

She looked up, grinning. A guy about her age was reclining against a table, watching her. "I'm Colt." He grinned and walked over to where she stood.

"I'm Julie." She popped the top on the Dr Pepper and took a

sip. "And you're right. It's ice cold." She smiled.

"So, what's your story?" he asked. "I haven't seen you around. Are you working as a seasonal?"

She furrowed her brow. "No. I'm staying with my aunt for the summer. She's a ranger." She shrugged. "I'm babysitting my cousin."

"Sounds fun." The yellow Hollister T-shirt he wore emphasized his tanned skin. Well-worn jeans and leather flip-flops completed his look.

Julie shot him a look. "It is fun."

Colt laughed. "Actually, I meant it." He took a sip of Coke. "I love kids. I have four younger siblings." He leaned closer to her, his dark eyes gleaming. "I'm working for the summer in the maintenance department. It's hard work. So babysitting actually sounds like a pretty good deal to me." He chuckled.

She felt herself relaxing. "I see. Does your family live here?"

"Yep. My dad is a law enforcement ranger, and Mom teaches at the elementary school." He reached down and pulled a Coke from the cooler. "We actually live just down the street from here."

"So you go to school here, then?"

"I just graduated. I'm headed to college in the fall, and I can't wait." He smiled. "I'll take a dorm room any day over sharing a room with my younger brother."

She laughed. "I'm an only child, so I'm actually not looking too forward to the dorm. I just graduated, too." Even though Julie and Claire planned to share a room, it would be an adjustment to have to share space. Julie hoped it didn't strain their friendship.

"Cool. So where are you planning to attend?" He raked his fingers through his coal black hair.

"Northern Arizona University. In Flagstaff." She couldn't help but notice how cute he was. Her friends back home would be so jealous.

"Awesome," he exclaimed, his eyes widening. "That's where I'm going, too."

"Seriously?" Julie smiled at his obvious excitement.

Colt nodded. "Most of my friends are going to Arizona State. I was beginning to think I was going to be the only person at NAU." He nudged her. "But now I'll know somebody."

Julie thought of Heath for a brief second then pushed him from her mind. There was no harm in making friends. Even if the prospective friend happened to be gorgeous. "Do you know what you're going to major in?"

He shook his head. "No idea." He grinned. "Do you want to sit down? I see an empty table." He motioned his head toward a card table in the corner of the yard.

"Sure." She felt his hand on her back as he directed her to the table and marveled at the shiver of excitement that ran through her at his touch.

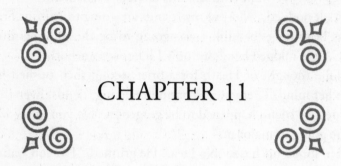

CHAPTER 11

One of the things I love the most about living at the Grand Canyon is the people. Around two thousand people live on park grounds—employees from the park service and the organization that runs the concessions, as well as their families. Your dad and I used to throw these fantastic cookouts for our group of friends. We had a volleyball net up in our backyard, and after dinner, we'd all play. Those games got pretty rowdy. And your dad was always the best athlete out there. I loved to watch him play.

Jake knew he'd never keep so many names straight. It seemed like over the past hour he'd met every single person who could possibly work at the park. And they were all so welcoming. He appreciated the sense of community here. It was a sharp contrast to the city.

"Jake, you'll have to stop by sometime for dinner," Edie said. "My youngest son is an avid hiker, so I'm sure you guys can find something to talk about." She looked wistful. "He's my last one at home. I don't know what I'm going to do when he goes to college next year."

He grinned at the older lady. "If you're anything like my mother, I'd guess you'll redecorate."

She laughed. "That sounds like a good plan."

Ainsley walked by just then, carrying Faith. The little girl was nestled against her mother's chest. "Well, I think we're about partied out." She smoothed Faith's wispy reddish hair. "It's time to put my girl to bed."

"It's wonderful to see you outside of work," Edie said. "I was just telling Jake that he needs to come over for dinner soon. That goes for you, too." She reached out and stroked Faith's smooth cheek. "And Faith and Julie."

Ainsley grinned. "Thanks." She scanned the crowd. "Speaking of Julie, I need to go try and round her up. Then we can find Dustin and thank him for playing host."

"I can look for Julie," Jake offered. "I mean, if you want me to."

She gave him a grateful smile. "Thanks. That would be great." She hurried off toward Dustin, who lingered near the grill. Jake watched the exchange between them and wondered about their history.

"He used to be her best friend," Edie said after a moment.

Jake cringed. Had he been that obvious?

"Dustin and Ainsley were inseparable her first couple of years here. He's actually the one who introduced her to her husband, Brad. He and Brad grew up together—I think they'd been friends since they were in Boy Scouts." She laughed. "Total opposites, though. After Brad moved here, he and Dustin lived together. I used to get such a kick out of listening to them. They could've been the Odd Couple."

"Was Brad a ranger, too?" Jake asked, his eyes still on Ainsley and Dustin.

She shook her head. "Firefighter. He was killed on the job." Her gaze followed his to where Ainsley and Dustin stood. "It was a hard adjustment for Dustin, his two closest friends exiting his life at the same time."

Jake was quiet.

"And now she's back," Edie said, more to herself than to him. She seemed lost in thought.

Jake cleared his throat. "It was wonderful to meet you, Edie," he said. "I'm sure I'll see you again soon."

"You, too, Jake. I hope you enjoy it here." She clasped his hand.

He hurried off, scanning the crowd for Julie. He finally spotted her sitting at a table, deep in conversation with a dark-haired guy. "Julie," he said uncertainly. They looked like they were having such a good time, he hated to interrupt.

She looked up in surprise. "What's up?"

"Ainsley sent me over. She said it was time for Faith to go to bed." At the crestfallen look on her friend's face, Jake couldn't hide his grin. This guy was smitten. He held a hand out to the guy. "I'm Jake McGuire."

The teenager jumped up from his seat and clasped Jake's hand. "Colt Keller." His grip was strong.

Jake glanced at Julie. "Listen, do you want me to just tell Ainsley that you'll be home later?" He glanced at his watch. "It's only eight."

She and Colt exchanged glances.

"I could walk you home," Colt offered. He looked at Jake. "I mean, if that's okay."

Jake shifted his weight. He had no authority over Julie. Although, if she stayed with Colt, it might give him some time alone with Ainsley. "You should probably ask your aunt," he said to Julie.

She grinned. "It will be fine. I'm nearly eighteen, after all." She held up her cell phone. "I have my phone if she needs me. Will you just tell her I'll be home by ten?"

Jake nodded. "Will do." He nodded at Colt. "Nice to meet you, Colt."

He headed toward Ainsley and Dustin.

"Thanks for having me," he said to Dustin. "I met a lot of great people."

Dustin gave him a once-over. "Good." He turned his attention back to Ainsley. "Let's get together soon, okay?"

Ainsley nodded. "Tell Lindsey it was nice to see her."

A shadow crossed Dustin's face. "I told you. . ." He glanced at Jake and stopped. "Sure."

Dustin excused himself and left them alone.

"Julie is hanging out with a new friend. Some kid named Colt. Said she'd be home by ten."

Ainsley looked confused for a second. "Colt Keller?" she asked finally.

Jake nodded. "That's right. Is that okay? I told her she should probably ask you."

Ainsley smiled. "It's fine. He's a good kid. I've known him since he was a little boy." She glanced up at Jake. "I should really get going. You're welcome to stay here, though. Don't feel like you have to leave on account of me."

He laughed. "Are you kidding? I feel like I've barely gotten to talk to you all night."

They made their way over to the gate, where the stroller sat. Ainsley carefully put Faith into the stroller and strapped her in. She barely stirred.

Jake held the gate open for her, and they set off down the street. "I'd be glad to walk you home," Jake said. "If you're okay with it." He glanced over at her. "I mean, I know we just met, and I'm sure you probably like to wait until you've been around someone a few times before letting them know where you live."

She laughed. "Is that the standard rule?"

"I just don't want you to feel like I'm forcing you to let me go to your house or anything." He grinned. "Maybe I was a cop for too long, because I expect everyone to be suspicious of people they've just met."

Ainsley was quiet for a moment. "First of all, I've been living in my parents' basement for the better part of two years. I haven't been out meeting people, and therefore haven't been in danger of them finding out where I lived." She shook her head. "But given the fact that you've just met all of my neighbors, and since there are a lot of people out tonight, I think it will be fine for you to walk us home." She motioned at the sleeping child. "Besides, I really need to get her into bed."

"Edie told me about your husband's accident. I'm sorry."

She sighed. "Thanks. It's been a difficult time." She gave him a determined look. "But I'm glad to be back."

"When you say 'back' you don't just mean back to the canyon, do you?" he asked softly.

She shook her head. "It's almost like I've been living someone else's life these past couple of years. I'm starting to feel a bit more like me." She shrugged. "I'm not over it by any means. But I had fun tonight. There was a time not that long ago that I didn't know if I'd feel happy again."

Jake glanced over at her. "Baby steps, right?"

"Exactly. At first, it was a victory if I just got out of bed in the morning." She laughed. "I think that's why God gave me a child. Because after she was born, I had to face the day. When someone else is depending on you, you don't have a choice."

"Well, I know that you don't know me very well. So this won't mean much." He smiled. "But I think you're doing a great job."

"Thanks." She sighed. "But enough about me." She shot him a sideways glance. "How did you go from cop to hiking guide? That seems like quite a transition."

Jake tensed. He didn't want to tell her the truth. It made him seem weak. And if there was one thing he wanted to prove to her, it was that he could take care of any situation.

CHAPTER 12

One of the things that's been the hardest for me since your dad's accident is having to be responsible for everything myself. I guess independence was never as exciting for me as it was for Vickie or Kristy. They've both told me how important it was for them to accomplish things on their own—Kristy used to travel alone and Vickie bought a home for herself. I don't think I have the same independent streak because I absolutely loved making decisions with Brad. We would talk things out and reach a conclusion together, whether it was about new furniture or which movie to see. I miss that.

Ainsley watched Jake from the corner of her eye. Emotions played across his chiseled face.

"Technically, I'm still a cop." He frowned. "I'm just on a leave of absence right now."

They slowed down to let a truck pass.

"For how long?" Ainsley asked.

He met her gaze. "Indefinitely. I hadn't taken a real vacation in a couple of years. My boss thought I needed some time to recharge." He raked his fingers through his hair. "But honestly, I don't know if I'll ever go back."

"I have to say, you've picked a great place to recharge." She hoped to lighten his mood. "A lot of people think there's a peace here like nowhere else." Ainsley placed herself in that number. Something almost magical about the canyon made her feel relaxed.

Jake nodded. "That's what I'm hoping. I used to come here every year with my family, and we had such great times. I guess I was hoping to recapture some of those good feelings."

Ainsley understood perfectly.

He continued. "See, I was known in my department for being a good negotiator. I have a way of talking to people, making them feel at ease." He swallowed. "My partner, Dwight, and I went out on a domestic call. The neighbors phoned in a complaint that they could hear this guy yelling, saying all kinds of crazy stuff. It wasn't the first time we'd been called to this particular house."

Ainsley reached over and placed a hand on his arm. She could see how difficult telling the story was for him. At her touch, he looked up in surprise, although she was probably more surprised at her forwardness than he. "You don't have to talk about it if you don't want to," she said softly.

He smiled. "It's probably about time I tell someone." He continued, "Anyway, by the time we got there, this kid, Tommy— he was barely twenty—had pulled a gun on his girlfriend." Jake shook his head.

"That's awful," Ainsley whispered, thinking of Julie and her relationship with Heath.

"It gets worse," Jake said grimly. "I tried to be the hero. Thought I could talk the guy down." He grimaced. "It had worked the last time. I tried to reason with him, but he was clearly on something."

Ainsley gripped the stroller tightly, not sure she wanted to hear what came next.

"The girl, Gina, was a mess. Can't blame her. She was hysterical, begging me to help her." He shook his head. "Still, I tried reasoning with him. Dwight thought I was being overly cautious. He said we should go after Tommy and let the chips fall where they may. But I wanted a peaceful resolution."

"Of course you did."

"In a split second, Tommy shot her. Dwight shot him before he could do any more damage."

Ainsley let out the breath she'd been holding. "That's awful."

Jake shuddered. "Even worse, once we got inside, we realized they had a baby. A little boy. Almost a year old."

Ainsley glanced down at her sleeping daughter. What a horrible story. "But it wasn't your fault."

"Yes, it was. I still can't sleep without seeing Gina's eyes, begging me to save her. I let her down. And now, that little boy is growing up without either of his parents."

Ainsley stopped as they reached her driveway. "But you did what you thought was the right thing." She clutched his sleeve. "That's all you can ever do."

He managed a weak smile. "Now I've totally brought you down from what had been a great night."

She shook her head. "I'm glad you told me. If there's one thing I've learned, it's that keeping things bottled up only makes them eat away at you even more." She motioned her head toward the house. "Here we are."

"Thanks so much for inviting me tonight," he said as she fished her keys from the diaper bag. "I'll just make sure you get inside; then I'll be on my way."

"Um, actually. . .could you do me a favor?"

"Of course."

"Walking into an empty house kind of freaks me out. Can

you come inside for a second and just check it out?" She was embarrassed at her request but knew she'd be a nervous wreck otherwise. It had been years since she'd lived alone.

"I'd be glad to." Jake smiled. "Here, let me get the stroller." He carefully lifted the stroller with Faith inside onto the porch.

Ainsley glanced at her daughter. "Wow. She didn't even wake up." She grinned at him. "Nicely done."

He laughed. "My sister always puts me on stroller duty."

Once they were inside, Jake glanced around the living room. "Do you mind if I just do a quick walk-through?"

"Please," she said as she turned her attention to Faith. "Hey, baby girl," she said softly as Faith's eyes fluttered open. She picked Faith up and relished the feeling of her daughter burrowing closer into her arms.

"It's all clear," Jake whispered from the hallway.

She smiled broadly. "Thanks," she said softly.

"I'll let you get her to bed." He crossed the small living room but stopped. "Can I maybe get your phone number?" He grinned, flashing his dimple. "I'd love to have another chance to talk to you. And I promise not to completely depress you next time."

◈

Ainsley collapsed onto the front porch swing. What a night. She glanced down at the baby monitor in her hand to make sure it was turned up. It was. She held it to her ear and made out the faint sound of Faith's breathing. She couldn't help but smile. Her daughter had done so well tonight. Only a couple of cranky moments, both quickly fixed with food and a diaper change.

A lone figure hurried up the driveway, and for a moment Ainsley froze. As the figure got closer to the porch, she recognized Julie.

"Hey," she said softly. "I'm in the porch swing."

Julie climbed the steps onto the porch. "It's a good thing you said something," she said, smiling. "Otherwise you'd have scared me to death." Julie sank down beside her aunt. "What are you doing out here in the dark?"

Ainsley leaned her head back against the swing. "Thinking." She held up the monitor. "But don't worry. I can hear everything going on in the house."

Julie smiled. "Tonight was fun."

"It sure was." Ainsley looked over at her niece. "I figured Colt would walk you home."

Julie shrugged. "He wanted to, but I told him I'd be fine." She gave Ainsley a tiny smile. "Sometimes it's nice to be alone, you know? I guess I have a lot on my mind."

Ainsley nodded. She needed to remember that Julie was an only child. She was used to having her own space.

They sat in silence for a moment.

"Do you think people can change?" Julie finally asked. "I mean, really change. Not just say they have."

"Are you going to think it's a cop-out if I say it depends?"

Julie grinned. "Not if you explain that."

"Okay. I think people can change, but only if they want to." Ainsley put her arm around her niece. "I think sometimes people think they can change someone. A lot of women in particular that I've known have dated guys and thought they would be able to change things about them. But from what I've seen, that's only possible if he actually wants to change. And it goes both ways."

"Mmm." Julie leaned her head against the swing. "That's kind of what I thought." She was quiet for a moment.

"I don't want to pry, but is everything okay?"

Julie shrugged. "It's fine." She glanced over at her aunt. "I know Mama has probably told you a lot of bad stuff about Heath."

There was no point in pretending otherwise. "She's told me a little."

"He isn't all bad. He has a temper problem, but it's gotten better."

Ainsley thought about Jake's story. That was scary stuff. "You shouldn't have to be scared of someone who loves you," she said softly.

Julie wrinkled her nose. "I'm not scared of him. It makes me mad when he acts like that. But I don't think he'd ever really hurt me or anything." She heaved a great sigh. "But I talked to him earlier, and all he wanted to talk about was how he was going to spend the summer partying with his friends."

"And you don't like that?"

"No. I just wish he had more ambition than that. He's just out for a good time."

So there was trouble in paradise. Rachel would be thrilled. "Are you at least glad you're here? I know finding out you were spending the summer in the middle of nowhere wasn't exactly welcome news."

Julie's mouth quirked into a smile. "I'm dealing with it better. I love hanging out with you and Faith." She was quiet for a minute. "And it's cool that I met Colt. He's going to be at NAU this fall. So it will be fun to already have a friend."

Ainsley wondered if Colt had anything to do with her niece's sudden change of heart about Heath. Although, at seventeen, feelings could change on a dime. One good conversation or sweet text message from Heath, and he'd likely be back in Julie's good graces. "I've known him since he was a little boy."

Julie giggled. "He told me. His dad works with Dustin."

At the mention of Dustin's name, Ainsley couldn't help but feel a pang of regret. She'd hardly had the chance to talk to him at all tonight. There had been so many people around, and it seemed like each time she'd been free, Lindsey had been by his side.

"Colt's a good guy."

"He seemed nice. He asked me if I wanted to hang out again sometime soon." With that news, Julie stood. "I should go to bed. I'm beat." She paused. "But your friends were nice. Dustin. . .and

Jake." She raised an eyebrow but didn't say anything.

Her niece might be a little too perceptive. "I'm glad you had fun."

Julie went inside, and Ainsley was alone again, the darkness surrounding her. Had she been out of line, giving Jake her number? It seemed so odd. But it would be nice to have a friend.

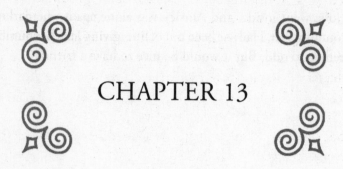

CHAPTER 13

Right after your dad and I met, we double-dated with Dustin and this girl named Lindsey. She and I couldn't have been more opposite. One time, I joked with Dustin that he'd managed to find the anti-me. He didn't think it was very funny. Your dad told me once that Lindsey used to hit on him whenever she got the chance. I never had the heart to tell Dustin in case he really liked her, but sometimes I wonder if I should have. The fact that your dad was always honest with me, no matter what, was one of the things I loved the most about him.

Dustin tried to shake off his frustration with the way things had gone at the cookout. He felt helpless watching Ainsley leave with Jake. It should have been him walking her home, laughing and talking and reconnecting. But instead, he'd been left to clean up behind his guests.

"Everything is finished outside," Lindsey said. "All clean. Is there anything else I can do?"

"No." He raked his hands through his hair. "Thanks for all of your help. It means a lot."

She grinned. "See? I am good for something." She held up a full trash bag.

He took the bag from her and tied it up. "I guess you are." He walked her to the door. Maybe he'd been too hard on her.

Lindsey paused in the doorway. She regarded him with serious blue eyes. "I'm sorry it worked out this way," she said. "If it's any consolation, I think you're much cuter than that Jake guy." She winked. "Although I can't say I'm sad. Just surprised."

"Surprised? Why?" he met her gaze.

She shrugged. "I guess I figured Ainsley would be really happy to see you, that's all."

He winced.

"I mean not that she wasn't happy to see you, it's just. . ." She blinked innocently.

Dustin shook his head. He'd been right on the money about Lindsey. She'd always been at her best when she was causing trouble. "She's been through a lot, Linds. She just needs some time."

Lindsey smirked. "Whatever gets you through the night." She pulled him to her in a tight hug. "Call me," she whispered. And with that she was gone, leaving behind the faintest trace of her perfume.

Dustin sank onto his couch. A picture on his end table caught his eye. He picked it up and looked at the image of him and Ainsley the day they'd gone skydiving. Those were happy days. He knew his friendship must still mean something to her. He'd just have to be patient and do everything he could to let her know how much he cared about her.

◎◎

Jake thanked the group of hikers for entrusting him to be their guide. He glanced at his watch. "There's still plenty of daylight left. I encourage you to find a good spot and watch the sunset."

"Where do you suggest we go?" an older gentleman asked. He pulled his wife to him. "This is our first time to visit the canyon. The hike was fantastic, but now we'd like to find a romantic spot to watch the sunset."

Jake thought for a moment. Although he didn't spend much time thinking about romantic spots, it had crossed his mind that Hopi Point would be a pretty spectacular place to visit with Ainsley. "You might try Hopi Point. You can walk along the rim or catch a shuttle." He grinned at the couple. "Enjoy."

They hurried off, leaving Jake alone. He tried to contain his excitement. He'd gotten up the nerve and called Ainsley last night, and she'd agreed to have dinner with him. He had just enough time to go to his camper and get ready for their date. If you could call it a date. He wasn't totally sure what she thought, but he knew what he wanted it to be.

An hour later, he stood nervously outside of her house. He rapped lightly on the door and waited.

The door swung open. Julie stood in the doorway. "Hey, Jake," she said. "Come in. She's almost ready. We had a little mishap here, so she's running a little late."

Jake took a seat on the couch. "Is everything okay?"

Julie laughed. "Oh, everything is fine. Somehow, Faith got her hands on some lipstick. Let's just say that she's going to be quite the little makeup artist someday."

"I hope there are pictures," Jake said, chuckling.

Julie held up her phone. "I've got enough evidence to totally embarrass her someday if need be."

He glanced around the living room. The boxes that had been stacked in the corner Friday night were gone. The only out-of-place item left in the room was a red backpack. "You guys have been busy, haven't you?"

Julie nodded. "It's starting to come together. I think there are only a few boxes left before it will be done."

"Sorry to keep you waiting." Ainsley rushed into the room, her face flushed. "It's just been one of those days."

Jake smiled. Even frazzled and at the end of a busy day, she still managed to look beautiful. She wore only a hint of makeup, and her dark red hair was pulled back into a low ponytail. He appreciated her low maintenance vibe. It was a refreshing change from some of the women he'd known back in Phoenix. "At least you had the day off, right?"

Ainsley nodded. "And thanks to Julie here, we've gotten nearly everything unpacked." She patted her niece on the back. "I'm pretty sure I owe you big-time for today. I know it would have been much more fun to explore the park than to help me get organized."

Julie beamed at the praise. "I didn't mind. It will make my life easier when I'm babysitting if everything is in its place. Besides, I'll have plenty of time to explore, later."

Jake thought he caught the slightest twinge of frustration in her voice but couldn't be sure. "Well, are you ready?" he asked. They were going to the Bright Angel, which was no more than five minutes away, but it was prime dinnertime, and there'd likely be a wait. After many meals alone, he looked forward to having company.

Ainsley nodded. "Yes, I'm starving." She glanced at Julie. "Faith is finally asleep, and hopefully she'll stay that way. If you need me, call."

"Will do." Julie collapsed onto the sofa and flipped on the television.

Jake held the door open for Ainsley. "After you."

She flashed him a smile. "Thanks."

He couldn't help but appreciate the way her dark jeans and green sleeveless top clung to her body in just the right places.

They walked in silence for what seemed like an eternity. Jake racked his brain for a good conversation starter. It had been so long since he'd gotten to know someone new, he was embarrassed at his rusty skills.

"So, I hear there was a lipstick incident," he said finally. The easy back-and-forth they'd had the other night after the cookout seemed to be missing.

She nodded. "Faith pulled it out of Julie's purse. Ever since she started walking, she's into everything." Talking about her daughter visibly relaxed her.

"Did you enjoy your days off?" Ainsley had a four on, three off schedule. She'd explained to him that the schedule was to accommodate trips to a larger town for supplies and appointments.

"I did. We should've gone to Flagstaff for a grocery run and to visit the family, but instead, we worked around the house." They stopped at the shuttle stop. "After church yesterday, we had lunch with Edie and a few of her neighbors."

He grinned. "I'll bet Julie's new friend Colt was there."

Ainsley laughed. "He was, along with a couple of his siblings. I'm just glad Julie has made some friends. I know this transition has been difficult for her." She explained the situation with Julie and her boyfriend.

Jake wrinkled his brow. "Hopefully this summer will be good for her, then. Once she's in college, she probably won't think twice about Heath."

"That's what we're hoping. Ever since you told me that story the other night, I've been worried." She shook her head. "I just hope Julie will come to her senses soon."

Great. He didn't want to cause this woman any more grief than she already felt. "I'm sorry. I should've kept that story to myself."

Ainsley grabbed his sleeve. "No. I'm glad you shared it." She gave him a tiny smile.

They caught the shuttle and rode in companionable silence. "Here's our stop," Jake said, once the shuttle reached the Bright

Angel Lodge. The main lodge housed an information desk, along with a museum, restaurant, bar, and gift shop. Nearby were the other Bright Angel buildings that contained guest rooms.

Jake held the door to the rustic building open for her and inhaled as she passed by him. The faintest scent of raspberry reached his nose, and he smiled. Just knowing he got to spend the next few hours with her was enough to make him happy.

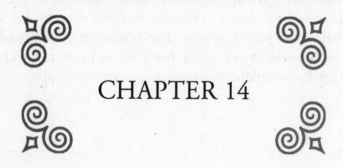

CHAPTER 14

There are days when I imagine that I dreamed the last two years. Especially now that I'm back at the canyon, it's like I can feel Brad's presence. I expect him to walk through the door just like he used to. But I know that isn't going to happen.

Jake pulled the chair out for Ainsley, and she was touched by his thoughtfulness. She'd only been around him a few times, but each time, he seemed to go out of his way to take care of her and make her feel special.

"Thanks," she said, smiling. She glanced around the full restaurant. She recognized a couple of families, but the establishment was mostly full of tourists.

Jake sat down across from her. "Are you ready to go back to work tomorrow?"

"Honestly, I'm a little nervous." She plucked a sugar packet from the holder and turned it over and over in her hands. "I'm scheduled for ranger programs later this week." She shook her head. "Public speaking always takes a little while to get used to." There was more to her nerves than that, but she wasn't sure if she wanted to tell him.

"Oh, I'm sure it will go fine." He smiled kindly. "As soon as you start talking and answering questions, it will all come rushing back."

She swallowed. "It's more than just the public speaking that has me worried."

Jake drew his brows together. "What's wrong?"

"This is going to sound crazy." She met his gaze. "Believe me, I know. But I keep thinking about the rim of the canyon."

"The rim?"

She nodded. "Up until now, I've managed to stay away from the rim since I've been back. But the day I moved in, I was suddenly aware of the rim and the deep drop-off into the canyon." She shook her head. "I've never been afraid of heights. Until now." She dropped her eyes. It was almost as if she'd brought a whole new set of fears with her when she returned to the canyon.

"Are you afraid of falling?" he asked.

Ainsley shrugged. "That's just it. I lie awake at night thinking of all the scenarios that can go wrong. Me tripping on a rock and falling right over the side. A visitor on one of my programs backing up too much for a picture and falling. Julie losing control of Faith's stroller and it going over the edge." She sighed. "And it goes on and on."

"Maybe it will just take you a little time to get reacclimated," he suggested. "If you think it will help, we can go walk along the rim trail after we eat."

She tensed. He was probably right. Better to face it tonight than tomorrow with a bunch of strangers. "That's a good idea."

The waiter swung by their table. "Can I get you guys something to drink?"

Jake nodded his head at Ainsley. "You first." He smiled.

"I just want water," she said.

"Coke for me, please."

"I'll be right back with your drinks and take your orders." The guy didn't look much older than Julie.

"Thanks," Jake said. "So, other than dreading your ranger program, are you glad you're back?"

Ainsley thought for a moment. "On the one hand, it's nice to see some familiar faces." She paused. "But on the other hand, there are memories lurking around every corner. I didn't expect that."

She'd known coming back would be tough, but these past days it seemed like every landmark she passed held a long-forgotten memory of Brad. This morning, it had been while on a quick trip to the park's grocery store. She'd rounded the potato chip aisle and Brad's favorite flavor caught her eye. She'd laughed at the memory of them standing on that very spot, having a playful argument over which flavor to buy. But at least she was able to feel happy about the memory. For so long, remembering had been so painful she'd tried her best not to look back. But today, for the first time, she felt like she could look back fondly.

"I'm sorry. I can't even imagine."

She quirked her mouth into a smile. "The other night, it was you bringing the conversation down. Tonight, I guess it's my turn."

The waiter returned and set drinks in front of them.

"Saved by the waiter." Jake grinned.

They placed their orders and sat in silence for a moment. "Why don't you tell me more about yourself?" Ainsley finally asked. "Besides being a cop and all."

Jake took a sip of Coke. "Well, I've already told you that I have a sister. She and her husband live in Phoenix with their two kids. My mom also lives nearby." He shrugged. "I hang out with them a lot."

"Does your dad live there, too?"

A grimace flashed across his handsome face. "My dad died not too long ago. Our family is still adjusting to life without him."

She caught his eye. She understood that pain all too well. And sensed that this wasn't the time to inquire more about it. Neither of them spoke for a long moment. "So what do you like to do in your spare time?" Ainsley cringed inwardly. Getting to know someone seemed a lot more awkward than it used to be. Thankfully, Jake didn't seem to notice.

"I play a lot of golf." He grinned. "Are you going to hold it against me if that's my only hobby?"

She shook her head. "Golf is a good hobby. Not that I've ever played or anything." She smiled. "I'm more of a putt-putt kind of person I guess." Although it had been years since she'd even done that.

The waiter set plates of steaming food in front of them. Ainsley had chosen a burger but was suddenly aware of how messy it would be to eat in front of someone. She glanced over at his chicken, which could be eaten with a fork. Would he think she was unrefined if she picked her burger up?

"It looks yummy," she said, smiling.

"It sure does," Jake picked up his knife and fork. "Enjoy."

Ainsley closed her eyes and said a silent prayer of thanks before she dug into her meal.

◎◎

"Thanks for dinner," Ainsley said as they left the restaurant. "It was delicious."

"You're welcome." Jake grinned. "Are you still up for a walk along the rim?"

She hesitated. "Just a short one. I need to get home." Besides that, her knees had already begun to quake at the thought of being so close to the edge of the canyon.

Jake held the door open for her, and they stepped outside. Despite the darkness, the courtyard was well lit, and several people were milling about.

"Let's walk toward the El Tovar," Jake said. "We can catch the shuttle there and head back to your house." He motioned toward the paved trail that ran alongside the canyon rim.

Ainsley's mouth was drier than a desert. "Great." They walked in silence for a moment. Ainsley focused on her breathing. *Just put one foot in front of the other and focus on the solid pavement.*

"How are you feeling?" Jake asked finally. "Do you want to stop for a minute?" He pointed toward a bench just off the trail.

She nodded. "Let's sit." She sat on the old wooden bench and gripped it for support. She gazed out into the canyon, thankful its depth was masked by the darkness.

"Did you ever have this kind of reaction in the past?"

She took a deep breath. "Never. In fact, I used to run along this trail in the morning before work." She glanced over at him. "I'm okay right now, sitting down. I feel like as long as I hold on to something, I'll be fine." She managed a tiny smile. "But as soon as I stand up, it's like the earth might shift at any minute and send me straight into the canyon."

"I'm sorry. I think we should turn around and go back to the Bright Angel. We can catch the shuttle from there."

"It's okay. We can keep going. As long as you stay between me and the canyon, I should be fine."

He reached over and took her shaky hand. "Of course. Whatever it takes to keep you feeling safe."

They stood and gingerly walked toward the El Tovar. "This doesn't bode well for my ranger program, does it?" Maybe she should ask Edie to assign her programs to someone else. Although, if she had to do that, what was the point of being here?

"I have an idea," Jake said, grinning. "I think I know a way for you to handle your first program without anyone finding out about your phobia."

Ainsley brightened. "You do?" Whatever his plan was, she hoped it would work. Because a Grand Canyon ranger who was scared of the Grand Canyon didn't have much job security. And in spite of everything—the memories, the fear, the uncertainty—she wanted to stay at the canyon more than anything. So she'd do whatever it took to conquer her fears and rid herself of the helpless feeling that came over her whenever she stood at the rim.

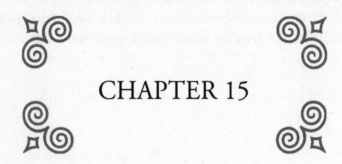

CHAPTER 15

Having Julie here this summer is a real blessing. She's wonderful with you, and you love her so much. It makes it so much easier for me to go to work every day, knowing that you're happy. I have a feeling August is going to come way too soon.

What's your deal?" Heath asked, his voice tinged with anger. He was on his lunch break and had called Julie to check in with her.

"I don't know what you're talking about." Julie wiped Faith's mouth with the "My Mommy Rocks" bib she wore. She tried to coax the little girl to eat another bite of pureed sweet potatoes. Ainsley painstakingly made her own baby food because she thought it was more nutritious. After watching the ritual for a few nights, Julie had already decided that when she had kids someday, they were going to eat the regular Gerber stuff. Making all that food seemed like an awful lot of trouble.

"Don't you miss me? Because you're sure not acting much like it."

Someone must've gotten up on the wrong side of the bed. Or stayed out too late. "I'm trying to feed the baby. I can't help it that you happened to call at a bad time."

"I can fix that. How about I just hang up and find someone else to talk to?" His veiled threats were beginning to wear on her. She'd never pegged him as a cheater, but now that she was far away, she wasn't so sure.

She put the spoon down on the high chair tray and sank into a chair. Faith would be fine for a few minutes. "Come on, Heath," she said softly. "You know I want to talk to you." She ran her fingers through her hair, only to find that they'd had the remnants of sweet potato puree on them. Great. "Tell me how things are going with you."

"I'm thinking about going camping this weekend with a bunch of people." He let out a loud sigh. "This summer sure would be more fun if my girlfriend was here to go camping with me," he said in a pitiful voice.

"I wouldn't get to go with you even if I were there. You know my parents wouldn't allow that."

He snorted. "You could tell them you were staying with Claire." He was quiet for a moment. At least he'd calmed down some.

"That would be a bad idea. I don't want to lie to them, and it would put Claire in a bad position."

Julie jumped at the sound of loud knocking. "There's someone here." She quickly ended their conversation and glanced at Faith, who beat her sweet potato–covered hands against the tray as if answering the door knocks. "I'll be right back," Julie said.

Could it be Colt? At the thought, Julie's stomach fluttered. Without even bothering to check the peephole, she flung the door open.

"Hey, Julie." Dustin stood awkwardly on the porch. "I guess Ainsley is at work, huh?"

She nodded, fighting the wave of disappointment that it wasn't Colt standing on the porch. "Yep." She motioned toward the kitchen. "I'm feeding Faith. You want to come inside?"

He followed her in and sat down at the table. "Sorry for just stopping in. I'm off today and thought I'd check in here."

Julie washed Faith's face with a cloth and removed the potato-covered bib. "We're happy for company." She picked Faith up from the high chair and set her on the ground. She took off running through the house.

"She's got a lot of energy to be so small," Dustin said.

Julie chuckled. "More than you could ever imagine."

"Did you finally get to see some of the sights?" he asked.

"Not yet. We spent most of the weekend getting everything unpacked and all." Every time she'd mentioned to Ainsley that she'd like to get out and see the canyon, her aunt acted funny. Julie wasn't sure what that was all about, but it was annoying. "And I've been busy with Faith since then."

"I've got some free time." Dustin grinned as Faith swooped into the room, a book in her hands. "How about we head over to the ice-cream fountain? You can get a good view of the canyon from there."

Julie was dying to get out of the house. "That would be great," she said, smiling. "Today is Ainsley's first ranger program of the year. She was pretty nervous when she left this morning." Nervous was an understatement. Her aunt had practically been shaking when she walked out the door. "Maybe we could stop by and see her."

"Do you know where she's stationed today?"

Julie laughed. "I know where she is every minute of every day." She pulled a paper from underneath a refrigerator magnet. "Ainsley wants to make sure I can get in touch with her if there's an emergency." A little overboard, considering Ainsley had a cell phone with her, but Julie tried not to question her aunt.

Dustin let out a low whistle. "Wow."

At the sound of his whistle, Faith stopped in her tracks and cackled.

Julie giggled. "You never know what she's going to think is funny. Guess today it's you."

⌀

Dustin whistled a second time and watched as Faith giggled. "Do you think I'm funny?" he asked. "I'm Dustin, and someday I'm going to tell you lots of stories about your mommy and daddy." He grinned and turned back to Julie.

"She's at Verkamp's Visitor Center today," Julie said.

"Well, what do you say? Let's head over to Verkamp's to see her; then we'll stop for ice cream. The ice-cream fountain is right beside the Bright Angel Lodge."

Julie considered the offer.

"Ainsley won't mind. She and I go way back." Although considering Ainsley had been at the canyon for a couple of weeks already and hadn't made an effort to see him, that might be hard for Julie to believe.

Finally, the teenager nodded. "Okay. We can't stay too long though, because Faith has to take a nap soon."

"Fair enough." Dustin was thrilled. Ainsley would be so happy to see her daughter and niece—and hopefully that happiness would translate into her warming up to him.

The backpack he'd gotten for Ainsley to carry Faith in was still in the same spot in the living room. Guess she hadn't had time to use it yet. He adjusted the straps and put it on his back. "If I kneel down, can you put Faith in?"

"Yep." Julie picked up the little girl. "You wanna go for a ride, little miss?"

Faith responded with a string of words Dustin didn't understand. "I'm going to take that as a yes." He grinned.

Once Faith was settled, Dustin headed toward the door.

"Hang on," Julie said before he could get outside. "I have a little problem."

"What's wrong?"

She made a face. "I don't know where the spare key is." She sighed. "It's on a keychain that has a little flashlight on it." She picked up the throw pillows from the couch and looked underneath them.

"Is there another key anywhere?"

She nodded. "I guess we'll just use the one that's hidden outside." She followed him onto the porch and closed the door behind her. "It's underneath the mat." She snagged the key from its spot and put it in her pocket. "Not the best hiding place, huh?"

He chuckled. "Probably not."

They headed down the street. It was a gorgeous, sunny day. "Hope you brought your sunglasses," Dustin said.

"I did." Julie pulled oversized dark sunglasses from her bag and slipped them on. She glanced up at Faith. "She seems happy. That backpack is cool."

"Thanks. Ainsley and Brad used to do a lot of hiking, so I figured she'd get a lot of use out of it."

Julie nodded. "I like that shade that goes over her head. Because trying to keep sunglasses on a one-year-old is an impossible task." She laughed. "And that's one of Ainsley's rules. Sunglasses and sunblock for Faith if we so much as step a toe outside."

He sensed Julie's frustration. Funny, Ainsley didn't used to abide by any rules. Maybe motherhood had changed her outlook on life. "Better safe than sorry, right?" he asked.

Julie shrugged, suddenly engrossed in her cell phone.

An incoming text, perhaps? "Be glad you get service out here. It used to be really spotty, but it's gotten a lot better."

She tapped away in silence. Finally, she glanced over at him. "Huh? Oh. Yeah. That's what Ainsley said."

He sighed. Here he'd thought females were supposed to be

better communicators than males. That's what every woman he'd ever dated seemed to think. He was beginning to think they might've been wrong. "Check it out," he said, pointing at a corral. "That's where they keep the mules who take visitors down into the canyon."

Julie wrinkled her nose. "Shoo. They're way stinky." She looked up at Faith. "Do you see the mules?"

Faith bounced in her carrier and patted Dustin on the head. "Shoo," she exclaimed, mimicking Julie.

They passed the mule corral and stopped at the main road to wait for a truck to pass. "We could've taken the shuttle, I guess, but I figured you'd rather walk and see the place."

"This is better," Julie agreed. "I'm happy to be outside. Especially on a pretty day like this." They crossed to the other side of the street. "I'd like to do some hiking at some point. And maybe camp or something."

Dustin nodded. "Sounds fun."

They walked through the Bright Angel parking lot to the sidewalk that led to the rim.

"Whoa," Julie breathed. "I've been here before, a couple of years ago." She shook her head. "But it's just so amazing."

Dustin gazed out into the canyon. The vivid colors ranged from lightest pink to terra cotta, depending on the sunlight's angle. He never tired of looking at it. "It's indescribable, huh?"

"No kidding." She held up her phone and snapped a picture. "I'm not even sure pictures do it justice."

He agreed. Over the years, some of the most famous photographers in the world had taken beautiful pictures of Grand Canyon. But even so, they could never convey the feeling of standing at the rim and looking at the canyon. "You ready? We'll walk the rim trail over to Verkamp's, so you'll get to see some different views." He grinned. "Maybe even an elk or two. You never know."

She nodded. "Sounds good."

They passed by a throng of tourists, all of them trying to photograph the canyon at just the right angle. The bevy of languages never ceased to amaze him. People from all over the world came to stand at the rim. He wondered if they all went home and had trouble explaining it to their friends. He'd come to realize it wasn't just the beauty of the canyon that was hard to describe, but the feeling you got standing near it. It always left him with a deep appreciation for God's gifts. He'd dare anyone to gaze out into the depths and not feel a spiritual connection.

"There's Hopi House," he told Julie as they passed. "There's a lot of history there. The Hopi Indians inhabited the canyon years ago, and that is a replica of the kind of home they lived in." He was leaving out so much, but there'd be time for her to learn the history later. Today would just be an overview. "Now it's a gift shop."

"Cool," said Julie.

"And right up here is Verkamp's Visitor Center," he explained. "It used to be a store, but a few years ago, it was transformed into a visitor center."

"Is it the only visitor center?" she asked.

He shook his head. "Nope. There are actually three visitor centers. The main one is huge. It's near Mather Point, which you will definitely have to see sometime."

They walked up the stairs to the visitor center.

"I hope she's glad to see us," Julie said nervously.

"Me, too," he admitted, holding the door open for her. The woman at the desk smiled as they walked in. She must be a seasonal worker, because Dustin didn't recognize her. "Hi." He smiled. "We're looking for Ainsley Davis."

The woman looked puzzled for a second. "Oh, you mean the new park ranger?" she asked. "She's just started a ranger program." She pointed. "If you hurry, you can probably catch part of it."

This was turning out even better. Dustin felt certain Ainsley would love having their support on her program. What a great surprise.

They hurried out the door and continued along the trail. Dustin could see the group gathered around the speaker. That must be them.

Ainsley didn't see them as they approached, her concentration centered on the visitors.

"Let's just stand here until she gets through," he whispered to Julie, motioning at the trail. "I don't want to distract her."

Julie nodded, a funny look on her face. "Hi," she said to someone over his shoulder.

He turned to see who she was greeting and came face-to-face with the last person he expected to see.

Jake McGuire.

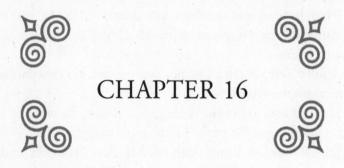

CHAPTER 16

When people tell you that doing something you haven't done in a while is just like riding a horse or a bicycle, I don't understand what they mean. Because I assure you, if I hadn't ridden a horse or a bicycle in a long time, it would make me a little nervous to hop on. I've decided that sometimes, people just say what they think you need to hear. It used to be that this didn't bother me, but I'm tired of well-meaning advice. It seems like everyone and their brother knew exactly what I needed after your daddy died. Some would try and get me to talk about him. Some wouldn't mention him at all. Some would say things like "he's in a better place" or "only the good die young." After hearing every "feel good" line in the book, I've determined that there's no such thing. It used to get on my nerves, but now I understand that they're only trying to help. At least, I try and remember that.

T he Grand Canyon has played an important role for many different groups of people." Ainsley wiped her palms on her green uniform pants. If she could've given this talk indoors, maybe at the visitor center, it would be going better. Instead, the canyon loomed. And although Jake had a wonderful plan—she'd keep her back to the canyon, and he'd stand between it and her—she was still aware of its presence.

Jake had assured her no one would know he was there on purpose. They'd think he was another random tourist. Just one in a million. But she knew he was more than that. Today, he was the person who'd given her the courage to do her job. And she was very thankful.

"In closing, I encourage you to write your own stories while you're here. Each of us takes away a different experience from the canyon. It's time for you to go out and find yours." She smiled at the group around her.

"Ma–ma," a familiar voice said from behind her. She glanced over her shoulder. Faith was bouncing in the backpack on Dustin's shoulders, her face scrunched up in a grin. Ainsley felt the blood drain from her face. They were so close to the edge. Two steps back and Dustin and Faith would go tumbling.

She sent a panicked look in Jake's direction. Thankfully, he caught on quickly and motioned for Dustin to join the tour group. With each step, Faith got closer and Ainsley's heart rate slowed. She turned to the group of tourists, most of whom were watching her with interest. "Thanks for your attention, and I hope you have a wonderful day." No way she was opening up for questions like she should. If they had questions, they could go back to the visitor center.

Dustin reached her, and it was all she could do not to rip Faith from the backpack. "What are you doing here?" she asked, not bothering to hide her anger.

He jerked back like he'd been slapped. "We thought we'd come see you." He motioned toward Julie, who was chatting with Jake. "She hadn't seen the canyon yet, and I figured it would do her some good to get out."

Faith patted his head and babbled.

Dustin laughed. "And this little angel loves her new ride." He cocked his head and glanced up at Faith. "She's been jabbering nonstop since we left. And, of course, playing drums on my head."

Ainsley had to admit to herself that seeing Faith get along so well with her old friend was a cute sight. But not enough to make her forget her earlier fear. "You shouldn't have brought them here."

He looked confused. "We're not going to stay long. I told Julie we'd grab an ice-cream cone from the Bright Angel and then head back. I know Faith needs to go down for a nap soon." He almost sounded responsible. But she knew him well enough to know better. "That isn't the point. I'm her mother. You shouldn't just bring her out here without asking me."

"Touché. I'm sorry. I figured you'd be happy to see her in the middle of the day." He glanced to where Jake stood at the rim. "I see your *friend* is here." The word dripped with uncertainty. Or maybe jealousy, she couldn't be sure.

She glared at him. "Jake's just making sure I'm okay." As soon as the words left her mouth, she wished she could retract them. Dustin was the last person who needed to know about her phobia. Her luck, he'd tell Lindsey, and then the whole park would know. It was bad enough that they all pitied her; she didn't want to be a laughingstock, too.

He took his sunglasses off and stared at her with crystal blue eyes. She used to tell him his eyes were the same color as the Mediterranean and must be the reason he was so popular with women. Because he reminded them of a dream vacation. "Why wouldn't you be okay?" he asked softly. "Ainsley, what's going on? You've avoided me like the plague since you got here." He rubbed his jaw, his eyes never leaving her face.

She shrugged. "I'm just having trouble adjusting to things, that's all." She was determined not to tell him about her fears. "Jake's just offering moral support."

Hurt flashed in his eyes. "I should be the one offering you support. I've known you since you were barely older than Julie."

A pang of guilt hit her. He was right about that. But she wasn't the same girl he used to know. She was a widow. With a child. She had responsibilities and problems that someone like him would never understand. She couldn't ride off into the sunset on the back of his motorcycle like she had when she was twenty-two. Times had changed, and so had she. "He knew how nervous I was about my first program back. He's just here to be a friendly face in the crowd." And to stand between her and the canyon.

Dustin sighed and slipped on his sunglasses. "I guess we should go."

The sharpness in his voice stung her for a minute. But she knew she deserved it. He'd been offering her his friendship since the day she'd returned. And she was determined to keep him at arm's length. He couldn't possibly understand how complex her life had become. No matter how close they'd once been. Ainsley reached up and took hold of Faith's hand. "Hey, baby girl." She smiled at her daughter. "Be good for Julie, okay?"

Faith waved her arms and patted Dustin's head.

Ainsley laughed. "I think she likes you. But then, you always did have a way with the ladies."

Dustin groaned. "Don't start."

"It sure is beautiful here," Julie said, trotting over. "Jake just said he'd take me hiking sometime if I wanted to go."

Ainsley met Jake's eyes, and he shrugged. "She asked," he explained.

"We'll talk about it later," she said to her niece. "In the meantime, I think you guys are due for some ice cream."

Julie grinned. "That sounds great to me."

Ainsley watched as the three of them headed toward the Bright Angel. It was all she could do to keep from running after them to make sure they stayed safe.

Jake came and stood beside her. "They'll be fine. He knows what he's doing, and Faith is snug in her little backpack." He placed a hand on her arm. "How'd you feel giving your first program?" he asked. "Was it just like riding a horse?"

"Yeah, a wild one that hasn't been trained yet." Dustin showing up out of the blue with Faith and Julie had thrown her off. She'd been so focused on them, she wasn't even sure if she'd finished her program.

"I think it went well. You're a natural with visitors, and it's easy to see that you're a great park ranger." He grinned, his brown eyes sparkling. "Did it help for me to stand between you and the canyon?"

She nodded. "Knowing you were there made all the difference to me. So thanks." Ainsley quirked her mouth into a smile. She knew if he hadn't been standing there, she never would have been able to leave the visitor-center porch. In fact, she'd probably still be there, frozen, and today's visitors would think she was crazy.

Ainsley glanced in the direction of the Bright Angel, hoping Faith was okay. She'd call Julie in a few minutes and make sure they were safely home. Otherwise, she'd be useless the rest of the day.

☙◌☙

Jake had to admit, Dustin was the last person he'd hoped to see in attendance today. Not that he had any claim on Ainsley, at least not yet. But the way he saw it, Dustin was one thing standing between the two of them. He knew Ainsley was exactly the kind of woman he'd been looking for: smart, funny, and caring. Not to mention beautiful. He'd let enough women get away. But not this one. He'd do whatever it took to make her fall for him. "You know it was my pleasure." He smiled. "Before you know it, you'll probably be running the rim trail again."

She laughed. "I'm not so sure about that. But I'll be happy if I can just do my job without having a panic attack." Her hazel eyes clouded over. "I don't have any more programs today. And I'm at the main visitor center the next few days. But I'll probably have another program at the rim again next week."

"Name the day, and I'll be here," he said earnestly. His schedule was flexible. And he planned to use it to his advantage.

"Oh, I couldn't ask you to do that." She perched on the wooden bench she'd been standing next to and crossed her arms.

He sat down beside her, a little closer than necessary. He couldn't help himself—he just wanted to be close to her. Her creamy skin didn't have the usual freckles he'd always associated with redheads. It was so smooth, it reminded him of the porcelain dolls his sister used to keep on display in her room. "You aren't asking me. I'm offering." He grinned. "What can I say? I'm happy to help."

"Have you always been so helpful?" She cocked her head and glanced at him.

He shrugged. "Guess it depends on who you ask. I kind of like rescuing a damsel in distress."

She was quiet for a minute. "My life is certainly no fairy tale, that's for sure."

He leaned over and bumped her shoulder with his. "You never know. I have a feeling, you might be surprised by a happy ending."

Ainsley cast a hopeful glance his way. "Doubtful." She glanced at her watch. "I'd better get back to the visitor center." She stood to go. "Thanks again."

"See you soon," he said, watching her walk off, red ponytail swishing. He remained on the bench, lost in thought. They'd had only one date. He couldn't count the cookout at Dustin's house. It was time to kick it into high gear. Maybe later this week, he could convince her to have dinner with him off park grounds. Williams, perhaps? Flagstaff would be too far to drive. There was no way she'd leave Faith for that long.

His cell phone buzzed in his pocket. "Can you do an overnight hike?" Shane asked once he'd answered. "I had another guy scheduled, but he's got a family emergency."

So far, Jake had only led day hikes. An overnight adventure could be fun. "Sure. What are the details?"

"You'll leave Wednesday and camp two nights. If you can do it, we have permits for you that you'll need to pick up." The park service required anyone camping in the canyon overnight to have a backcountry camping permit. Jake knew these permits had been applied for far in advance. "It's a family of four that you'll be leading."

"Where will we be camping?" Jake asked.

"Indian Gardens. You'll hike down the Bright Angel Trail to Indian Gardens Thursday and spend the night. Get up the next morning and hike down to Phantom Ranch. Return to Indian Gardens for one more night, then up early Friday morning and hike back to the trailhead." Shane sighed. "Can you handle it? I know it's a lot to ask, but I'm in a real bind. This hike has been scheduled for a long time, and with us being short staffed already. . ." He swore under his breath. "My brother ought to be ashamed of himself."

"It isn't a problem." Jake had been looking forward to a multiday hike. He'd expected to do it alone, but a group could be kind of fun. "I'll swing by later today and pick everything up. You gonna be at the store?"

"I'll be here till around six." It was only a fifteen-minute drive to the small town of Tusayan, so Jake had plenty of time. In addition to hiring out hiking guides, Shane's store also carried outdoor equipment for sale or rent. As far as Jake could tell, it was a successful business. And if he decided to leave the police force for good, one that he thought he'd be happy to be a part of.

"See you in a bit." Jake clicked off his phone. This did throw a kink in his plans to ask Ainsley out for another date. For a minute, he considered backing out. His being away for a couple of days might give Dustin the chance to reconnect with his old friend. But from what Jake had observed, Ainsley wasn't giving Dustin much of a chance to rekindle their friendship. Jake wasn't sure what was holding her back, but he hoped the situation stayed that way.

After the excitement of seeing her mother and having ice cream, Faith went down for her nap without a fuss. Julie considered a nap of her own but decided against it. If she napped now, so late in the afternoon, she'd never get to sleep tonight. And since sleep hadn't been coming easy for her lately, she couldn't risk it. Since she'd been at the canyon, she and Heath had fallen into a pattern of texting to say good night. But the past few nights, his response had been delayed. Last night especially, it had taken him two hours to text back. She couldn't help but wonder what he was up to. And if it was something she'd approve of.

She grabbed her phone and the baby monitor and stepped out onto the back deck.

"Julie?" Claire's uncertainty came through the line as the call connected.

"I had a few minutes of peace while Faith is sleeping, so I thought I'd see how your new job is going." Julie felt a pang of regret. Claire was like the sister she'd never had. Or at least she had been until recently. She should've called her friend days ago to see how she liked waitressing.

"My feet hurt." Claire chuckled. "But my tips have been good enough to justify getting a pedicure later in the week, so that'll make them feel better."

"Are you trying to make me jealous?" Julie teased. "I'm out here practically in the middle of the wilderness. Not a chance of a mani-pedi for me."

"Yeah, I guess not." Claire was quiet for a moment. "Um. Have you talked to Heath lately?"

"Not since yesterday, why?" She didn't dare admit that yesterday's conversation had only been a couple of random texts. Claire didn't need any more convincing that Heath was the worst boyfriend ever.

"He was at the restaurant last night. Not at one of my tables or anything." She sighed. "He was with a group, but it looked to me like he was acting pretty flirtatious with that girl Miranda. You know. The one with the big hair."

Julie knew. Miranda happened to be Heath's ex. She was pretty sure Claire knew it, too, but just didn't want to say it. "Yeah. Heath and Miranda are friends." She sighed. "But that's all. Just friends."

Claire didn't say anything for several seconds. "Well, they sure looked pretty friendly last night, that's for sure."

"Don't jump to any conclusions, okay?" Julie begged. "He isn't a bad guy."

"So you're saying you trust him?"

Julie swallowed. "He would never hurt me."

"Jules, I don't understand you." Claire sighed. "But I hope for your sake that you're right about that."

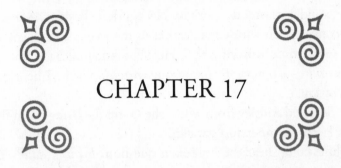

CHAPTER 17

Not that I expect you to see this journal as me giving you advice or anything. But if you choose to heed a couple of warnings, that would be great. So here goes: Sometimes it's easiest to judge those relationships you aren't a part of. I've learned this lesson more than once, but most recently, this summer with Julie. I wonder what she'll be up to by the time I let you read these summer musings. Anyway, Julie has this boyfriend back home. To those of us looking in from the outside, we see an immature young man with a quick fuse and a penchant for partying. But she clearly sees something else. I'm not sure what. But something. Otherwise she wouldn't hang on so tightly. Right?

J ulie grabbed her favorite American Eagle hoodie from her closet. The days might be hot, but nights at the canyon could be cool. Must have something to do with the elevation. She quickly tied the yellow jacket around the waist of her orange tank. Even though Claire always said her legs were her best feature, she was covering them up with jeans. After all, she wasn't trying to impress Colt. She'd agreed to go with him into Tusayan for dinner. Nothing fancy. Just fast food.

It would be nice to be off the park grounds for a bit. He'd mentioned coming back and taking a walk along the rim to see if they could spot any deer or elk. No big deal. Besides, ever since her conversation with Claire earlier in the week, she'd spent way too much time worrying that Heath was falling back into old habits with Miranda. Hanging out with Colt would be a good distraction.

"So," said Ainsley from where she sat on the living room floor with Faith. "Dinner and a walk?"

Julie could hear the unspoken question. *Is this a date?* "Yep. Just a burger and fries. I don't want to get spoiled by all of your veggies, I guess." She grinned.

"You need some 'real' food, right?" Ainsley laughed. She turned the page on the book she and Faith were looking at. "See the puppy?" she asked as Faith babbled. "It's just like Bo Bo." She pointed at the worn, stuffed dog Faith carried everywhere she went.

Julie sank down onto the sofa. "We won't be out late." She paused. "And this is *not* a date. I love Heath." She wanted to be clear. Although maybe Ainsley would've passed the news of a date along to her parents, and then they'd be off her case. "Besides, Colt knows I have a boyfriend."

Ainsley raised an eyebrow. "I didn't ask. What you do is your business." She caught herself. "Within reason, of course." She grinned.

Julie smirked. "So no wild parties or fast cars?"

Ainsley ran a hand through her wavy red hair. It was still damp from the shower. "Right."

"You know, you should wear your hair that way more often," Julie said. Her aunt wore her hair up or pulled back so much of the time that it was easy to forget how beautiful it was.

"How? Tangled? Wet?" Ainsley grinned. "I'd catch my death of cold," she drawled.

Julie rolled her eyes. "No. Down. Loose and wavy." She smiled. "It looks really pretty like that."

An odd expression came over Ainsley's face. "I like it better pulled back. Keeps it out of my way." She motioned toward Faith. "Besides, she has a tendency to pull it when it's down."

As if to prove her mother's point, Faith chose that moment to tug on a lock of red hair. "Book," she exclaimed, grinning.

Ainsley flashed a "see" look at Julie and pried her hair from Faith's chubby fingers. "That's right. Book." She kissed Faith on the head. "You're my smart girl."

Julie glanced out the front window. "There he is. I'll be home soon. By ten, I promise. Maybe earlier." She grabbed her bag and headed outside.

"Be careful," Ainsley called. "Call me if you need anything."

Julie shot her a quick smile and closed the door.

☙◓

Two hours later, Julie and Colt sat on the stone wall next to Kolb Studio. The faintest hint of light from the quickly fading sun made the canyon seem almost mystic.

"Sometime we'll have to catch the sunset from a different vantage point," Colt said. "It's amazing how different the canyon looks depending on where you're standing."

Julie glanced over at him. Clad in a green polo shirt and khaki shorts, he gazed out into the canyon. "Was it fun growing up here?" she asked, gesturing. "I mean, are you used to this scenery? Or can you ever be used to it?"

Colt was quiet for a moment. He furrowed his brow. "It was lots of fun, I guess. We moved here when I was about ten. So I guess I'm used to it now, but I realize not everybody gets to live next to something so beautiful." He gave her a sideways look. "How about you? Where did you grow up?"

"A small town called Cottonwood." She shrugged. "It's okay.

It just gets old having people in my business all the time." That was true. It seemed like everyone from the local librarian to her former kindergarten teacher knew every move she made. It drove her crazy.

Colt chuckled. "I understand completely. Living here has its downfalls. It's kind of a fishbowl, too."

"I'm sort of enjoying not knowing many people here just for that reason." She sighed. "Everyone back home seems to think they know what's best for me." Claire had called this morning, partly to talk about plans for the dorm room they planned to share, but also to make sure Julie hadn't seen Heath since leaving town. She knew her friend was only concerned, but the fact that no one seemed to trust her judgment really bugged her.

"Yeah?" Colt swung one leg over the wall and turned to face her. "Why's that?" He grinned. "Does it have anything to do with this mysterious boyfriend you mentioned?" She'd offhandedly mentioned Heath the other night at the cookout, mainly so Colt would know she wasn't available.

Her face grew hot. "I guess most people don't understand what I see in him."

"So tell me." He met her gaze, his brown eyes serious. "What *do* you see in him?"

She bit her lip. "Besides the normal stuff—he's cute and funny—there's something else. But it will make me seem crazy." She shrugged. "I guess partly I think I'm a good influence on him. It's like I keep him on the right path." It was true. Heath had straightened up some since they'd been together. She liked the thought of changing his life. Then someday when they were old, he'd tell their kids how he used to be a wild man until she came along and tamed him. That thought kept her hanging on to him, even against her better judgment.

"Doesn't seem so crazy I guess. As long as he knows he's a lucky guy." Colt picked up a stray rock and tossed it back and forth in his hands.

"Well, he tells me all the time that I'm the only good thing he has going in his life. So I think he does." She met his gaze. "But I guess you could say he's a little rough around the edges."

Colt narrowed his eyes. "How so?"

Julie shrugged. "He kind of has a reputation for being a bad boy. And he's been in some trouble with the local cops. Needless to say, my friends and family can't stand him."

"I don't get it." Colt rolled his eyes. "What's the fascination with bad guys? Do girls just like to be treated like dirt?"

She was quiet for a moment. She'd only just met Colt. She didn't have to defend herself to him. But for some reason, the disgust in his eyes made her sad. "He doesn't treat me like dirt. He can be really sweet." She sighed. "Plus, he needs me. That's the reason I can't walk away, even when he does dumb stuff."

Colt raked his fingers through his dark hair. "He needs you? That's pretty lame."

She scowled. "I've only dated one other guy besides Heath. He was Mr. Perfect, you know? And he could take me or leave me. But Heath. . .he says I'm the only person who can save him."

Colt widened his brown eyes. "Sounds like a lot of pressure to me." He tossed the rock out into the canyon and stood. "You ready to walk home?"

His abrupt action startled her. She'd hoped to learn more about him tonight but instead had been on the receiving end of the questions. "Sure." They headed toward the park's residential area in silence.

◉

Jake finished packing his sturdy backpack. Funny how many memories the old, faded LL Bean pack held. He'd first broken in the pack on a trip across Europe ten years ago. After that, there'd been various hiking trips through more national parks than he could count. He liked nothing more than being outdoors.

Except for being a cop. He'd only been away from his job for a few weeks, but already he was itching to know what was going on in the precinct. So far, he'd refrained from calling Dwight, but he'd already decided to call and check in when his hiking trip was over.

He set the backpack on the floor of the camper and looked around. The old camper was the same one he and his dad had used for many years. After Dad had died, Jake took ownership. They'd had so many good times on their camping trips. Jake sat down at the built-in table and gazed out the little window. So many families here, having adventures they'd remember forever. Had he made a grave mistake choosing work over relationships all these years? He thought about his old girlfriend, Sharon. They'd dated for a couple of years, and everyone expected them to marry. But he'd let her slip away, always choosing work over her.

The ringing of his phone startled him. "Hey there," his sister said. "Just thought I'd see if you were enjoying yourself."

He grinned. "Wow. It's great to hear your voice, Marie. How is everyone?"

"We're good. The kids miss their Uncle Jake, though." She laughed. "And of course, Mom is ready for you to get yourself back home." She was quiet for a minute. "You are coming back home, right?"

"I haven't made any plans yet."

Marie's disappointment seemed to seep through the phone. "It's not the same without you around here. . . ." She paused. "But I know you need to sort some stuff out. So no pressure." She laughed. "I'll try not to send you on a sisterly guilt trip."

Jake chuckled. "Thanks a lot. I do have some decisions to make. I guess if I'm not coming back to the force, I'm not sure I want to be back in Phoenix."

"Do you really think you can give it up? I know you feel like you made a mistake, but remember, you are the reigning officer of the year."

Images of last summer's banquet flashed in his head. His entire family had been there to see him get the award. "I'm not sure. Maybe."

"Well, you do whatever you think is best. You'll have our support no matter what." A noise sounded in the background. "Oh, I need to run. The kids are chasing the cat."

"Tell them Uncle Jake said hello and I love them." He laughed. "And to leave the poor cat alone." He hung up and tossed the phone back on the table. Was it normal for thirty-five-year-old men to be homesick? Jake wasn't certain. He glanced at his watch. It was time to go meet the hikers. At least the activity would take his mind off the uncertainty of his future.

And when he returned, he'd call a certain red-haired park ranger and see if he could take her out to dinner. Just the thought of spending time with Ainsley made his day brighter. He slung his backpack over his shoulder and headed toward the shuttle.

CHAPTER 18

Sometimes I feel like I've lived two lives. There was the "me" I used to be—free-spirited, always laughing, and never stressed—and the "me" I am now. This new me, she gets on my nerves sometimes—and quite possibly on everyone else's, but they're just too nice to say so. These days, I feel so much stress and tension. Like I'm always on edge. I can't help but wonder if this is just what happens when you get older or if it's something else entirely. Did someone steal my personality? Because I'd like it back.

Consider it done," Edie said, grinning. "I'm so glad to have you back, I'd give you just about anything you ask for."

Ainsley breathed a sigh of relief. She'd thought her heart was going to pound out of her chest when she'd gone to Edie's office to ask for a schedule change. "I can't tell you how much I appreciate it." For the next several weeks, she'd be stationed at the main visitor center, which meant her programs would take place away from the rim of the canyon.

Edie shook her head. "Don't give it another thought. I want

you to be happy here. I can only imagine what the past couple of years have been like for you. If we need to ease you back in to things here, it's not a problem."

Thank You, Lord. Ainsley knew she was blessed to have such an understanding supervisor. It would've been completely within Edie's right to say that if Ainsley didn't feel she could handle things, she should look elsewhere for employment. The sense of family here was just one of the reasons Ainsley had decided to come back. "Easing back in sounds great."

Edie nodded. "Tell you what, I can probably give you a month at the main visitor center. You think that will be long enough to get yourself in order?"

Ainsley hadn't told her boss that she was struck with fear each time she got near the rim. Instead, she'd just asked for time at the main visitor center until she got used to working full-time again. Rangers there spent more time indoors, answering questions and handing out brochures, than they did leading programs. She wasn't sure she could conquer her phobia in a month, but at this point, she'd take any time she was given. "A month sounds wonderful."

"So, not to change the subject or anything, but how's that sweet baby doing?" Edie's kind blue eyes twinkled. Changing the subject was exactly what she was doing.

Ainsley grinned. "Growing like a weed. She's getting into everything she can reach. And I caught her trying to climb onto the coffee table the other day." She sighed. "I wish I could just wrap her in bubble wrap and protect her forever." If only that were possible.

Edie chuckled. "I wish it were that easy." She shook her head. "All you can do is raise them the best way you know how and say a lot of prayers."

Wasn't that the truth? Ainsley figured she'd prayed more since Faith was born than in all the rest of her life combined. Motherhood and prayer went together hand in hand. "Believe me, I know."

"I guess Dustin's glad to have you back," Edie said matter-of-factly. "He's been such a loner these past couple of years."

Ainsley couldn't keep the smirk off her face. "If I know him, he's found plenty of beautiful women to keep him company. I can't imagine he stayed lonely for long."

Edie furrowed her brow. "I think you're wrong about that, honey. But maybe you should ask him." A knock on the door stopped her from saying more.

"Ms. Barrett?" A young woman poked her head around the door. "The chief ranger is on the phone for you."

"I'd better take this," Edie said. "I'll check in on you again soon to make sure everything's going okay. And I'd love to have your family over for dinner again soon." She paused with her hand on the phone receiver. "You can bring Dustin, too," she said with a wink.

Ainsley walked along the sidewalk outside Edie's office, relieved that things had gone so well with her boss. The cell phone buzzed on her hip, and she pulled it from the holder. Her mouth formed a broad grin at Kristy's name on the screen. She didn't have to be at the visitor center for a little while, so the call was perfect timing. Especially since she and Kristy had been playing phone tag for the past couple of weeks.

"Hey," Ainsley said. "I was beginning to think I wouldn't get to actually talk to you until we were at the beach." She perched on the nearest bench and stretched out her legs.

Kristy chuckled. "I know. You know how summertime is, though. It seems like I'm running in a million different directions."

"So much for lazy summer days, huh?"

"What I wouldn't give to be ten years old again for about a week." Kristy laughed. "Nothing but swimming in the river and chasing fireflies."

"You sound like a country song."

"Funny." Kristy was silent for a moment. "So I have a question for you. I debated about whether to ask you or not, but I finally decided it was okay."

"You didn't ask Vickie? She's the reigning etiquette queen, after all."

Kristy burst out laughing. "Okay. You know me too well. You know what a habit I have of sticking my foot in my mouth. So yes, I ran it by Miss Manners first."

Ainsley couldn't keep from grinning. She missed her friends something fierce. E-mails and phone calls were no substitute for seeing them often. "If it got clearance from her, it must be fine. Ask away."

"How did you know you were ready to be a mom?"

Ainsley exhaled loudly. "My sister always told me that if I waited until I was a hundred percent ready, I'd never have a baby." She chuckled. "And I guess in some ways she was right about that. Brad and I had a small list of things we wanted to do pre-baby. Travel, pay off student loans. . .you know the drill."

"So you completed your list and then went for it?"

"Not exactly. I think in the end, we just decided that whenever it happened, the timing would be perfect. And it was. . . . I'm thankful to have Faith. Having her to concentrate on helped me through my grief."

"Ace and I have been talking about it for a long time." Kristy sighed. "I'm pretty sure we're ready, but I guess part of my reservations have to do with my job."

"What do you mean? Do you think anyone at the park would have a problem with you being on leave for a little while?"

"Nothing like that. They'd all be thrilled for me. It's the decision of whether to keep working or not." Kristy let out a loud sigh. "I love what I do. I'm not ready to give it up."

"No one says you have to," Ainsley said gently. "You will be a wonderful mother, no matter what."

"What made you decide to go back to work? And don't answer

that if it's too personal." Kristy added the last part quickly.

Ainsley grinned. "Don't be silly. I don't think there is any such thing as too personal between us. Brad and I had always planned for me to stay home once the baby was born. Not that we thought there was anything wrong if I didn't. Just that that was our plan."

"I know."

"But after spending the better part of two years at my parents' house, I decided that my going back to work would be the best thing for both me and Faith. I felt so isolated—and I know a lot of that was my own fault for not getting out of the house. But I didn't want to bring that isolation on my baby. Once Julie leaves, Faith will start day care here. Even though that's going to be a little hard for me, I think she'll enjoy being around other kids."

"Do you have a hard time leaving her each day?"

"I guess it's easier now because I know how much Julie loves her and I know she's well taken care of. Plus, I can run home at lunch to check on her, so that makes it easier. But I'm not going to lie to you: It is difficult."

"Are you still happy with your job? I know how much you used to love it."

Ainsley shifted the phone to her other ear. "I'm happy I came back. My perception has changed, though. I'm much more aware of balancing life and work now than I was. And I think juggling motherhood and work has also made me use my time more wisely."

"That makes sense." Kristy was quiet for a moment. "Thanks for sharing all of this. I guess I just started panicking at the thought of a major life change." She chuckled. "You know me. I've always been resistant to change, even when it meant something good happening."

"Motherhood is definitely life changing." Ainsley grinned. "But you'll just learn what works for you as you go. And I know

Ace will be so supportive."

"He's thrilled at the prospect. Of course he says it's my decision whether to stay home or keep working. I guess I should just consider myself blessed to have the choice."

"True. And anytime you have questions or just want someone to talk to, please call me."

"Will do," Kristy said.

After Ainsley disconnected the call, she sat on the bench for a moment longer. As hard as it could be, she'd meant what she'd said to Kristy. She was glad she'd decided to return to her job at the Grand Canyon. Despite the fear that washed over her at times, she knew she was right where she was supposed to be.

☙◗☙

Dustin wiped the sweat from his brow. He should've known better than to put off yard work until the heat of the day. All week long, he'd promised himself he was going to get up at daylight and get it done. And all week, he'd managed to oversleep. He let go of the lawnmower's handle and the motor sputtered off.

"You can come do ours next," a familiar voice called from across the street.

He grinned and glanced up at Colt. "I'm good, thanks."

Colt jogged over, still in his maintenance uniform. "You sure? 'Cause I'd be glad to give up the job." He grinned.

Dustin took a long swig of bottled water. It had been outside so long, it was lukewarm at best. "What are you up to? Big weekend plans?"

Colt made a face. "No plans to speak of." He sighed.

Over the past year, Dustin had gotten to know the teenager pretty well. Colt was quiet, but he was a good kid. Since Dustin had been leading devotionals on a semi-regular basis, he'd been making an effort to get to know more of the teens in the neighborhood. In fact, he liked to think of himself as somewhat of a mentor. "Everything okay?" he asked.

Colt shrugged. "Yeah. I'm just. . .Did you ever like a girl even though you knew she liked someone else?"

He should've known. What else would be on the mind of an eighteen-year-old guy besides trying to figure out women? Too bad Dustin didn't have the answers, especially when it came to matters of the heart. "Yes," he said simply. "It's not the best position to be in."

Colt made a face. "You know that girl Julie? Ainsley's niece?"

Of course. He'd noticed Colt and Julie hanging out at the cookout. Dustin nodded. "She likes someone else?"

"She has a boyfriend back home. Sounds like a real loser." Colt frowned. "Normally if I liked a girl and she was seeing someone, I'd just back off." He sighed. "But I hate knowing he doesn't treat her well."

Dustin nodded. "Tough situation, man. I'd say your best bet is just to be her friend. Maybe she'll have a change of heart once she gets to know you better and sees what a nice guy you are."

"Yeah," Colt said glumly. "I'm always the guy that ends up the friend. It stinks."

Dustin chuckled. "Don't be too hard on yourself. You'll figure out someday that friendship is the best starting-off point for a relationship." Not that he knew from firsthand experience, but at least he'd seen it happen.

Colt shot him a wry smile. "I guess." He sighed.

There had to be a way to cheer him up. Julie must really be under his skin. "I've got an idea," Dustin said. "How about a little later tonight, we go pick up a couple of pizzas and take them over to Ainsley's?"

Colt considered his offer. "You think they'll mind?"

Dustin grinned. "I'll call Ainsley and make sure they're not busy. Leave it to me."

LOVE IS GRAND

"Don't worry about thawing out the chicken." Ainsley said, stepping into the kitchen.

Julie looked up from the cookbook she was reading. She'd volunteered to cook dinner tonight, even though cooking wasn't exactly her talent. But she hated for her aunt to feel like she always had to cook the meals. "I just set it out a minute ago," she said, motioning over to the counter. "So it's probably still frozen. What's up?" She hoped her aunt was going to suggest going out for dinner. It had been a long week, and Julie was aching to get out of the house. She'd kind of thought Colt might ask her to hang out, but he hadn't called since their trip to Tusayan earlier in the week.

Ainsley crossed the small kitchen and put the package of chicken back into the freezer. "Dustin called."

Great. Was Ainsley going to ask her to stay with Faith while she went out to dinner with Dustin? Not that Julie minded necessarily, because she loved Faith. It was just that she was hoping for a night where she wasn't responsible for anyone but herself. "Are you going somewhere with him?"

"No. Actually, he's picking up a pizza for dinner." She grinned at Julie. "And he's bringing Colt with him."

Julie shut the cookbook with a snap. Colt? She glanced down at her faded running shorts and old T-shirt. A random stain on the front of it remained from earlier in the day when Faith had decided spitting out her apple juice like a fountain was more fun than drinking it. "What time are they coming over?" She tried to keep the panic out of her voice. She wasn't a high maintenance girl, but she hated to look like a complete slob in front of Colt.

"They're just going to the general store," Ainsley explained. "I don't guess you've been over there yet, but there's a deli inside that has pretty good pizza."

123

Julie scooted her chair back. "I'm just going to go change clothes." She gestured at her mismatched outfit. "I wasn't expecting company."

"I guess I should've asked you first if it was okay," Ainsley said with uncertainty. "I can call and tell them we don't feel like having company if you want."

"Oh. No. It's fine." Julie was thrilled to have something to do. And the fact that she thought Colt was all kinds of cute made it even more fun. Not that she had any interest in him or anything. She loved Heath. But it couldn't hurt her to have a friend. And after the way Colt had left things the other night, she'd been afraid she wouldn't see him again. She headed into her room to find something that was cute but not obvious. She grinned to herself, happy to have plans on what would've otherwise been a boring Friday night.

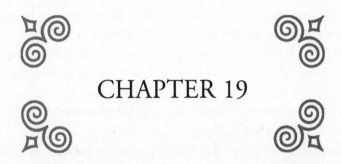

CHAPTER 19

After keeping myself isolated for so long, sometimes I think I've forgotten how to be social. Sure, I spent time with my parents and siblings, but I didn't go out very often. Sometimes your Aunt Rachel would come over and insist that I go to dinner and a movie with her. But mostly I was content to hang out with you. The funny thing is that I can see now how much you love being around people. You remind me so much of your daddy in that way. Even at fifteen months, you're happiest when you have an audience. And I'm such a proud mama, I want everyone to dote on you like I do.

At the sound of the doorbell ringing, Faith's brown eyes widened.

"We have company," Ainsley said, setting the container of baby food on the table. "Mama's going to go let them in." She left Faith in the high chair and went into the living room, glancing down the hallway. Julie must still be primping.

She opened the wooden door to a smiling Dustin and Colt.

"Come in." She stepped back to let them inside. "The pizza smells great," she said to Dustin. "And what's that you have?" she asked, nodding toward the box in Colt's hands.

He looked sheepishly at Dustin. "He, uh, gave it to me to carry. It's a game. Pictionary."

Dustin laughed. "It's the one and only board game I had at my house. I think I've had it since I was in college, believe it or not." He shrugged. "I thought it might be fun."

Ainsley nodded. "Sure." She motioned toward the dining room. "Put the pizza in there."

Dustin walked into the dining room. "Hey there," he said to Faith. "Looks like it's suppertime for somebody."

"She's just about finished." Ainsley held the last bite of food up to Faith's mouth.

Dustin sat down at the table. "I hope pepperoni is okay." He grinned at Ainsley. "Oh, and a veggie for you. I'm guessing you're still as health conscious as you always were."

She laughed. "I'm not sure that pizza can be considered 'health conscious,' but yes, veggie is still my favorite." She marveled that he remembered her little quirks. Of course over the years, she and Dustin had shared hundreds of pizzas. She still knew that pepperoni was his favorite. And if memory served her right, Coke was his drink of choice. It was funny how many memories a simple meal could bring back. And as much as she'd been trying to pretend otherwise, she knew she'd missed having him in her life.

Julie walked into the dining room, clad in khaki shorts and a purple T-shirt. Her hair hung in loose waves, and she had on the slightest hint of makeup. Cute, but not like she'd tried too hard. Ainsley fought back a grin. For someone who claimed to be totally in love with a boy back home, her niece sure was trying to impress Colt. And from the look in his eye, she was doing a good job of it.

"Dig in." Ainsley passed out plates. "Anybody need a fork?" She stepped into the kitchen to get a roll of paper towels. "Where's the hand towel?" she asked. "I just put a new one out this morning."

Julie looked up from putting a slice of pizza on her plate. "It was there at lunch." She laughed. "I used it during the apple juice fiasco."

"Oh well." Ainsley set a roll of paper towels and a handful of forks on the table. "Sorry there aren't more drink options. I'm due a trip to the grocery store." She smiled. Finding time to get groceries proved to be a lot harder now that she worked full-time and had a child. "There's bottled water and apple juice."

Julie jumped up. "I'll get the drinks."

"Water is good with me," Colt said.

Dustin nodded. "Me, too."

Julie passed out water bottles and sat down next to Colt.

"How about I offer the blessing?" Dustin asked once their plates were full.

Ainsley glanced over in surprise. He'd always hated praying out loud. "That would be great," she said, turning to Faith. "Faith, can you put your hands together for a prayer?" She smiled as her daughter put her little hands together and closed her eyes. Maybe she was doing at least one thing right as a mother.

Dustin said a quick prayer, thanking God for food and friendship. Once he'd finished, he smiled. "Dig in, everyone. I hope it's good."

Faith banged on her high chair tray. "Down. Down."

Ainsley put a cookie on her tray. "Here's a cookie. You can get down in a minute."

"She sure communicates well considering she isn't talking yet." Dustin observed.

"If she's anything like me, it will happen all of a sudden. Mom says I was a one-word kind of baby until all of a sudden I started using complete sentences. She says the house was never quiet again."

Dustin laughed. "I've never asked my parents when I started talking." He was quiet for a moment.

Ainsley knew he'd never been that close with his family. His parents split up when he was young, and he'd never seen eye-to-eye with his dad. She'd always thought that was part of the reason he and Brad were so close. Dustin had practically been raised as Brad's brother. She wondered if he'd been in contact with Brad's parents over the past couple of years. If she hadn't been so caught up in herself and in Faith, she would know. "So, Colt," she said, "are you as excited as Julie is about college?"

He wiped his mouth with a paper towel and grinned. "I can't wait. I'm going to miss everyone here and all, but I'm pumped about living in a city."

Julie giggled. "No doubt. Can you imagine what it'll be like to be able to run to the mall or a movie? And I'm dying here without having a Starbucks nearby."

"Oh, come on." Dustin groaned. "Someday you'll look back on living here and see it as one of the greatest experiences of your life."

Ainsley nodded. "He's right. I felt the same way at first." She'd only been five years older than Julie and Colt when she'd moved to the Grand Canyon for work. The isolation had been a real adjustment, but pretty soon, she'd figured out there were a lot of positives to living there.

"Whatever." Julie grinned. "I will say that my bank account is happy this summer." She laughed. "But by the time I get back to civilization, my wardrobe will probably be completely out of style."

"Any idea what you're going to study?" Dustin asked. "Either of you."

Colt shook his head. "I wish I knew. My dad's on my case about it right now. He's trying to get me to major in business, but I don't know. . . ."

"I'm leaning toward elementary education, but I probably won't declare a major until I've taken an education class." Julie grinned. "I've always wanted to be a teacher."

Ainsley cringed. Her niece had been living with her for several weeks now, and this was the first she'd heard of a potential major. She really needed to do a better job of communicating. "You'd be a wonderful teacher. Faith absolutely loves you, and I know you've been adding words to her vocabulary." It was true. It seemed like every day when Ainsley got home, Faith knew a new word. Today, she'd been surprised when she walked in the door and Faith lifted her arms and said, "Up."

"Let me give you guys some advice," Dustin said seriously. "Do some job shadowing. Make sure you're a good fit for whatever field you choose." He plucked another slice of pizza from the box. "I'm here to tell you that while work shouldn't be the most important thing in your life, it needs to be something you enjoy. You spend an awful lot of time doing it."

Ainsley grinned. "I had no idea you were such an insightful advice giver." The Dustin she'd known had always been asking for advice, not giving it.

A tinge of red crept up his face. She couldn't remember ever seeing him blush before.

"I try," he said sheepishly.

"That's a good idea," Julie said. "I'm sure I can find a teacher who'll let me sit in on their class for a day or two."

Colt nodded. "My mom would let you, I'm sure of it." He grinned. "She's teaching summer school right now."

"Cool." Julie shot Colt a dazzling smile. "That'd be great."

Dustin tossed his paper towel on the table. "The pizza was pretty good, huh?"

"It was," Ainsley took a small bite of her veggie pizza. "This reminds me of old times." She and Dustin had shared countless pizzas over the years. A wave of nostalgia swept over her. During her first couple of years at the park, she and Dustin had fallen into the habit of pizza and a movie on Friday nights. They'd never dated, but their fellow rangers had always given them a hard time about spending so much time together. Later, after she and Brad met, the three of them still carried on the tradition, although by that time, Dustin often had a new girl on his arm every week.

"Indeed." He looked at her thoughtfully.

Before she brought down the whole group with a walk down memory lane, she rose. "Let me get that for you." She held her hands out for Dustin's empty plate.

He shook his head. "Nope. I'll get it." He stood. "You just hang with your girl." He motioned at Faith, gnawing on her cookie. He collected everyone's plates and carried them into the kitchen. "Are the dishes in the dishwasher dirty?" he asked.

"Just leave them on the counter," Ainsley said. "I'll take care of it later." She wiped Faith's mouth and hands with a cloth. "Are you ready to get down?" she asked.

"Down," Faith agreed, grinning.

Ainsley set the child onto the ground.

Faith picked up her faded stuffed dog.

"Can you love the puppy?" Ainsley asked.

Faith hugged the stuffed animal to her and grinned.

"She takes that thing with her everywhere she goes," Ainsley said, laughing. "Someday, I'm going to show her a real puppy."

"She's never seen a real puppy before?" Dustin asked, removing the empty pizza box from the table.

"No. My parents' neighbors have a lab in their backyard, but he's fully grown." She smiled. "At least we have Bo Bo, the stuffed puppy, to keep her company."

Faith took off running toward the living room.

Colt laughed. "Man, she's a fast little thing."

"You have no idea. It's like she's able to be in three places at once." Julie grinned. "She certainly keeps me on my toes. By the end of the day, I feel like I've run a marathon."

Guilt washed over Ainsley. It seemed like Julie spent more time with Faith than she did these days. She'd started letting Faith stay up a little later than normal just to have more time with her. Edie had warned her about "mommy guilt," but she hadn't expected it to become a daily feeling.

Julie stood. "I'll go see what she's up to," she said.

Colt quickly followed her into the living room.

"You okay?" Dustin asked, coming over to stand by Ainsley's chair. "You look like you're a million miles away."

She managed a smile. "Just thinking." She shrugged. "Things don't always work out like you think they're going to, do they?"

He pulled out a chair and sat down next to her. "No. I guess they don't." He smiled kindly. "But you've always been able to roll with the punches."

"I don't know if I'm as resilient as I used to be." She sighed. "I don't feel like I've gotten to talk to you much since I've been back. How are you? Besides work."

He rubbed his jaw. "I guess I'm okay. Better now that you're here." He grinned. "I missed you."

She turned away from his piercing blue eyes, not wanting to see the hurt they reflected.

"Hey," Julie said from the doorway. "Are you two up for a game of Pictionary? If not, we're going to go for a walk."

Dustin and Ainsley exchanged a glance. On the one hand, a board game would let her exit the conversation. On the other, she owed Dustin an explanation for shutting him out these past couple of years. "I probably need to put Faith to bed in a few minutes," she said. "Why don't you guys go for a walk and maybe we can play some other time?"

Julie nodded. "Sounds good." She grinned. "Faith's reading to Colt right now, but we'll leave in a minute."

"Quite talented for only a year old," Dustin teased.

Ainsley met his eyes. "You'll have to get her to read you a book, too. It's mostly babbling and turning pages." She grinned. "But I happen to think she's a genius."

"With parents like hers, I don't doubt it." Dustin used to complain about always being in Brad's shadow academically. They'd graduated one and two in their high school class, though, and Brad always claimed that was only because Dustin hadn't applied himself. It had been one of their longest-standing arguments.

"She gets her brains from her daddy. I'm sure of it." Ainsley grinned. She stood. "Come on, let's go relieve them of babysitting duties."

"Thanks for having us over," Dustin said once they were alone. "I hated that we had to invite ourselves, but I figured I'd take a chance."

Ainsley sat down on the couch next to him and set the baby monitor on the coffee table. She'd put Faith to bed while he cleaned the kitchen. Everything in the house from the dishes to the furniture was so familiar to him. Yet it was almost like he was meeting her again for the first time. Despite the huge wall she kept around herself now, he'd started to catch glimpses of the girl he used to know. Becoming a widow and a mother nearly simultaneously had changed her, there was no doubt. But underneath it all, he was pretty sure his friend was still there somewhere. At least he hoped so.

"Thanks for the pizza. I'm pretty sure Julie was about to stage a rebellion if she had to eat vegetables again. Greasy pepperoni pizza probably kept me in her good graces for another few days." She sighed.

"I'm glad you have someone to help out," he said. "Although, I'll help you however I can. You know that."

She grinned. "I'm not sure you're ready for diaper duty, but thanks." She was quiet for a moment. "Listen. I want to apologize to you."

Dustin drew his brows together. "You don't need to." He knew he'd given her a hard time about her lack of communication with him over the past months. But he really didn't want her to feel bad about it. After all, she'd been going through something most people couldn't fathom.

She leaned over and nudged him with her elbow. "Yes. I do." She gave him a sideways glance. "I should've taken your calls and answered your e-mails. I missed you." Her voice grew husky. "But I couldn't deal with seeing your pain. I know that sounds crazy. I just. . .I had all I could handle with my own grief, and then Faith was born and life got really hectic." She sighed. "I didn't want to see that hurt in your eyes and know it was there because you missed Brad. I guess in some ways, it helped me to just pretend like you were fine. That was one less thing for me to worry about."

"I'm sorry for everything you've gone through." If he could take away her pain, he would. But history couldn't be rewritten. "I understand your not wanting to try and deal with my pain, too." He guessed he understood. But he didn't. Not really. He wished she would've let him help her get through it. Wasn't that what friends were for?

"Thanks for understanding." She gave him a tiny smile. "I was worried you might not forgive me. And believe me, there were a lot of times when I wanted to see you, to talk to you." She shook her head. "But I couldn't do it. I thought seeing you might make me too sad."

"And does it?" He was afraid of what her answer would be. Of course seeing him would remind her of Brad and all she'd lost. He had introduced them, and the three of them had hung out a lot. He'd even been the best man at their wedding.

That day had been so weird for him. On the one hand, he was

thrilled. He loved Brad like a brother, and it was nice to see him so happy. But there'd always been that little niggling idea in the back of his mind that Ainsley might've been exactly what he'd always hoped to find. Of course after she'd married his best friend, he'd convinced himself that he wasn't ready to settle down anyway. But still. For the first several months of their marriage, Dustin had been haunted by what Lindsey had called "what-might-have-been syndrome."

She grinned. "No. It makes me happy to see you. And these days, happiness doesn't exactly come easy. So I'm thankful to be here."

"Well believe me, I'm glad you're back. And I'm glad to hear that you're finding some happiness again." He motioned toward the baby monitor. "I can see that she brings you a lot of joy."

She grinned. "You have no idea. I love her more than I could have ever imagined. She's such a blessing."

"You're a great mother. Brad would be so proud." He was quiet for a minute. "And I know he'd be proud of you for coming back here. This was your place long before it was yours together. You know?"

Ainsley nodded. "I hope so. It's hard to make decisions alone and constantly wonder if I'm doing what he would've wanted." She pushed a stray strand of red hair from her eyes. Despite her tightly wound bun, one piece had escaped. "It's getting easier, though."

"I'm glad. How about work? Has that been a tough transition?"

She groaned. "Has it ever. I'm exhausted by the end of the day, but then I have to find the energy to be a good mom for Faith. It's impossible to find a balance." She sighed. "And my sister keeps telling me I need to find time for myself, but I don't know how to do that, other than get up at the crack of dawn."

"Well, since you've never been much of a sleeper, that shouldn't be a problem. Right?" he laughed. He used to tease her about being part vampire. But really, he worried about her troubled sleeping patterns more now than before. He saw the dark circles under her eyes, such a sharp contrast with her creamy skin.

She laughed. "I guess. It doesn't seem to be getting much better."

"Are you still running?" Years ago, she'd taken up running and found the daily exercise seemed to help her rest better.

"Not since I've been here."

Dustin glanced at her from the corner of his eye. "If you want to start meeting me in the mornings, we can do a run along the rim trail. Just like old times." He grinned. "Run along the rim trail, then grab a coffee at the Bright Angel before work." He raised his eyebrows in question.

She shook her head. "Oh, no. I couldn't." A shadow crossed her face. "I'd hate to ask Julie to be in charge any more than she already is."

"Wouldn't they be asleep that early?"

Ainsley's hazel eyes flashed. "I said no, okay?"

He bit his lip. How had he managed to upset her? "Okay. That's fine." He smiled. "Are you enjoying your ranger programs at least? I'm sure you're back in the swing of things there." Dustin didn't know how the interpretive staff did it. If he had to cover the same information day in and day out, he'd go crazy. He much preferred the law enforcement side of rangering. One day, he might help with a canyon rescue, and the next, he might have to pull over a tourist for speeding. He never knew what his day would hold. And he loved it.

"They're okay," she said quietly. "I'm going to be stationed at the main visitor center for the next month, so that should be fun."

Dustin cocked his head sideways. That wasn't normal. The interpretative rangers rotated to a different location each day. He didn't know if he'd ever heard of any of them staying stationary for a month. "What's up with that?"

She sighed. "Fine. I'll tell you." She shot him a serious look. "But don't make fun of me. You promise?"

He wrinkled his brow. "I won't. Just tell me."

"I seem to have developed some kind of phobia. Of the canyon." The desperation was evident in her voice. "I'm terrified of it. It's just one more item in the long list of things that keeps me awake at night." She looked at him frantically. "But don't tell anyone. Especially Lindsey. I can only imagine what she'd say about a Grand Canyon ranger who's scared of the Grand Canyon." She let out a snort. "It's the craziest thing you've ever heard, right?"

It was starting to make more sense now. He thought she'd acted funny the other day on her ranger program. And that guy, Jake, must've known about her fears. For a moment, the realization that she'd chosen to confide in some stranger before telling him caused his heart to sink. "No. Don't be so hard on yourself. You've been around here long enough to know that lots of people are frightened of heights at first." He bit his lip. "Maybe if you spend some time at the rim, you'll get used to it again."

She shook her head. "It makes me sick to think about."

Must be why she refused to go for a run along the trail. "Come on. You'll be fine." He grinned. "I'll go with you—remember, I'm trained in canyon safety. That should make you feel better."

"I don't think so," she said, her eyes bright with unshed tears. "I can't do it. But I'm afraid that if I don't get a grip on things in a month, I'm going to have to transfer to a different park."

After he'd just gotten her back? No way. "Tell you what. How about I try and help you conquer your fear? We'll start out running in the neighborhood. We'll gradually get closer to the rim trail. Before you know it, you'll be sitting on the edge, gazing out. I know that used to be your favorite thing." Ainsley used to love to sit near Hermit's Rest, reading her Bible and praying.

She'd told him once that she never felt as close to God as when she was sitting there, surrounded by peace and quiet and staring at one of His most beautiful creations. Over the past year, he'd started visiting that spot with his own Bible. He had to admit, there was much more peace in his life now.

She narrowed her eyes. "I don't know. Can I think about it?"

"Of course." He pointed at the backpack he'd gotten for Faith. It still sat in the same spot he'd put it after they'd gone for ice cream. "Guess you're not planning on hiking anytime soon either, huh?"

Ainsley made a face. "I know. I'm a big loser." She made an L shape with her thumb and index finger and held it up to her forehead.

Laughing, he reached over and pulled her close to him. "Don't talk about my old friend that way, okay?"

She buried her head against his chest. "Your old friend has some issues."

"Kid, we all have issues." He grinned, knowing what was coming next.

She pushed away from him. "Don't call me that." Her full lips were drawn into a scowl, but there was a joking tone to her voice that gave her away.

He laughed. "I'd have thought that you'd enjoy it now that you're in your thirties." When they first met, he'd liked to tease her about being just a kid. Not that his being four years older made much of a difference, but he'd always enjoyed teasing her.

"Ugh. Don't remind me." Her mouth twisted into a mischievous grin. "But maybe you can give me some pointers on old age, now that you're on the back side of thirty."

He winced. "I'm young at heart, though, and that's what matters." It was true. Just like the country song said, he still felt twenty-five. . .most of the time. Except that now his body ached a little more on days after he'd done yard work or lifted weights.

And he wasn't totally sure, but he might have a few gray hairs. But at least he still had hair, unlike some of his friends.

"I guess so." She narrowed her eyes. "And of course, I suppose dating younger women helps."

He knew if he told her he hadn't been on a date in at least a year, she'd never believe it. For some reason, she seemed to think that he was the same guy he'd been nearly ten years ago when they'd met. But he wasn't. His life bore little resemblance to the party-boy bachelor he'd turned into once she and Brad started dating. "Right," he murmured.

How could he ever confess to her that part of the reason he'd dated such a long string of women had been to help him forget that the one woman he'd thought he might actually have a future with had chosen to marry his best friend? It was too late now to own up to those old feelings. Even if they were still under the surface for him, he knew without a shadow of a doubt that she would never feel the same way, never be able to look at him without being haunted by memories. So he'd have to be content to just be her friend. As hard as that might be.

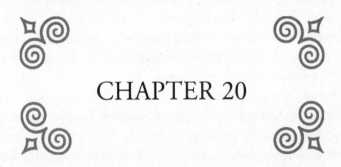

CHAPTER 20

I hope we're close when you get to be a teenager. I know it might be really uncool to hang out with your mom. But there's so much I want to be able to help you deal with. Thinking about you getting your heart broken someday just makes me sick, although I realize it's inevitable. Would you think I'm crazy if you found out I'm already praying about your future husband? Don't answer that. You're still in diapers, yet the other night I found myself asking God to make sure the man you'd someday fall in love with was worthy of your love. I know, I know. But a mother thinks about those things.

Julie and Colt sat in Ainsley's backyard, gazing up at the stars. It was amazing how many stars were visible. It reminded Julie of the school trip she'd taken to the planetarium in Flagstaff. Only better.

"I think I need to make a confession," Colt said finally.

Julie glanced over at his handsome profile. If he weren't so shy, he could be a movie star. Put him on the Disney Channel, and preteen girls everywhere would hang posters of him on their walls. And rightfully so. "My grandma says confession is good for the soul." She grinned. "So go ahead."

He sighed. "I get it." He looked over at her. "About your boyfriend, I mean." He propped himself up on his elbow. "I understand that we can only be friends. I'm not happy about it. But I'd rather be just your friend and get to hang out with you than to never see you at all."

She couldn't hide her smile. "Thanks. Hanging out as friends will be fun." And it would. It would be nice to hang out with a guy and not feel any pressure. Especially these past few months, it seemed like she'd spent half of their dates fighting off Heath's advances. She knew plenty of girls her age were sleeping with their boyfriends. But she wanted to save herself for marriage, something Heath didn't understand.

Colt smiled. "And by the way, I think you'll make an awesome teacher someday. I'll ask Mom if you can come by her classroom sometime soon."

"Cool. Probably a Monday would be best because Ainsley is off work. That way I won't have to bring Faith." She could only imagine the chaos that would ensue if she asked Ainsley if she could take Faith somewhere. Her aunt was really overprotective. She'd probably be scared Faith would get a germ from one of the students.

"I should probably get going soon," he said. "Besides, I'm pretty sure I've already wowed you with my knowledge of constellations, so my job here is done." Despite bragging that he'd taken an astronomy class, Colt hadn't been able to point out many constellations.

"Well, at least you got the Big Dipper. That's the main one, right?"

He laughed. "Right." He stood. "Hey, there's a devotional at Mather Amphitheater Sunday night at sunset. You want to go with me?"

"Sure," Julie said. "That sounds like fun." She participated in her youth group back home but over the past months had become less active. Heath thought the activities were lame, but Julie had always enjoyed them. Bowling, putt-putt, movie night... she missed that stuff. But she missed the devotionals most of all. She tried to be a good influence on Heath and hoped that someday he'd have a change of heart. But so far, he'd balked every time she asked him to attend one. It made her feel awful, like she wasn't doing a good enough job of sharing her faith. But she couldn't force him to share her beliefs.

"Good." He grinned. "And by the way, I was totally just trying to make you feel better about those constellations. I really know them all."

She rolled her eyes. "Yep. Whatever." Her mouth turned upward in a smile. "Just text me on Sunday and let me know what time."

"You know it." He pulled her to him in a quick hug. "I'm gonna go on now. I don't wanna wake Faith up. But tell Ainsley and Dustin I said thanks for the pizza."

He headed off down the street with a wave.

Julie sank down into the porch swing and watched him walk away. It would be nice to have a friend. Colt was a good guy. She knew he meant it when he said he just wanted friendship. He wouldn't cross the line.

⊚☜

"Did you and Colt have fun tonight?" Ainsley asked, taking a seat next to Julie on the porch swing.

Julie nodded. "Yep. We walked over and got ice cream and then came back to look at the stars." She giggled. "He acted like he was some kind of pro at finding constellations but then could only find the Big Dipper. It was hilarious."

Ainsley chuckled. "I'm glad you had a good time." She'd had a good time, too. Dustin had a way of making her feel like she was still that twenty-something girl who thought she could take on the world. It was nice to be around someone who believed in her so much. He thought she could beat her fears in no time and be the fearless woman she'd always been. She wasn't so sure about that, but it was nice to know someone had such faith in her.

Julie heaved a great sigh. "Colt promised me that he understands we're just going to be friends."

"Why do I get the feeling that you're not too happy about that?" Ainsley glanced at her niece from the corner of her eye.

Julie widened her eyes. "Oh, I'm totally happy about it. It's kinda nice to hang out with a guy and there not be any pressure, you know?" She shrugged.

"Right." Ainsley wondered what kind of pressure Julie was referring to. She had a strong suspicion she knew. "Does Heath pressure you to do things you aren't ready for?" She already dreaded Faith's teenage years, and they hadn't even reached the terrible twos.

Julie sighed. "Have you ever known somebody who made you feel all gooey inside?" Julie asked. "Like, I just want to melt into a puddle around Heath."

Ainsley smiled. "I do know that feeling."

"At first, I guess I was just in awe that someone like him was even interested in me," Julie explained. "I mean, he was a few grades ahead of me when we first met. He could've gone out with any of the older girls. But he liked me." Her lips turned up in a smile at the memory. "He had this convertible back then, and I remember once my sophomore year, he offered me a ride. I felt like I was going to die from happiness. The radio was loud, the air was warm, and he looked at me like I was the most beautiful girl in the world." She met Ainsley's gaze. "No one had ever looked at me like that before."

First love was powerful. There was no doubt about it. Ainsley still remembered the first boy she'd kissed, back when she was sixteen. There was something intoxicating about it; that was for sure. The first time she realized she had an effect on someone else, that she had the power to make his heart beat faster. Ainsley smiled. "I understand. I know I probably seem old and out of touch to you, but in some ways it seems like only yesterday that I was seventeen and riding in a car with a boy seemed like heaven on earth."

Julie laughed. "You don't seem out of touch." She twisted her mouth into a mischievous grin. "And only a little bit old."

"Ha." Ainsley grimaced. "Very funny."

"Actually, I like that I can talk to you." Julie sighed. "Mama doesn't ever want to hear about Heath. She only wants to tell me that he's all wrong for me."

Ainsley bit her lip. She was on the same page as Rachel on this one, but she hated to tell Julie. "Rachel just wants what's best for you. She wants you to be happy and safe." She reached over and patted Julie's bare leg. "And from what I hear, Heath might not be the most respectful of guys."

Julie was quiet for a moment. "He does have a temper. And he cusses sometimes. I hate that." She shrugged. "But he loves me."

Ainsley sighed. "Julie, maybe he loves you in his own way. But I know he yells at you. And I know about what happened on graduation night." She shook her head. "And I'm sure there's other stuff besides that. I get that you've fallen hard for him. But I promise you that there will be other guys. Guys who won't get mad and take it out on you. Guys who will put you first and who share your values."

"It's so complicated." Julie heaved a great sigh. "Heath needs me. I feel responsible for him, you know?" She shrugged. "He says I'm the only good thing he's got going in his life."

"You're going to get mad at me for saying this." Ainsley gave her niece a tiny smile. "But I'm going to take the chance. That's way too much pressure to put on someone. It kind of sounds to me like he's manipulating you into staying with him by taking advantage of your sweet nature."

Julie rolled her eyes. "That's pretty much what Colt said, too. Heath's not manipulating me, though. He loves me."

Which to address first? Colt or manipulation? Ainsley sighed. "I know this is a tough lesson to learn at seventeen. But sometimes, even people we love find ways to manipulate us. That doesn't necessarily mean they don't love us. It just means that's how they operate." She cringed inwardly. She was going to have to get much better at this if she wanted to be a good mother. "My friend Kristy used to date a guy who was that way. She was engaged to him actually." Kristy counted the fact that the wedding had never happened among her biggest blessings, as now she was married to a wonderful man. "He was kind of like that. He used her forgiving nature to his advantage and somehow he always made her feel like his happiness was her responsibility." She leveled her gaze at Julie. "But it wasn't. The same way you aren't responsible for Heath. You can't make him be a better person. You can't convince him to make better decisions. And you can't save him if he doesn't really want to be saved."

Julie's lower lip trembled. "But what if I'm the only chance he'll ever have of knowing God?"

Wow. This was so far out of her league. Ainsley's heart pounded with the difficult question. "Honey, he knows your beliefs, right?"

Julie nodded. "And I try and talk to him about coming with me to church, but he won't do it."

"You can't force him to have a relationship with the Lord." She shrugged. "All you can do is be true to yourself." She put an arm around Julie. "I'm sorry you're dealing with this. I know it's hard."

"It makes me so sad. I love him." Julie's eyes filled with tears. "But I know we have problems."

Ainsley nodded. "You're about to be off at college, and you're going to have lots of choices to make. Your parents aren't going to be calling the shots any longer." She smoothed Julie's hair. "You have to decide who you are and make sure you're making choices that reflect that person."

Julie managed a tiny smile. "As much as I hate to admit it, growing up might not be all it's cracked up to be."

"I have a feeling you're going to be just fine."

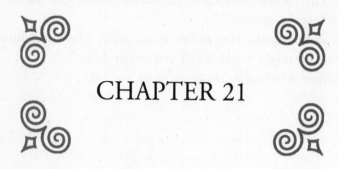

CHAPTER 21

I wonder if everyone questions their mothering skills. Does it get easier with the second child? The third? Or will I finally feel like I'm a good mother when you're a certain age? Sometimes I wonder. I asked my mom what she thought. She laughed at me. Laughed. She said she still worries sometimes that she gives me the wrong advice. I'm thinking this means I'll constantly question myself. But the more I see you learn and grow, the more I think I must be doing something right. The other night, you put your hands together for the prayer, and I wanted to jump up and down and cheer. I promise not to cheer every time you make a good decision, though. At least not out loud.

Jake stood at the Bright Angel Trailhead. It was a beautiful morning at the canyon. He'd caught the sunrise at Mather Point, followed by a hearty breakfast at the Bright Angel Lodge restaurant. So far, it had been a perfect morning, and he was looking forward to a short hike. His multiday camping trip had been successful but exhausting. The family he'd led was athletic and well prepared for their hike. Today, his group only wanted to hike down to the three-mile rest house. Shane had warned him it was two elderly woman hikers, so Jake was on the lookout for white hair and bifocals.

He glanced at his watch. Mavis and Mary Bunch were late.

"Ooh, are you our guide, young man?"

Jake turned toward the voice.

A tall woman with bright orange hair sauntered over to him. "I'm Mavis," she drawled, her voice dripping with Southern belle. "And my big sister Mary will be here in a minute. She's shopping over at the El Tovar gift shop. Said she needed a bandana for the hike." Mavis adjusted her oversized sunglasses.

Mavis was seventy if she was a day, so the thought of her referring to someone as her big sister made Jake chuckle.

A shorter woman with hair so dark it was nearly purple hurried up to where they stood. "Mercy, it's hot," she drawled, wiping her face with a blue bandana. "We may as well be smack dab in the middle of Georgia it's so steamy."

"We're from Daphne, Alabama," Mavis explained. "Right on the Gulf Coast. It gets hot there, but we have a nice gulf breeze to cool us down."

He shook hands with each of them. "I'm Jake, and I'm very pleased to meet you."

Mavis turned to Mary with a grin. "He might not be a Southern boy, but he's got good manners."

Mary giggled. "Sure enough." She batted her mascara-caked lashes at Jake. "Now go easy on us, Jake. We're not exactly professional hikers."

"Hiking into the Grand Canyon has been on my bucket list ever since my husband passed." Mavis dramatically wiped her brow. "My grandson came back from a trip out here with the most amazing pictures, and I thought to myself, Mavis, you need to go out there to Arizona and have your picture made down in the canyon." She grinned. "We're going to send it in to the newspaper back home."

Jake had been wrong with his expectations. These two were miles away from white hair and bifocals. "Have you been preparing for the hike?" They looked fairly fit, but it was a hot day. Hiking down might not be too hard, but coming up was brutal even for people half their age.

Mavis and Mary exchanged a glance. "We've been walking a mile every day," Mary said. "And taking a Zumba class at the YMCA."

Mavis wiggled her hips and waved her hands in the air. "We love that Zumba class. Makes me feel like I'm forty again."

"Oh, stop that, Mavis," Mary chided. "People are looking."

Jake glanced around. A young couple had stopped and were watching Mavis's dance with interest. He cleared his throat. "Okay, ladies. I'm glad to hear that you've been exercising in preparation for the hike." He gestured at the trail. "Tell you what. How about we start hiking and make plenty of stops to rest and take pictures?"

Mavis beamed. "Jake, you're a peach."

"Do you both have plenty of water?" He carried extra, just in case, but it would make his life much easier if they were prepared.

They nodded in unison. "We've been reading up on what to bring," Mary said. "We have water and salty snacks. That's what the guide books say to bring."

Jake grinned. "Sounds like you're ready." He tightened the strap on his backpack. "Okay, ladies, follow me."

ॐ

Jake leaned against a rock. "You two doing okay?"

Mavis plopped down on the rock. "I'm good." She turned to Mary, who was busy snapping pictures with her digital camera. "You okay, Mary?"

"Oh, yes." Mary took one final shot then sat down next to her sister. "I can't believe we've never been here before. It's so beautiful."

Jake took a swig of water. "President Roosevelt said that every American should see the Grand Canyon sometime in their life."

"Teddy or Franklin?" Mavis asked.

Mary rolled her eyes. "I told you this on the plane. It was Teddy." She grinned at Jake. "Right?"

"Maybe I was just checking to see if he knew which one," Mavis growled at Mary. She smiled sweetly at Jake. "But I'm sure a smart young man like you knew the answer."

Jake sighed. These two had been bickering ever since they began their descent into the canyon. "I did." No need to tell them the only reason he knew the fact at all was because he'd overheard Ainsley's ranger program. He wondered how she was doing. He should've called to check on her. But the truth was, he'd hoped she would contact him. He'd been the one to initiate things up to this point, so he'd been waiting a few days to see if she might send him a text or give him a call. But maybe she was a traditional kind of woman who expected the man to do the calling. He raked his hand through his hair and glanced over at the sisters. They were both staring at him like he'd grown horns.

"Are you okay, honey?" Mavis asked. "We asked you if you'd take our picture before we hiked farther, but you just sat there, staring out into the canyon." She giggled. "Is there a nekkid woman down there or something?"

"Oh, Mavis. Really." Mary shook her head. "Leave him alone." She held her camera out to Jake. "Here you go."

Mavis and Mary got situated with a minimal amount of arguing, and Jake snapped a few pictures.

"Just a little farther ahead is an awesome spot for a picture." He grinned. "It might be the one you want to send to the newspaper."

They walked slowly down the path, careful to stay near the canyon wall. The drop-off into the canyon looked menacing, even to Jake, who'd hiked it several times. A few minutes later, they came to the spot he'd mentioned.

"Ooh," Mary exclaimed. "It's incredible."

An arch had been carved into the rock, and hikers had to hike through the arch to continue on the trail. It was one of Jake's favorite spots.

Mavis dropped her backpack and began to shuffle through it. She came up with a tube of lipstick. "I want to look nice for this one," she explained. "Mary, help me make sure I get my lips painted on straight."

Mary groaned. "Vanity is unbecoming on you." She shook her head at Jake. "She's been this way all her life. I think Mama dropped her on her head when she was a baby."

Jake grinned. He doubted he'd have a more entertaining hike the rest of the summer. Finally, they were primped and ready for the photo.

Mavis leaned against the arch, Mary at her side.

"One, two, three," he counted. He clicked a few photos.

"Thank you," Mavis breathed.

"Excuse me, sir?" Mary asked a man hiking past. "Could you take a picture of all three of us?"

"Certainly," the man said.

Jake hesitated for a minute. He hated getting his picture taken.

"Come on, Jake. You can stand in the middle," Mavis called.

Jake took his spot between the sisters and smiled for the camera.

"Thanks," Mary said, once the picture was taken.

Mavis nodded. "That one might be the one we put in the paper. All the girls in our Zumba class will be so jealous." She chuckled and did a little wiggle in place.

Jake motioned for them to follow him through the arch. "If you'll look up toward the top of the canyon, you can see some markings." He pointed them out. "There's a lot of speculation as to how old they are or what group did them, but I think they're pretty neat to look at."

"Just like Egyptian hieroglyphics," Mavis said, clearly enthralled.

Mary shook her head. "No, no, no. Those are pictographs," she said in disgust. "I don't know why you didn't read the guide book."

"No matter what they're called, I think they're charming," Mavis said matter-of-factly.

By the time they reached the next switchback in the trail, both women were huffing and puffing. Jake motioned to a section of rocks just off the trail near the wall of the canyon. "Let's rest for a minute." He didn't want to hurt their feelings, but he was beginning to get worried. His job was to get them safely out of the canyon, and he wasn't sure how much farther down they should go.

The women took sips of water. Mavis stood up and looked out over the trail. "Wow. You can see how it curves and curves down there." She motioned at Mary. "Come see."

Mary pushed off the rock she was sitting on and went to join her sister. "Sure is a long way down there." She pointed at something down the trail. "Look how tiny the hikers look from up here. And are those mules?"

Jake joined them at the overlook. "Yep. The mules carry people down into the canyon and then back up. It's a fun trip, but I prefer to hike down."

"I hope y'all won't get mad at me," Mavis said, fanning herself. "But I don't think I can go too much farther."

Mary breathed a big sigh. "Oh, thank goodness. I can already tell it's going to be hard going to hike back up to the top."

"Good idea," Jake said. He pointed at a spot a few yards away that would give them more space to sprawl out and rest. "How about we make it down to those rocks, then we'll sit and wait for the mules to pass?"

Mavis squealed with delight. "Oh, that would be wonderful. We can take pictures of the mules, too. That way, everyone will know we've really been down into the canyon."

They made their way carefully down to the rocks and sat down.

Mary passed a granola bar to Mavis then glanced over at Jake. "Do you want one?" she asked.

He shook his head. "I'm good right now, thanks."

She opened her bar and took a bite.

"So, Jake," Mavis said, "are you married?"

Mary shot her a look. "Don't be so nosy."

"I'm just making conversation," Mavis said in a hurt voice.

He laughed. "It's okay. No. I'm not married. I guess you could say I might be a bachelor for life."

"You could go on that TV show," Mavis said. "Except that those girls seem a little trashy to me, so maybe you should find one the old-fashioned way."

Mary groaned. "Just ignore her, Jake. I've spent my whole life having to do that."

"I don't think I'm quite ready to go on national TV to find a wife." He grinned. "But thanks for the suggestion."

"So you aren't even dating anyone?" Mavis continued. "Because I have a granddaughter about your age. You'd have to move to Alabama, though." She grinned. "Because I don't think she'd leave her job, even for an adorable thing like you."

"He doesn't want to move to Alabama," Mary said. "Can you imagine having this in your backyard?" She waved her arm at the canyon.

Mavis wrinkled her nose. "We have the gulf. It's pretty beautiful, too. Plus, we have wonderful weather. Hardly any winter." She grinned. "I know it gets cold here during the winters. That's why we waited until summer." She jerked her head in her sister's direction. "I didn't want to take the chance of Mary falling and breaking a hip."

Mary grimaced. "That isn't true, and you know it." She glared at Mavis and turned her attention toward Jake. "We didn't come during the winter because Mavis thinks winter clothes make her look fat," she said conspiratorially.

Jake looked at his watch. This was turning into one long day. "Here come the mules, ladies. Get your cameras ready."

The women scrambled for their cameras and poised them for shooting. "That first mule looks a little bit like Burl Hanks," Mavis whispered.

A laugh escaped Mary's mouth, but she clapped her hand over her lips to keep it in. "You shouldn't say such things." She leaned over to Jake. "Burl took Mavis to a Mardi Gras ball last year." She clucked her tongue. "It was a disaster."

The mule train plodded past.

"I'm glad we didn't try that," Mary said. "I'd be a nervous wreck."

Jake laughed. "It isn't that bad. After a few minutes of hiking uphill, you might wish for a mule to come by and offer you a ride."

"I'll take my chances," she retorted. "My own legs have been carrying me for more than seventy years. I think they'll do okay." She turned to her sister, whose mouth was already open for a reply. "Don't you say a word."

Jake slowly stood. "Well, ladies. Are you ready?"

They nodded.

"We won't go too fast, and if either of you need to rest at any point, just say the word." He sighed. It was going to be a long hike out of the canyon. The only bright spot was knowing that once he got to the top, he was going to call Ainsley to see if she wanted to have dinner again one night soon. He might not want to go on TV to find romance, but at least he could put forth some effort.

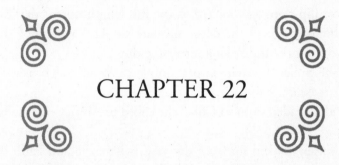

CHAPTER 22

I wish I could tell you that I knew I was going to marry your daddy from the moment we met, but it didn't quite happen that way. Sure, we hit it off, but I wasn't sold on him romantically for a few weeks. His form of flirting was to make fun of me and if there's one thing I hate, it's feeling stupid. But eventually, he won me over because he was just so sweet. He'd bring me flowers and leave me the corniest love notes. I still have those saved if you ever want to see them. Of course, it helped that he was adorable.

Once we started dating in earnest, I never looked back. It taught me an important lesson, though—make sure you give everyone a chance. If I'd have written him off after that first meeting, we never would've married and I wouldn't have you. Believe me, the world would be a sad place without you in it.

Julie flipped through her closet. For the millionth time, she wished she'd brought more clothes. Or at least less junky clothes and more cute ones. It hadn't occurred to her that she might actually go out and do things here, so she'd mostly come prepared for hanging out at home with a toddler. She finally settled on a faded pair of jeans and a turquoise tank top. She stepped into a pair of flip-flops and looked in the full-length mirror that hung on the back side of the door. She sure wouldn't win any fashion awards, but she didn't look terrible, either.

She pulled her hair into a simple ponytail and brushed on some mascara. Not bad.

"I'm headed to meet Colt," she called to Ainsley out the back door.

Ainsley looked up from the yard, where she and Faith were playing peekaboo. "Have fun. Call me if you need me," she said.

Julie grabbed her bag and stepped outside. The heat washed over her, and she was glad she'd put her hair up. She quickly walked to the shuttle stop where she was supposed to meet Colt. Maybe meeting her at a generic location was his way of making sure she knew he was taking their "just friends" agreement seriously.

He stood up as she approached. "Hey there," he said, grinning. "You want to take the shuttle, or do you want to walk?"

She thought for a minute. "Let's wait a few minutes on the shuttle. If it doesn't come soon, we'll walk." She didn't want to get there and be all sweaty if she could help it.

"Fair enough." He grinned. "You can meet some of my friends tonight. If you want to, I mean." He stuck his hands in the pockets of his cargo shorts.

Julie blinked. Heath hardly ever let her around his friends. He always said they'd think she was a baby. "Meeting your friends sounds fun." She glanced down the road at the approaching bus. "Looks like we get to take the shuttle after all."

"Perfect." He stood aside and let her board first.

"Do many people attend these things?" she asked, once they were seated.

He shrugged. "It depends. There'll be a handful of locals and probably some park visitors, too."

Fifteen minutes later, they were at the Shrine of the Ages, a multipurpose building. Ainsley had mentioned giving ranger talks there in the winter, and it was also where they attended church services.

"There's a trail right over here," Colt pointed at a wide path. "This goes to Mather Amphitheater. It's kinda in the middle of the woods but isn't a bad walk." They set out on the trail.

At a searing pain in her foot, Julie stopped. "Ouch," she said, raising her foot. A sharp rock had found its way into her flip-flop.

"You okay?" Colt asked. He pointed at her feet. "We can slow down if you need to."

"Are you kidding? I could run a marathon in these things," Julie said, grinning. "Just a rock or something, no big deal." She was touched that he offered to slow down for her, though. Colt really was a sweetheart.

"Here it is," Colt said as they came to a large amphitheater. Wooden seats faced a bare stage. "Ranger talks are given here every night in the summer," he said. "I'm surprised Ainsley hasn't brought you here yet."

Julie made a face. "Are you kidding? I've barely been out of the house. I really want to hike the rim trail sometime soon, and I'm dying to go down into the canyon." She grinned. "Even if I just go a little ways down, I want to be able to say I hiked part of it."

"Definitely. And sometime soon, we'll hike the rim trail all the way to Hermit's Rest. It's my favorite place to watch the sunset." He laughed. "Actually, my favorite place to watch the sunset is wherever I happen to be when the sun is setting."

"I like that attitude." She couldn't hide her smile.

Colt introduced her to a few of his buddies, who were sitting together. "There's Dustin," he said, pointing to a spot near the stage.

"I didn't know he'd be here," she said. "We haven't seen him at church these past weeks." She knew her aunt had noticed, too, because she'd commented about it earlier in the day as they were leaving the service.

"Oh, that's because he works some Sundays and on the Sundays when he doesn't work, he drives Mrs. Whittaker to Williams to go to church with her nephew's family."

"That's nice of him."

Colt nodded. "Yeah, he's a good guy. He's probably leading the devotional tonight." He shrugged. "He's as close as we have to a youth minister here."

Julie was surprised. Ainsley had never mentioned that. "Cool."

A hush fell over the small crowd, their cue to be seated. As a man in the second row stood up to lead a prayer, Julie glanced over at Colt. His eyes were closed. She'd never noticed how long his eyelashes were before. Any girl would kill to have lashes like those.

Colt opened his eyes and shot her a look.

She felt a blush creeping up her face and quickly closed her eyes and bowed her head. How embarrassing.

As soon as the prayer was over, he leaned over. "Were you just checking me out?" he whispered teasingly, his breath hot against her ear.

She wrinkled her nose. "Of course not. I was. . .I thought there was a bug on you." Okay, she was in trouble for telling a white lie at a devo, but she couldn't tell him the truth. That she might've been checking him out just a little bit.

He grinned. "Try and pry your eyes away from me and concentrate," he said, chuckling.

"Don't flatter yourself," she said from the corner of her mouth.

Dustin stood just then and smiled at the crowd. "Thanks, everyone, for coming. It's a beautiful night to worship our Lord."

A couple of people in the crowd shouted, "Amen."

"As most of you know, I often come up with these devotional thoughts as a result of things that go on in my own life," he said, pacing in front of the stage. "These past few days, I've been thinking about making decisions."

Julie shifted on the uncomfortable wooden bench and brushed against Colt.

"Can't stay away from me, huh?" he murmured.

"Zip it," she hissed. But she couldn't squash the giddy feeling rising up. They might be just friends, but maybe it was okay to be a little flirtatious. She turned her attention to Dustin. *After* the devo.

⊚⌀

Ainsley stood over the crib and watched her sleeping daughter. They'd had such a wonderful day, laughing and playing. It was almost scary how fast Faith was growing. It seemed like just yesterday when she'd been a tiny baby. Now her personality was starting to blossom. It was hard to believe she was already fifteen months old. Just in the few weeks they'd been at the canyon, Faith had grown and changed. She rarely lost her balance anymore when she walked.

The ringing phone sounded from the kitchen, and Ainsley hurried out of Faith's room to grab it.

"Did I catch you at a bad time?" Jake asked.

Ainsley walked into the living room and sank onto the couch. "Nope. I just got Faith down for the night, so all is finally quiet here."

He chuckled. "Time for you to relax now, huh?"

As if. With Faith finally in bed, maybe now Ainsley could start on the mountain of laundry that needed to be done. She didn't want to bore him with the details of her life, though. "So what are you up to?"

"Doing a little relaxing of my own. I've spent several days hiking." He sighed. "Anyway, I just thought I'd check to see how you were doing."

"We've had a nice weekend. We had lunch at Edie's after church and spent the rest of the afternoon playing and napping."

"That sounds nice," he said. "Especially the napping."

"Yeah, that sort of goes along with having a toddler. If she doesn't get an afternoon nap, she's prone to a meltdown." Faith had gotten cranky after lunch, disproving Edie's theory that she never cried. Screamed was more like it. There was something about wrestling with a screaming toddler that always made Ainsley feel like a failure of a mother, but Edie had assured her otherwise.

He laughed. "I've seen a couple of those with my niece and nephew. Not a pretty sight."

"Definitely not."

"So I thought I'd see if maybe you wanted to grab dinner one night this week. I'd love to drive into Tusayan—you know, get off of park grounds for a little while."

She hesitated. She hated to make plans at night. It wasn't that she didn't want to see Jake, it was just that her time with Faith was precious. "Well, I'd need to check with Julie to make sure she doesn't mind babysitting one night. You know, she's here all day with Faith—I want her to have some time off, or at least time where she isn't in charge of a child."

He sighed. "Oh. Sure. I understand."

Ainsley almost suggested taking Faith with them but thought better of it. If that were something he wanted to do, surely he would've mentioned it. "She's gone right now, but I'll ask her when she gets home. Is there a particular night you had in mind?"

"How about Wednesday or Thursday? Whichever works best."

"I'm sure one of those will be fine. I'm not sure what time she'll be home tonight, but I'll call you tomorrow."

"I'll be looking forward to it."

She clicked the phone off and rested her head on the back of the couch. Jake was a nice guy. He seemed very genuine, and she appreciated that trait. But she wasn't certain he understood that her daughter had to come first. For a second, she thought about Dustin and his constant offers to help. While she didn't expect that of Jake, considering they were still getting to know one another, she couldn't help but make the comparison. Ainsley tossed the phone onto the coffee table.

The mountain of laundry would wait no longer. In fact, it seemed to have grown during her phone conversation.

Twenty minutes later, she'd started a new load and returned to the living room with a basket of Faith's clothes that Julie had managed to wash and dry.

Just as she started folding Faith's clothes, a key turned in the door, and Julie walked in, her high ponytail bouncing. Someone must've had a good night.

"Hey there," Ainsley said quietly, not wanting to startle her.

Julie smiled. "I'm surprised you're still up. I didn't mean to stay out so late."

Ainsley glanced at the clock above the couch. It was nearly eleven. She hadn't even realized Julie was out later than normal. She really needed to get better about this whole supervision thing. "Oh, you know me. If I were in bed now, I'd just be tossing and turning." She grinned. "Besides, I'm running a Laundromat here."

Julie sat down and started folding. "Here, let me help. I'm too wound up to go to bed, anyway."

"Did you have fun tonight?"

"Yep. I met some of Colt's friends. We ended up hanging out after the devo, just talking." She grinned. "He's so funny. He's always giving me a hard time about stuff I do or say." She giggled. "And I think it surprises him when I give him a hard time back."

161

Just friends, huh? Ainsley decided to keep her opinions to herself. Might be better to just let things play out the way they were supposed to. "How was the devo?"

Julie tossed a pair of folded socks into the basket. "It was really good. Dustin talked about how every time we have important decisions to make, we should make them prayerfully." She met Ainsley's gaze. "He gave lots of examples from the Bible of people who were making decisions or going through tough times, and the thing that tied them all together was the fact that they prayed first."

Ainsley was too stuck on Julie's second sentence to even begin to digest the rest of her words. "*Dustin* was the one who gave the devotional talk?" That couldn't be right. He'd always shied away from those. Brad used to be in charge of weekly devotionals, and the most he ever got Dustin to do during them was thanking everyone for coming.

"Yep. Colt says Dustin's kind of like the youth minister around here." She grinned. "I can totally see that. He'd make a great youth minister. He seems to really care about Colt and his friends. He knew all about them and what's going on with them and stuff." She shrugged. "Plus, he's funny, and that's always a good characteristic for a youth minister."

Ainsley tired to wrap her head around the information. She sank down onto the couch next to Julie. "I didn't even know if he went to church anymore," she said weakly.

"Oh, about that," Julie piped up. "Colt says that on the Sundays he doesn't have to work, he drives some lady to Williams so she can go to church with her nephew." Julie wrinkled her nose. "Mrs. Whitten or something like that?"

Ainsley's eyes widened. "Mrs. Whittaker?"

"That's it." Julie nodded. "Why? You know her?"

"She's the librarian." The librarian who'd once upon a time warned Ainsley to stay away from the likes of Dustin.

Julie yawned. "Okay. I think I'm going to bed." She leaned toward Ainsley. "Are you okay?"

"What? Oh. Good night." She gave Julie a half smile.

Ainsley sat in silence. People rarely surprised her anymore. But the news about Dustin and his ministry was a shocker. What else did she not know about her old friend?

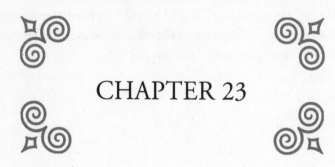

CHAPTER 23

*I used to think those people who went on and on about
their kids were tiresome. But now I understand. The other
day, I actually took my phone out of my pocket and showed
your picture to a group of tourists I met in the visitor center.
It was like an out-of-body experience. I couldn't believe
I'd turned in to one of those mothers. But I'm so proud to
be your mom. I want everyone to know how special you
are. And you have my word that if I ever get into a relationship with anyone, he will understand that we're a package
deal.*

Jake stood nervously on Ainsley's porch and waited.

The door swung open, and Julie stood, grinning. Faith was
on her hip, a stuffed dog in her hand. "Come in. She'll be ready
in a minute."

"Running late again? Was there another lipstick incident?"
He chuckled.

Julie shook her head. "Nope. Nothing like that. She got in
from work late and wanted to be the one to feed Faith." She

shifted the little girl to her other hip. "Can you love the puppy dog, Faith?"

Faith grinned and hugged the dog to her. "Mmm," she said.

Ainsley breezed into the room, wearing a yellow shirtdress that tied at the waist. Her hair was pulled back in a low ponytail, but one dark red strand had already escaped. "Okay, I'm ready," she said, grabbing her bag from the coffee table. She leaned over and kissed Faith on the cheek. "Be a good girl, okay? I love you."

Jake held the door open for her, and they stepped out onto the porch. "You hungry?" he asked.

"Very," she said. "Lunch seems like a long time ago."

They got to the end of the path, and Ainsley stopped. She cast one more glance back at Faith and Julie, who stood on the porch, waving.

She waved. "Bye, sweet girl," she called. "Julie, I have my phone if you need me."

He'd never dated a woman who had a child. Something about seeing the look in Ainsley's eyes as she looked back at Faith made him think he should offer to let her just stay home. He hadn't considered that she'd been away from her child all day and it might be difficult to leave again so soon. "So how would you feel about a little change of plans?" he asked.

"How so?" She wrinkled her forehead.

He grinned. "I know I mentioned driving into Tusayan, but I made reservations at the El Tovar Dining Room instead." The restaurant at the exclusive El Tovar Hotel advertised itself as the only fine dining on park grounds. Jake had heard wonderful things about both the food and service, so he figured it was a good way to impress a date.

Her hazel eyes widened in surprise. "The El Tovar?" she asked. "That sounds wonderful."

"And this way, I didn't have to get my truck out, either. We can just take the shuttle." He grinned. "Those things sure do come in handy."

She nodded. "I save so much money on gas." She shrugged. "I rarely have to get my car out, unless we're going into Williams or Flagstaff."

They climbed onto the packed shuttle and rode in silence to the El Tovar stop.

Jake glanced at his watch. "We're a few minutes early for our reservation," he said. "Do you want to sit outside or go ahead and go in?" The El Tovar sat right on the rim, so he figured she'd want to go on inside rather than be so close to the canyon. But he wanted to give her options.

"Have you ever been inside?" she asked.

He grinned. "It's been years. I think my dad took our family there for breakfast once."

"Let's go on in. The interior is really beautiful, and there's plenty to look at while we wait."

Jake held the door open for her, and they stepped inside. The main lobby managed to combine elegance with rustic charm. It gave the appearance of a cozy hunting lodge with stuffed animal heads on the walls and gorgeous dark wood finish.

"I'll let them know we're here," he offered. He waited in line at the hostess station. "McGuire, party of two," he said once it was his turn. "We have reservations."

The young hostess nodded. "It will be just a couple of minutes." She handed him a buzzer. "Take this, but stay close. We should be able to seat you momentarily."

Jake made his way through the crowd to where Ainsley stood. He held up the buzzer. "It'll be just a few minutes."

Ainsley nodded. "That's fine. The food here is definitely worth waiting for." She smiled. "How were your hikes? Do you have any more overnight trips scheduled?"

"The hikes were fine. The overnight trip was great. It was this family who'd been preparing for their hike for the past year," he explained. "The one I led on Saturday wasn't as great. It was these two old ladies from Alabama." He shook his head. "They were like characters out of a sitcom, bickering and cutting up."

Ainsley grinned. "Sounds like a fun time to me."

He rolled his eyes. "They were ridiculous. Putting on lipstick and snapping pictures. One of them did a dance at the top of the trailhead."

She burst out laughing. "How old were they?"

"In their seventies, I think."

"That's awesome." She smiled. "I love the variety of people who come through here. Meeting people from so many different backgrounds is one of my favorite things about my job."

He scowled. "People kept staring at us. All the way down and then back up." He shook his head.

"Did they at least have a good time?" she asked.

"They told me it was the best trip they'd ever been on, including the time they went on a singles cruise last year." He gave her a tiny smile. "And they took a picture of the three of us to submit to their local newspaper."

She giggled. "You're going to be a star in Alabama."

"Well, I have been waiting for my big break." He grinned. "Oh, it looks like our table is ready." He held up the flashing buzzer. "After you," he said, motioning toward the hostess station.

☙❧

Ainsley followed the hostess to their table. She glanced around, hoping Lindsey wouldn't have any reason to come out of the kitchen. Maybe this wasn't a "meet the chef" kind of night.

Jake pulled out her seat.

"Thanks," she said. His gentlemanly ways never failed to impress her, although dining at the El Tovar was a little fancier than her normal fare.

Jake picked up a menu. "What's good here?"

It had been a long time since Ainsley had eaten at the El Tovar. She, Brad, Dustin, and a few of their friends had celebrated Brad's birthday there. Tears sprang into her eyes. His very last birthday, now that she thought about it. She took a breath. "Everything's good here." She grinned. "You can't go wrong with anything on the menu."

"I've been wanting a good steak." He grinned.

She nodded. "I've never tried one here, but I've always heard good things about them." She glanced at the menu. "I think I'll stick with chicken, though."

Once they'd placed their order, Jake leaned forward, his eyes twinkling. "So you know those ladies I was telling you about?" he asked.

She nodded.

He motioned toward the far wall. "They're sitting over there. One of them has orange poufy hair."

Ainsley followed his gaze. She spotted the two older women, laughing and talking. "They look like tons of fun." She grinned at him. "Don't you want to go over there and say hello?"

He shrank down in his seat. "No way. They'd cause a scene if they saw me." He shook his head. "They told me hiking down into the canyon was on their bucket list."

She nodded. "I hear that all the time. People all over the world have the Grand Canyon on their bucket list."

Jake frowned. "I don't have a bucket list."

Ainsley widened her eyes. "Really? There's nothing you want to make sure you see or do?"

He shook his head. "I guess I just try and live in the moment." He shrugged. "How about you?"

"I have about a million things on mine." She grinned. "Of course, I've checked a lot of things off: skydiving, going to the top of the Eiffel Tower, skiing in the Rockies. . . . But there are plenty of things I still want to see and do. Someday, I want to go to Egypt. And Ireland." She pointed at her hair. "I'd like to go over there and see where my ancestors came from." She grinned.

"You went skydiving?" he asked in surprise.

She met his gaze. "Yes. That was before I was such a 'fraidy cat." She and Dustin had both gone. It had been just before he'd introduced her to Brad. Jumping out of a plane still ranked as one of the most exhilarating feelings she'd ever had. But there was no way she'd have the courage to do something like that again.

"So how's all that going?" he asked. "With work, I mean? I expected you to call me so I could come be the barrier between you and the rim." He grinned. "I haven't been replaced as your safeguard, have I?"

She explained the agreement she had with Edie. "So you're off the hook for now. And I've got a month to get it together." She sighed. "I'm afraid if I don't, I might have to think about transferring to a different park."

Jake shrugged. "There's nothing wrong with that. If it makes you feel safer to be somewhere else, then that's what you should do." He grinned. "Maybe you could transfer to one close to Phoenix."

Ainsley couldn't hide her surprise. She'd expected him to encourage her to stay, not encourage her to give up. "But I love it here," she said softly.

He narrowed his eyes. "Do you really? Or do you just like the security of a familiar place?" He leaned back. "I don't want to tell you what to do or anything, but it seems like a fresh start in a new place might be good for you." He pursed his lips. "It's worked wonders for me."

She pondered his words. It wasn't like she hadn't thought of that. A new place without any old memories did have a certain appeal. But the people here were like family to her. And she'd already left them once. "We'll see," she said finally. "I guess I don't have to make any decisions yet."

The waitress brought their food and set it in front of them.

"This looks delicious," Jake said, grinning. "Do you need anything else?" he asked her.

She shook her head. "Everything is perfect." And it was. This man was nice. He was good-looking. He seemed to care about her well-being. But she missed her daughter. And that put a huge damper on her night.

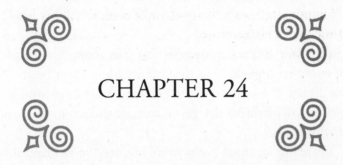

CHAPTER 24

Did you know your daddy proposed to me at the Grand Canyon? We'd gone on a hike all the way down to the bottom of the canyon to Phantom Ranch. The weather was perfect. It was early fall, so it was warm but not too warm, and the trees were so pretty. Anyway, the Colorado River runs right through, and we were sitting by the river, talking. One minute, we were sitting side by side, and the next, he'd dropped to his knee. I joked that the weight of the diamond caused me to be slower than normal when we hiked back to the top. The thing that struck me that day wasn't just that I was marrying the man I loved, but I was marrying the man who had become my best friend.

The ringing phone startled Julie. She'd been reading a book on the couch, and she must've dozed off. These days, when Faith napped, she did, too. Keeping up with a toddler was exhausting. She turned the book upside down on the coffee table to keep her place.

She fished her phone from her bag and glanced at the screen. Heath.

"Hey there," she said.

"Somebody sounds sleepy." He chuckled. "Did I wake you up?"

She yawned. "Yep. Faith's asleep, so it's allowed."

"Sleeping in the afternoon must be nice. I wish my boss gave me time off for a naptime."

Julie made a face. She was sick of him acting like keeping a baby wasn't hard work. "For your information, we've been on the move all day. I've been trying to get some stuff done around the house so that when Ainsley gets home, all she has to do is spend time with Faith."

"You're just an angel, aren't you?" His deep voice dripped with sarcasm.

Julie didn't respond.

"No really," he said softly. "I mean it. You are an angel. I miss you, baby."

Her anger subsided at his tender tone. "I miss you, too." Although, if she were honest with herself, she missed him less and less each day. She knew her budding friendship with Colt probably had something to do with it.

"Do you really? You promise?"

She grinned. "Silly boy. You know I do."

"I'm just making sure. I'm ready to see you." He'd been asking her for the past few weeks when he could come for a visit, but she kept putting him off. She wanted to see him. She just wasn't sure how she could keep his visit a secret from everyone. Ainsley, Dustin, Colt. . .the likelihood of running into one of them was pretty good. Unless he came over during the day while Ainsley was at work, but Faith took up all her attention.

She sighed. "Me, too."

"Why don't you come for a weekend soon?" he asked. "Your parents don't have to know. You can stay with me."

"Don't you think my aunt would mention it to my parents?" It was easier to pass the blame than to tell him for the millionth time that she didn't want to stay at his apartment. She knew she should just be honest, but she wasn't in the mood for another argument.

"Sorry. I forget that your family communicates all the time," he complained. "I just miss you so much."

"Well, I do have some news." She grinned. "My aunt is going on vacation next week. So I'm going to be home for the entire week."

"Awesome," he exclaimed. "I can't wait to see you, baby. You know even far away you're still the best thing in my life."

His words rang in her head long after the conversation ended. If she really was the best thing in his life, what would happen to him if she wasn't part of it anymore? The thought caused her heart to hurt.

❦

Dustin paced the length of his living room. His house was spotless. He'd even spent one of his days off this week scrubbing the kitchen tile. In his world, that was serious cleaning. Ainsley, Faith, Julie, and Colt were on their way over for dinner, and he wanted things to be perfect. Ainsley hadn't come inside the house the night of his cookout, so he really wanted to impress her tonight. He'd even decided not to grill. Instead, he had a casserole in the oven. Mrs. Whittaker had given him the recipe and assured him it was easy and delicious. The elderly woman had become somewhat of a surrogate grandmother to him over the past couple of years, and he trusted her judgment about cooking.

Dustin glanced out the window and saw Colt coming up the driveway. He opened the door.

"Hey, man."

Colt grinned. "Thanks for the invite. Julie just texted me and said they're just now on their way. Something about lost keys I think."

"Dinner's not quite through yet, anyway." Dustin motioned toward the kitchen.

"There they come," said Colt, looking out the window.

Dustin peered out from behind Colt's shoulder. Ainsley pushed Faith in the stroller, and Julie plodded alongside them. They seemed to be deep in discussion. He hoped nothing was wrong.

He opened the door. "Hey there. Let me help you with that."

Ainsley grinned. "Thanks." She lifted Faith out of the stroller.

Faith clutched her stuffed dog and grinned.

"Wow, your place looks great," Ainsley said, stepping inside. "Much different than the old place you used to live in." She laughed. "Your furniture actually matches."

Dustin grinned. "When I moved into this place, I had a big yard sale and got rid of all that mismatched stuff." He'd gone to one of those "buy the whole room" stores and bought a whole package. He hoped it made him look like he had more style than he really did.

"Dinner isn't quite ready," he announced to his guests. "But I do have a surprise for Faith." He could barely contain his excitement. "It's in the backyard."

Ainsley's eyes widened. "A surprise? What is it?" she asked.

He shook his head. "Nope. You'll just have to come see."

Ainsley picked Faith up and followed him to the back door.

They stepped into the backyard, and a tiny brown puppy bounded over to them.

Faith squealed with delight.

"A puppy," Julie exclaimed. "Oh, it's so cute."

Dustin reached down and picked the puppy up and brought it over to Ainsley and Faith. "I know how much she loves her stuffed dog. I just thought it was time she saw a real live puppy."

Faith reached her hands toward the animal. "Be gentle," Dustin said. He stroked the puppy gently to show her how to do it.

She tentatively reached for the puppy.

"Gentle," Ainsley said.

As her tiny hands made contact with the wiggly dog's fur, she giggled and looked at Ainsley with wide brown eyes.

"This is Max," Dustin said. "I borrowed him from one of my neighbors. He's part lab, part something else. They adopted him from a nearby shelter." He'd always thought rescued dogs made the best dogs. They seemed to try a little harder to please. It kind of reminded him of himself—not really wanted at his original home, so he'd tried hard to fit in with Brad's family.

Julie and Colt came over to play with the dog.

"Let's put them down and let them play." Dustin grinned at Faith. "Faith, do you want to play with Max?"

Ainsley hesitated, her brow furrowed. "Are you sure it's safe? Does he bite?"

"He lives in a home that has a couple of kids," Dustin explained. "He's used to them."

Ainsley gingerly put Faith on the ground next to the puppy.

She plopped down and laughed as Max sniffed her. He licked her arm, and she laughed louder.

Julie and Colt knelt down next to Faith and Max.

Dustin grinned and glanced at Ainsley, expecting to see smiles. Instead, she stood frozen. Tension oozed from her body.

"You okay?" he asked.

She nodded. "I'm fine."

"He's so cute," Julie said. "Faith, can you love the puppy?"

Faith picked up the puppy, giggling with each wriggle.

Julie grinned. "Hug him softly."

The little girl hugged Max to her. "Mmm." She grinned.

Ainsley stepped forward. "Okay, that's enough." She took Max out of Faith's grasp and set him on the ground. "We'd better wash her hands before we eat."

Faith wailed, reaching for the puppy.

"We'll see him later." Ainsley lifted Faith into her arms. "And your Bo Bo is inside the house. He's probably wondering where you are."

Faith quieted down, her eyes still on Max.

"Sure. I'll show you where the restroom is." Dustin held the door open for Ainsley and Faith. He glanced back at Julie and Colt. Julie had picked Max up and was cuddling and cooing at him. At least his surprise had gone over well with someone.

"Down the hall and to the right." He pointed to the hallway.

The casserole was finished anyway. He grabbed a pot holder and pulled it from the oven. Mrs. Whittaker would be proud. He stared down the hallway after Ainsley.

How had he managed to upset her again?

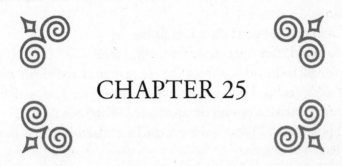

CHAPTER 25

You might not believe this, but I used to be really adventurous. Nothing scared me. Skydiving? Count me in. Rafting a river? The more rapids, the better. I guess you could say that I love adventure. Brad called me fearless. But now? Everything scares me. Since the accident, I see danger all around. The world is a scary place, and your mama has turned out to be a big chicken.

Ainsley held Faith up to the bathroom sink. "Rub your hands together and get them all soapy," she directed.

"Wash," said Faith.

"That's right, sweet girl. Now hold them under the water and rinse off."

Faith splashed the water around in the sink. She'd loved water since she was a tiny baby in her first bath.

Ainsley laughed. "Don't splash too much." She turned off the faucet and sat Faith on the counter. "Sit still," she said, pulling a yellow hand towel from the rack. "Dry off."

Faith patted her hands on the towel and grinned.

"You liked that puppy, didn't you?" she murmured. She'd

loved seeing Faith enjoy herself with Max, but what if he snapped and bit her? A toddler and a puppy were both unpredictable. Even if Max was used to kids, he could still be dangerous. That was a reasonable argument, right?

"Are you hungry?" she asked Faith.

Faith nodded and rubbed her belly. "Yesh."

She picked Faith up from the counter and carried her down the hallway to the kitchen. "It smells so good," she said, watching as Dustin stirred a pot on the stovetop. "What's for dinner?"

He grinned. "We're having a chicken casserole, green beans, and rolls."

"Wow," she exclaimed. "I didn't know you could cook anything that didn't include firing up the grill."

Dustin laughed. "Aren't you ever going to learn that I'm full of surprises?"

She supposed she should have learned that lesson by now, especially after the recent revelation that he led regular devotionals for the area teens. "I guess I'm not a very fast learner."

Julie came into the small kitchen. "Here, let me take Faith. We'll watch Max from the window." She reached her arms out for Faith.

Faith grinned and went smoothly to Julie. "Ju Ju," she jabbered.

"That's right." Julie grinned. "She's finally learning my name," she said, her face pink with delight.

Ainsley watched the two of them walk away and turned to Dustin. "Is there anything I can do to help?" she asked, leaning against the counter.

"Nope. Just keep me company while I finish up here." He grabbed plates from the cabinet next to the refrigerator.

She looked around the kitchen. The countertops sparkled, and no dirty dishes cluttered up the sink. "This is a far cry from your old kitchen."

"A man can only live on frozen pizza and burgers for so long."

He winked at her as he began to put ice in the glasses. "Besides, as you said the other day, I'm on the 'back side' of thirty." He shrugged. "I was tired of paper plates and mismatched plastic souvenir cups." He waved an arm around. "Even though I live alone, I want this house to be a home." He dropped the final ice cube in the glass with a flourish. "I have groups over a lot, too."

She met his eyes. "For devos?" she asked.

He flushed. "Julie told you, huh?"

Ainsley nodded. "Why didn't you tell me?"

Dustin pulled a pot holder from the drawer next to the stove. "I wasn't exactly sure how to work my renewed beliefs into conversation. Besides"—he glanced at her—"I didn't want to upset you. I remember when Brad led most of the teen devotionals. I was afraid it would just bring back memories."

She gave him a small smile. "I'd like to come to one of your devos sometime if it's okay."

He set the casserole on top of the stove. "Sure. Anytime." He grinned. "Now, make yourself useful and grab those plates."

She obliged and followed him to the dining room table.

Thirty minutes later, they were stuffed. "Amazing," Dustin said. "I slave over a hot stove for half the day, and in half an hour, the food's gone."

Ainsley laughed. "I have to admit, it was pretty good." She narrowed her eyes at him. "You haven't been taking lessons from the resident chef, have you?" That would explain it. She'd bet that Lindsey was behind his newfound culinary skills.

"What?" Dustin looked at her, confusion etched all over his face. His eyes widened as he realized what she was getting at. "No. I haven't." His words were clipped. "This recipe actually came from Mrs. Whittaker, thank you very much."

Colt and Julie exchanged glances.

Ainsley blushed. She shifted Faith in her lap. "Well, it was delicious." She'd always been one to jump to conclusions. Would she never learn? Dustin had told her multiple times that he and Lindsey were no longer an item, but she couldn't quite accept it. Maybe he'd been telling the truth, though.

"We'll clear the table," Julie said, standing.

Dustin glanced over at Ainsley. "Any chance you and Faith want to go back outside and check on Max?"

"Sure." She set Faith down and watched as her daughter took off. "She's getting steadier and faster every day."

"Must be hard to let her grow up so fast, huh?" he asked.

She nodded. "It seems like just yesterday when she was a tiny baby who couldn't even crawl. Now it seems like she has a new skill every hour."

They stepped outside and Faith ran to Max.

"Be gentle," Ainsley called. Her body tensed as the puppy licked Faith's leg.

The little girl shrieked with delight.

Dustin touched Ainsley on the back. "She's fine," he said softly. "But you aren't. What gives?"

She shook her head. "It just worries me. Every new experience she has scares me, and I think of all the things that could go wrong."

Faith waved her arms and bounced in place as Max scampered around her.

"But look how happy she is and how much fun she's having," he said. "Surely that counts for something."

Ainsley turned away. "Right. I do love to see her have fun. I mean, look at that face."

Faith threw back her head and giggled as Max rolled over on his back. She knelt down and poked his round belly then looked up at Ainsley and grinned. "Gentle," she said clearly.

"That's right, be gentle," Dustin echoed. He glanced at Ainsley. "Why do I get the feeling that your fears are directly related to what happened to Brad?"

She blinked away the tears that sprang into her eyes. "Because he was doing something that made him happy, too. He was just doing his job, doing what he loved." She bit her lip. "And look how it turned out."

Dustin reached over and pulled her to him and planted a kiss on her forehead. "I know, kid. I know."

Julie stepped out onto the patio. "We're thinking about going to get some ice cream. Do you guys want to come?"

Ainsley stepped out of Dustin's embrace. "I don't think so." She motioned at Faith. "She certainly doesn't need ice cream right before bed. She's excited enough without dealing with a sugar rush." She grinned.

Dustin cleared his throat. "Do you think you and Colt could take Max home on your way to the ice-cream fountain? The Brewsters just live a couple houses down. Colt knows them."

Julie nodded. "Sure."

"Thanks for dinner, man," Colt said, joining them.

"Do you know where the Brewsters live?" Dustin asked him.

Colt nodded. "Yes."

Julie walked over and picked Max up. "We're going to take him back to them on our way to get ice cream." She snuggled the puppy against her chest and rubbed her face against his soft fur.

"Sounds good." Colt grinned at Julie and the puppy.

Faith began to scream and tug at Julie's shorts.

Dustin picked Faith up. "Faith, can you tell Max bye-bye?" he asked.

Faith's screams subsided as she once again came face-to-face with the puppy. "Bye-bye," she cooed, leaning close to him.

Max licked Faith on the cheek, and she cackled with delight.

"Bye-bye, Faith," Julie waved one of Max's paws in Faith's direction.

"Faith, do you like to fly?" Dustin asked. He raised her over his head, and she giggled.

Ainsley was impressed. He'd sensed a distraction was the best way to handle the departing puppy. She smiled as Dustin let Faith "fly" all over the yard.

"I'll just see you at home later," Julie said to Ainsley as she and Colt turned to go. "Is that cool?"

Ainsley nodded. "Sure thing. Have fun."

◎◎

Dustin sank onto his plush red couch next to Ainsley. "Thanks for coming over." He picked up a throw pillow and hit it against her knee. "You upset about me borrowing the puppy?"

She grinned and shook her head. "No. I'm not mad at you." She sighed. "I know it seems like I'm unreasonable where Faith is concerned."

He looked at the little girl sleeping soundly on the love seat. She clutched her stuffed dog to her side. "It isn't unreasonable to worry." He met her gaze. "But it is unreasonable to let your worry rule you."

"I know you're right." She grinned. "You were great with her, by the way. She seems to really take to you."

"Maybe she can sense that I'm a good guy." He chuckled. "Babies, animals, and elderly people. They seem to be my fan base."

She shook her head. "You're too much." She leaned her head against the back of the couch. "Did you think this was where you'd be at this point in your life?"

He thought for a moment. "I don't know how to answer that. Things have happened along the way that have surprised me, that's for sure. I think I've learned to keep myself open to the opportunities God puts in front of me, though." He grinned. "If you'd have told me even a year ago that I'd be leading devotionals for teenagers and they'd be confiding in me and asking my advice about stuff. . .I'd have thought you were crazy."

"You seem happy, though."

He nodded. "Losing Brad was tough for me. It made me stop and take stock of my life." He reached out and touched her leg. "Is it okay for me to tell you that?"

"Of course. It's nice to talk to someone who knew him well. And I know what you mean." She sighed. "I've been taking stock of things in my life, too." She met his gaze. "Can I tell you something awful?"

He drew his brows together. "Sure. Shoot."

"I was so angry at God after Brad died. After his funeral, I stopped going to church. I stopped praying. I even put my Bible in storage with my furniture."

Dustin watched the emotions play across her face.

She continued. "For a long time, I wished I'd died, too." Her voice grew husky. "I know that's crazy. But I just couldn't understand how things had turned out the way they had."

"What changed?"

Ainsley gave him a tiny smile. "The day I went into labor, I was furious. I screamed at God in my parents' basement. Seriously screamed. I couldn't believe He was actually going to make me go through it alone. I guess up until that point, it almost felt unreal." She motioned toward her sleeping child. "We got to the hospital, and I made everyone leave the delivery room. My mom and Rachel tried to talk me into letting one of them stay, but I said no."

He listened, mesmerized.

"But the moment I heard the baby cry, I started sobbing. I was so incredibly *thankful*. Just this enormous amount of awe I had for the gift I'd been given. I can't tell you how sorry I felt. I'd turned my back on God for those months, but He hadn't turned his back on me. He'd given me this perfect little child who was part of me and part of Brad."

He glanced over at the little girl and back at Ainsley. "Is that how she got her name?"

Ainsley wiped a tear from her face. "Yes," she said softly. "I named her Faith so I'd have a constant reminder of the faithfulness of God. He never left me. I might've been able to push Mom and Rachel out of that room, but He never budged."

"Wow." He scooted closer to her and pulled her against him in a hug. "I think you're incredibly brave, kid."

She chuckled. "Don't start that again. And you know I'm not."

Dustin stood and grabbed a framed picture from the end table. He sat back down and handed her the picture. "See that girl?" He pointed at the picture of the two of them on the day, years ago, that they'd gone skydiving.

She groaned. "Yes. I see her. But I don't even know who that is anymore." She furrowed her brow. "And I'm sure she wouldn't recognize me."

He met her hazel eyes. "Don't be so hard on yourself. I think that fearless girl is still here, right in this living room." He tipped her chin upward. "And she's doing an amazing job of having a career and raising a daughter."

She caught his hand. "Thanks. I needed to hear those words tonight."

Before he could stop himself, he leaned over and removed the clip that held her hair in place. It tumbled over her shoulders in loose waves.

"Dustin," she whispered.

He swallowed. His heart was pounding so loudly, he was sure she could hear it. "You always have it pulled back these days. I miss seeing it down."

Ainsley self-consciously touched her hair. "It's so out of control when it's down." She took the clip from him and quickly twisted her hair back into a bun. "Plus it just seems more practical to have it put up."

"Practical is overrated sometimes." He grinned.

She motioned at Faith. "I should get her home and into her own bed."

Ainsley rose from the couch and began to gather the toys Faith had scattered. She stuffed them into the diaper bag.

"Why don't you let me walk you home?"

She grinned. "I was actually going to ask you if you would." She jerked her head toward the stroller. "I'd rather carry her instead of waking her up and putting her in the stroller. So I kind of need you to push the stroller. If you don't mind, I mean."

They walked slowly toward her house.

"Did I tell you I'm going on vacation next week?"

He glanced over at her. "Vacation? That sounds wonderful. Where are you going?"

"You know my friends Vickie and Kristy? We're meeting up for a few days."

He'd met both of them over the years as they'd come to Arizona to visit. "Vickie's the quiet one who lives in DC. Kristy looks like a blond Sandra Bullock. And she's really competitive."

Ainsley laughed. "That pretty much covers it. I didn't know if you'd remember."

He remembered everything that had anything to do with Ainsley. But there was no way to explain that to her without sounding creepy. "When Vickie came out for a visit, she barely said a word to me. And we all went bowling when Kristy was here. She won." He laughed. "Where are you headed?"

"Believe it or not, I'm beach bound. We've rented a condo in Florida." She grinned. "So pretty soon, I'm going to have my toes in the sand and just relax for a few days."

"That sounds amazing." He was quiet for a minute, wondering if he should tell her he knew the significance of the week. "I know that will be a much-needed break for you. Next week would be tough for you here."

She widened her eyes. "Can you believe it will have been two years?"

He shook his head. A lot had changed in two years. "I think a beach trip will be just what the doctor ordered for you." He grinned. "Is Faith going with you?"

She shook her head. "She's spending part of the week with my parents and part of the week with the Davises."

He kept in touch with Brad's parents on a regular basis. It was through them that he'd been able to keep track of how Ainsley was doing. He knew they'd be excited to spend a few days with their granddaughter. "It will be good for her to spend some time with her grandparents. And probably good for you to have a few days of no responsibility."

"I'm really excited about the trip. I haven't traveled much lately. Faith and I went to Tennessee last year for Kristy's wedding, but other than that, I've pretty much just stayed home."

Travel used to be one of her favorite things, so he knew the upcoming trip would be just another step to getting her life back. And he was proud of her for that.

"My house keys are in the pocket of the diaper bag. Can you find them and unlock the door?" She shifted Faith in her arms. "My hands are a little full."

He chuckled. "Not a problem." He unlocked the door and walked inside. "Looks like Julie isn't home yet."

"Will you check the house to make sure everything's secure while I put Faith in bed?"

Dustin grinned. "Sure thing." He lifted his leg and arms in a *Karate Kid* pose. "Anybody here is gonna have to deal with this."

She chuckled and shook her head. "You're too much." She carried Faith into the baby's bedroom.

Dustin checked all the rooms and made sure the back door was locked.

"All clear," he said as she walked into the living room. "I'm going to hit the road." He paused. "Unless you want me to stay until Julie gets here."

She shook her head. "We'll be fine. She should be home soon." She grinned. "Thanks for dinner and everything."

Standing close to her, his pulse started to race again, just like it had earlier on the couch. He thought those old feelings were gone. He'd packed them away years ago when she'd first met Brad. But it seemed like they were rising to the surface. Dustin pulled her into a quick hug. "I'm glad you're back."

"Me, too," she murmured against his chest. "Hanging out tonight was fun."

He stepped back. Hanging out. That's all it was. Hanging out. He needed to get a grip. "It sure was." He stepped out into the night air and headed toward his house. The moment he thought they'd had on the couch must've been in his mind. And even if it wasn't, he never should've let there be a moment in the first place. She was his friend. Just his friend. She'd been married to his childhood friend who'd been like a brother to him. And even if she was ready to move on, he knew there was no logical way she would be able to move on with him. Too many memories of Brad lingered between them.

So he'd do the one thing he could to keep himself in check. He pulled out his cell phone and dialed.

"Hey, Lindsey," he drawled once she picked up. "How about we have dinner one night next week?"

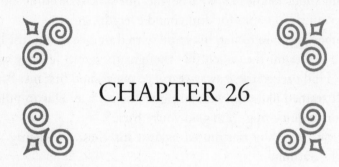

CHAPTER 26

Watching you the other night with the puppy that belongs to Dustin's neighbor made me so happy. You were so good. I'm amazed at how well you understand directions. Even though you aren't talking much yet, I can tell you're starting to understand what's being said. You were gentle with the puppy, and I have a feeling at some point we're going to have to adopt one of our own. But not until I get a better handle on being a single mom.

It seems like the list of things that need to be done never ends. It's the little stuff that I didn't think about before. Mowing the yard. Getting the oil changed. Finding time to get groceries. Just so many responsibilities. I hope I'm doing okay handling it all on my own. Even though I didn't plan on life turning out this way, I wouldn't trade it for anything—because of you. You keep me going on the days I'm so tired that I want to sit on the floor and cry instead of fix dinner or do laundry. One look at your sweet face, and I find enough energy to read you a story or play peekaboo.

Jake McGuire sat on a bench outside of the main visitor center.

Visitors filled the courtyard between the park bookstore and visitor center. A couple walked past him holding hands and laughing. They sat down on a bench across from Jake, so wrapped up in each other he could tell they were oblivious to everything else around them.

It would be a perfect time for a criminal to snatch her purse. *Really, McGuire? You aren't a cop anymore. At least here you're not.*

He sighed and put his head in his hands. It was time to start thinking about what he wanted to do next. Living in the camper had been fun at first, but he was beginning to miss his home. And his friends and family. He hung out with Shane some and really enjoyed spending time with Ainsley. But Shane had a wife and kids to tend to, so his time was limited. And Ainsley. . .she was tough to figure out.

She had a lot on her plate right now, but she wouldn't ask for help. At least not from him. Yet he'd found himself daydreaming more than once of swooping in and playing the hero. He could take her away from her problems. That was one reason he always wanted to take her out for dinner instead of just casually hanging out. She deserved to be treated to something special.

He glanced at his watch. It should be nearly time for her lunch break unless park rangers were on some kind of weird schedule and didn't eat at noon. He'd take the chance.

Jake walked past the large displays that told about the various trails and upcoming ranger programs. He stepped through the door into the large visitor center. The sun shone so brightly outside that the room seemed dark. He blinked a few times to adjust. Ainsley wasn't at the ranger desk; instead a male ranger stood there, answering an elderly couple's questions. Had she already left for lunch?

He glanced around. On the far right wall, a large map of the United States beckoned visitors. Jake crossed the large room to look at the map. It was labeled with all the national parks. There sure were a lot of parks he'd never visited. He and his family had traveled to some of the larger ones, but he still had several he'd like to see for himself.

"Planning a trip?" a cheerful voice said from behind him.

He turned to face Ainsley, decked out in her ranger uniform. She must be the most beautiful park ranger in the whole park service. "Hey there." He grinned.

She pointed to Tennessee on the map. "That's where I got my start with the park service."

"Really?" He knew her family lived in Flagstaff, so this news came as a surprise.

She grinned. "I went to college in Tennessee. I started working as a seasonal ranger at Shiloh National Military Park, not too far from my school. Shiloh is a Civil War battlefield."

There was so much he didn't know about her. "I'll bet that was really interesting. I always love watching shows on the History Channel that visit the different battlefields."

She nodded. "I enjoyed my time there. I've never been much of a history buff myself, but I learned so many interesting things." She chuckled. "If you ever need to know the steps involved in firing a Civil War–era musket or cannon, I'm your girl."

He joined in her laughter. "I'll keep that in mind. I'm surprised though, to hear that you aren't a history buff. I figured that was a commonality among all park rangers."

"Two of my best friends who are rangers at other parks are both really interested in history. But the thing that drew me to the park service was the opportunity to be outdoors. That's a huge reason why the Grand Canyon is such a perfect fit for me. A lot of my ranger talks center around the environment. I love getting to talk to people, especially children, about conservation and taking care of the earth for future generations."

"Wow. I didn't even think about those things being part of a park ranger's duties."

"We're a multitalented group." She laughed.

He grinned. "I'll say." He fell silent, trying to muster up the courage to ask her to lunch.

"So are you just out exploring? Or are you getting ready to lead a hike?"

"Actually, I stopped by to see if you have lunch plans."

Her eyes widened. "Oh. Um, I don't have anything planned. I was just going to head over to Market Plaza and grab something."

Market Plaza was a major shuttle stop at the huge park. The Canyon Village Marketplace served as the main grocery and general store for locals and tourists alike. It contained a little deli at the front of the store that served pizza and sandwiches. Jake popped in there frequently. There was also a cafeteria nearby. "Well, would you like some company?" he asked.

"Sure." She looked at her watch. "My break starts in fifteen minutes." She grinned widely. "Technically, this isn't a break." She motioned between them. "Because I'm educating you about the park service."

He laughed. "That you are." He nodded his head toward the door. "I'll be outside, checking out the displays. Just come find me when you're ready."

⊙⊙

"Okay, ma'am." Dustin shook his head at the older woman behind the wheel of a white van. "I'm gonna need you to watch the speed limit, okay?"

"I'm sorry." She shot him a smile. "I promise I'll watch it."

He walked back to his patrol car. Today had been one for the record books already, and he hadn't even had lunch yet. He pointed the car toward the general store. He had time to grab a quick bite before he went back out on patrol.

Dustin walked through the double doors into the store.

"Good afternoon, Brenda," he called to the woman at the nearest checkout line.

"Hey, Dustin." She grinned. "Enjoy your lunch."

He made his way over to the deli and stepped up to the counter.

"Can I help you?" A teenage boy asked.

Dustin scanned the daily specials. "Let me have a chicken sandwich. And a Coke."

"For here or to go?"

He glanced around the tiny deli. There were only a handful of tables, but it was mostly empty. His gaze landed on a couple near the window. Ainsley's red hair, pulled into a low ponytail, caught his eye. She sat with Jake, who hung on to her every word. "To go," he said to the teenager. He couldn't stomach talking to Ainsley and Jake. Especially after the other night. He couldn't seem to keep his feelings in check where Ainsley was concerned. And the last thing he wanted was to see her with someone else.

Dustin picked up the bag and drink and turned to go.

"Dustin," Ainsley called. She grinned when he made eye contact.

He walked over to their table, noting the irritated expression Jake wore. "Howdy." He nodded. "Jake, it's nice to see you again."

Jake returned his nod. "You, too." His broad smile didn't quite reach his eyes.

"Why don't you sit down and eat?" Ainsley motioned to an empty seat. "We just got here."

He knew he should take his sandwich and leave. Seeing her with Jake set him on edge. Colt's words from the other night replayed in his head. *Did you ever like a girl even though you knew she liked someone else?* Dustin had already decided he couldn't pursue the feelings he had for Ainsley. But he could at least check this guy out. After all, what did they really know about Jake? "I'd love to. Thanks." He pulled out the empty chair and sat down.

Jake looked like he'd just eaten a lemon.

"I was just telling Jake about my upcoming vacation," Ainsley explained.

Dustin nodded. "It sure sounds like fun." The fifteen-year-old inside him wanted to turn to Jake and say, "Ha, I knew about it first," but the thirty-six-year-old won out. Instead, he took a bite of his sandwich.

Jake furrowed his brow. "Would you like me to drive you to the airport?" He glanced at Ainsley. "Because I'd be glad to."

Her pleased expression made Dustin want to throw up. Was this guy for real?

"That's so sweet of you. But I have to take Faith to Flagstaff and drop her off with my parents. Then Julie and I will go on to Cottonwood. I'm going to leave my car there, and my sister is going to drive me to Phoenix to catch the plane."

Jake nodded. "Well, let me know if you change your mind." He took a sip of his drink. "I know driving makes you a little nervous, so even if you just want me to drive you to your sister's, I'd be glad to."

Dustin managed to turn his snort into a cough. "Sorry. Sandwich went down the wrong pipe."

Ainsley reached over and patted him on the back. "You've always eaten your food too fast," she chided. "Do I need to cut your sandwich into little pieces like I do for Faith?"

He chuckled. "No. I'm good. Thanks."

She turned to Jake. "You know, I haven't even thought about driving. But I was fine on the drive here, at least until we entered the park." She shrugged. "So I should be okay. And if not, Julie can take over." Her lips turned up in a smile. "Thanks though, for offering."

Jake nodded. "I want to help if I can."

Ainsley nodded. "Speaking of help, that's Faith's latest word. She wants to help all the time. Last night, I was doing laundry, and she came over to help me fold clothes. Of course, she mainly liked to lie on them when they were warm from the dryer, but still, I thought it was pretty cute."

Dustin glanced at Jake from the corner of his eye. "How is Faith, anyway? After the other night, I'll bet she's still jabbering about the puppy." Yep. It was a low blow referencing something he and Ainsley shared, and he knew it. But he couldn't help himself. This guy needed to know that he couldn't just swoop in here and be Ainsley's go-to guy.

Jake widened his eyes at Ainsley. "A puppy?"

She explained about Max.

Dustin could see Jake practically shrinking in his seat. Remorse washed over him. There was no need to antagonize Jake. He seemed like a genuinely nice guy. Ainsley's moving on was a given. So if it wasn't with Jake, it would be with the next guy who came along. Dustin would have to accept it.

He stood. "I'm going to leave you two to finish your lunch." He motioned toward the parking lot. "I need to get back out there anyway." He pushed his chair back and stood.

"Nice to see you again," Jake said.

"I don't know if I'll see you again before I go to Florida," Ainsley said. "If not, I'll see you when I get back." She smiled.

He nodded. "Tell Vickie and Kristy I said hello." He wanted to kick himself. It was like he couldn't help but let Jake know he had a history with Ainsley. He could all but hear Lindsey in his head, accusing him of marking his territory.

At the thought of Lindsey, he immediately tensed. He never should've asked her to dinner. They were supposed to go out next week, and he was already considering canceling—although she wasn't the kind of woman who took kindly to being canceled on. Nope. He'd have to go through with it.

Dustin headed out to the patrol car without looking back. While he didn't think Jake was right for Ainsley, he planned to mind his own business. Even if it proved to be the hardest thing he'd ever done.

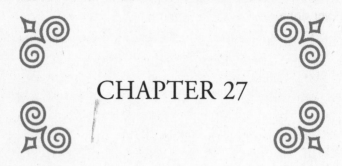

CHAPTER 27

I think this summer has been good for Julie. The responsibility that's come with taking care of you has helped her grow up. Not that she wasn't responsible before—trust me, if she hadn't been, I never would've let her keep you. But at the beginning of the summer, she wasn't nearly as happy as she is now. That sullen girl who lashed out at her mother on the day we left for the canyon is gone. She seems so content now. I can't help but think Colt has something to do with it, although maybe it's just that she's away from a toxic relationship. Either way, I'm thrilled to see her happy.

"Are you ready?" Colt grinned. "It's time for you to play tourist."

Julie laughed. "Yep. I can't wait to finally see more of the canyon." She returned his smile. "And I'm sure you're a great tour guide."

"Some might say the best." He waggled his eyebrows at her.

She chuckled. "I'm sure you are. Let me just tell Ainsley we're leaving." Julie opened the back door and stepped outside.

Ainsley and Faith sat on a blanket in the middle of the yard, surrounded by books and toys. "It's such a nice day, we decided to spend some time outside." Ainsley shaded her eyes with her arm.

"I don't blame you," Julie said, walking out into the yard. She knelt down and sifted through the pile of books. "I can't find the book I was reading the other day," she explained, catching Ainsley's questioning look. "It was in the living room on the coffee table. I keep thinking maybe it got picked up with some of Faith's books." She stood. "But it isn't here. Guess I'm just going to have to assume the main characters live happily ever after."

Ainsley chuckled. "I'm sure it will turn up."

"Hope so. Anyway, Colt and I are about to leave."

Ainsley furrowed her brow. "You sure you want to go on a hike?"

Julie sighed. Ainsley had been trying for the past two days to talk her out of going. "You know I do. We aren't even going into the canyon, just along the rim trail." She smiled. "We'll be fine. Stop worrying so much or you're gonna get all wrinkly."

Ainsley smirked. "Fine. Have fun. Don't forget to take some extra water."

Julie rolled her eyes. "Got it. And we packed lunch, too. We're hiking out to Hermit's Rest and having a picnic."

"You'll love it." Ainsley's eyes grew wistful. "It's beautiful out there and so peaceful." She sat up straight. "But be careful. There are rails at most of the viewpoints, but as you walk the trail, there aren't any. Just watch your step."

"Okay," Julie said.

"And watch out for your surroundings, especially for other people. Once you get past the Abyss, the Greenway Trail accommodates bicycles."

"The Abyss?" Julie widened her eyes.

Ainsley grinned. "It's one of the points along the way to Hermit's Rest. It's called the Abyss because from that vantage point, you're able to see just how deep the canyon really is."

"Cool." Julie could barely contain her excitement. She had her camera batteries charged and her sketch pad and pencils in her backpack. "You guys have fun, too." She bent down and kissed Faith on the cheek. "Bye-bye, Faith."

Faith grinned. "Bye-bye." She waved.

"Aww. I feel so special. She hardly ever waves at anybody." Julie turned to go.

"You are special. And don't you ever forget it," Ainsley called.

Two hours later, Julie sat down on the stone wall at Hopi Point. A group of tourists stood on the pavement below, posing for pictures. "Whew."

Colt collapsed beside her. "Well, what do you think so far?"

"It's awesome." She nodded toward the canyon in front of them. "Every point we stop at has a different view. This is my favorite so far."

He chuckled. "You say that every time."

"And I mean it every time, too." She looked over at him. "I didn't realize it would be a real hike, though."

"Just because we're on the rim and not down in the canyon doesn't mean it isn't a workout." He gave her a sideways grin. "Just wait till you do a canyon hike."

Julie took a sip of water. "I can't wait. I've been running in the neighborhood in the mornings to get ready."

"When are you planning to go?"

She shrugged. "I don't know. No plans just yet. Ainsley told me that I'd want to make sure I was in tip-top shape before I tried it." She sighed. "Although, I kind of think she'd make every excuse she could to keep me from going."

Colt furrowed his brow. "It's weird, because she used to hike nearly every weekend. I remember her and Brad and Dustin going together."

"You do?" Julie couldn't keep the surprised expression from

her face. It hadn't occurred to her that Colt would've known Brad.

He nodded. "Yep. Ainsley and Brad used to live across the street from us. They had a basketball goal in the driveway. Some of us guys would go over sometimes to play." He smiled at the memory. "Brad taught me a lot about the outdoors. He used to take a group of neighborhood guys on a camping trip every summer."

"Cool." She looked out over the horizon. Talking about her uncle made her sad.

Colt seemed to sense her feelings. He reached over and tugged on the brim of the baseball cap she wore. "Aren't you glad I brought an extra cap?" He grinned.

She'd been hesitant to put the cap on her head because she wasn't sure it was her best look. But Colt had seemed so eager for her to wear it. It was awfully sweet of him to think enough about her to bring an extra cap just to make sure the sun stayed out of her eyes. Plus, wearing something of his made her feel close to him. "Well, I don't normally think of myself as a baseball hat kind of girl." Her lips turned up in a smile. "But it does come in handy."

He laughed. "I think you look pretty cute in my baseball hat."

Julie felt the blush creeping up her face. At least she could blame it on the heat of the day and not his words. "You ready to keep going?"

He nodded. "We're not too far from Hermit's Rest." He grinned. "If *someone* didn't have to stop every few minutes for pictures, we'd already be there."

"That reminds me." She motioned toward a sign. "See that sign that tells the elevation of Hopi Point? I want to take your picture next to it."

He groaned. "Let me take one of you instead."

She dropped her backpack and kneeled beside the sign.

"Why don't you let me do that so you can both be in the shot?" An older woman passing by stopped and held her hand out for the camera.

"That would be great." Colt handed her the camera. He tossed his pack on the ground and knelt next to Julie.

"Can you get a little closer together?" the woman asked. "Why don't both of you get right behind the sign?"

Colt reached over and grabbed Julie around the waist, pulling her against him. "Sorry if I'm sweaty." He grinned.

His being sweaty wasn't a problem. But the fact that her pulse raced at his nearness worried her. "It's fine," she said weakly.

"Perfect," the woman exclaimed. "You two are just the cutest things. Such a good-looking couple."

"Oh, we aren't a couple." Julie jumped up and took the camera from the woman. "But thanks."

Colt raised an eyebrow in her direction. "You sure are quick to point that out," he said after the woman walked away. "You embarrassed for people to think we're together?"

"Of course not." Julie bit her lip. "Sorry." She didn't want to explain to him that lately, she'd been feeling guilty about spending time with him. It wasn't that there was anything happening. They were only hanging out. As friends. But she felt herself getting closer to Colt every time they were together. And she found herself sharing things with Colt she couldn't share with Heath. Stuff about her future plans and things she thought about God. It was almost like Colt knew a whole different side of her than Heath did. And she didn't know how to handle it.

"Good." He grinned. "Come on then. Next stop, Hermit's Rest and our picnic." He motioned toward the rim trail.

☙◦☙

"Okay, this place is amazing." Julie ran her hands over the rock arch. It reminded her of the arches couples stood underneath for weddings, except that it was made entirely of large rocks. In the very center was a large bell, and imprinted in one of the rocks were the words HERMITS REST.

"Let me get your picture underneath the arch." Colt snapped a picture as she smiled. "Do you want to look around first or eat first?"

"Let's eat." She motioned at a picnic table that overlooked the canyon. "I'm starving."

They pulled out the peanut butter and jelly sandwiches they'd made at Ainsley's.

"I never knew a PB&J could taste so good." Colt gazed at her with sparkling brown eyes.

Julie grinned. "No doubt. I'll bet nothing at the El Tovar would taste as good as this."

"I know the company wouldn't be as good." He took a sip of water. "Hey, I asked my mom about you shadowing her class. She said that'd be fine. So if you want to go on Monday, I'll let her know."

"I thought I told you. This is the week I'm going home. We're leaving after church tomorrow." She adjusted the baseball hat on her head. "Ainsley is going to the beach, so I'm going to be hanging out in Cottonwood."

Colt met her gaze. "Guess you're pumped to see your friends, huh?"

"Yeah. Claire and I are getting supplies for our dorm room." She grinned. "And Mama is going to take me shopping in Phoenix for some new clothes. We're going to go stay there a couple of days before we pick Ainsley up from the airport."

"That should be fun." He grew quiet, suddenly absorbed in his sandwich.

Julie hated to admit to him that she had mixed feelings about her trip home. She knew how he'd react. She sighed. "I'm looking forward to it."

He looked up from his food. "Are you going to spend much time with your boyfriend?"

No matter how many times she mentioned Heath by name, Colt always referred to him as her boyfriend. "If I can get away from my parents, I'm sure I will."

"You don't seem too excited." He leveled his gaze on her.

She shrugged. "Of course I am. Why wouldn't I be?"

"No reason. I just wondered, that's all." He stood. "You ready to look around here? Take some pictures?"

Julie rifled through her backpack. She pulled out a sketchpad and pencils. "Actually, I was thinking of sitting here and doing some sketches. Is that okay?"

He grinned. "I didn't know you were an artist." He came around to her side of the picnic table and began flipping through the sketchpad. "These are awesome." He stopped at a picture she'd sketched last week of Faith sleeping. "That looks just like her."

Julie blushed. She never shared her sketches with anyone. Claire had seen some of them in her room, but that was pretty much it. "Thanks. Lately I've been working on drawing faces. I'd like to do one of Faith and give it to Ainsley at the end of the summer. Faith's sort of been my model these past few weeks." She laughed. "But only when she's sleeping because that's the only time she's still."

Colt chuckled. "No doubt." He motioned toward the gift shop. "They sell ice-cream sandwiches and stuff over there. I'm gonna go get us a couple while you're drawing."

She appreciated him not standing over her and watching. It was like he understood that drawing was her private thing. "I'll show you my sketches when I'm through." She set to work, trying to capture the beauty of the canyon with her pencil.

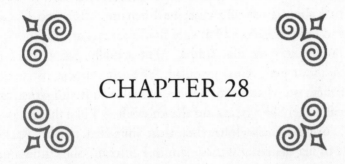

CHAPTER 28

I want to be the best mother I can be. It's first and foremost in my mind. I worry that I let you watch too much TV. Or that you aren't getting the right nutrition. I think about that fine line between raising you to be friendly and raising you to be too trusting of strangers. And I constantly wonder if my own idiosyncrasies are going to scar you for life. Do you pick up on my fears? Have I dealt with my grief in the right way? And someday, when you're grown, are you going to look back and blame me for your problems? Motherhood is much more complicated than I expected it to be. But I'm so thankful the Lord entrusted you to me. What is it they say? With great power comes great responsibility. I think that applies to being a mom.

Are you even listening to a word I say?" Rachel asked. They were on their way to Phoenix to the airport. They'd gotten a late start, and Ainsley worried she might not make her flight.

"Of course I'm listening." Okay, so she'd only been halfway listening. The dread that filled her seemed to have taken up residence in her ears, because mostly she could only hear her own thoughts. *What if the plane crashes? What if I have deep vein thrombosis and am killed by a blood clot I didn't know I had?*

Rachel shot her a glance from the driver's seat. "Are you worried about Faith? Because she'll be fine. Mom and Dad are thrilled to keep her, and I'm sure Brad's parents are, too."

If only it were that simple. "I'm actually not worried too much about her." Ainsley smiled. "I've left explicit instructions with them on what to do. Besides, if worse comes to worst, they can call Julie. She's great, and she knows how I like things done."

"I'm glad you've learned to trust Julie that much." Rachel's pride in her daughter was evident in her tone. "She's grown up a lot this summer."

Ainsley grinned. "Yes. But even so, I'll bet she's ecstatic about being home for a little while."

"I thought she was going to cry when she was reunited with her SUV." Rachel shook her head. "I'd daresay she probably wasn't even as excited at the prospect of seeing Heath as she was about driving again."

"There might be more to it than just the car." Ainsley filled her sister in on Julie's blossoming friendship with Colt.

"Why am I just now hearing about this?" Rachel demanded. "Julie mentioned Colt, but never let on that there might be something going on."

Uh-oh. Ainsley should've said something sooner. But she didn't want to get in the middle of things. She'd never been a meddler. "I'm sorry. And I may be way off thinking there may be interest there. I don't know for sure." She shrugged. "But Colt is a wonderful kid. If he was trouble of any kind, I would've told you."

"He's a good kid, huh?" Relief was etched in Rachel's voice. "Maybe he'll make her forget about Heath."

Ainsley nodded. "Maybe. . .although, I seem to remember someone else who had a penchant for bad boys when she was young."

Rachel's creamy skin turned pink. "That was a long time ago," she snapped. "And Jim was never even on the same level as Heath." Rachel's high school boyfriend was legendary in their family. The day he'd ridden up on his motorcycle, Ainsley had been sure Dad was going to have a heart attack.

"I'm just saying. Julie's a smart girl. I think she's been testing the waters with Heath. Hopefully, once she goes off to college, she'll realize he wasn't the right guy for her."

Rachel sighed. "Let's hope so." She veered off on the exit to Sky Harbor International Airport. "Are you excited?"

Ainsley tapped her fingers against the window. The closer they got to the airport, the more she was filled with dread. "I don't like to fly."

Rachel furrowed her brow but didn't say anything.

Thirty minutes later, Ainsley arrived at her gate. Because it was the middle of the day, security had been a breeze. She had plenty of time to kill. She glanced at her watch. Faith should be taking a nap, so she couldn't call to say good-bye. Normally when she had extra time, she'd call Vickie or Kristy. But they were both en route, as well. Jake had asked her to call him at some point during her trip. This was as good a time as any. She could certainly use a friendly voice right now.

"Hey," he answered on the first ring. "How are you?"

"Just sitting in your hometown, waiting for my ride." She smiled. "I just wish it was the kind of ride that would stay on the ground."

He chuckled. "Nerves getting to you?"

She explained her fears. "I seriously feel like I'm having trouble catching my breath." It was true. The more she sat and talked about her upcoming flight and all the things that could go wrong, the tighter her chest got.

"Don't go," he said gently. "I don't want you to fly if you're that scared. Your friends will understand, I'm sure."

She thought for a moment. It was true. Vickie already knew she was apprehensive about going. Of course, she thought her hesitation was mainly about leaving Faith, but still. She'd understand. And knowing her, she'd be able to convince Kristy to understand as well. "I don't know."

"I know plenty of people in Phoenix who can come pick you up. Heck, I'd come get you myself except that it would take several hours for me to get to you."

"Rachel's only been gone for half an hour." Was he right? Should she just back out?

"You could hang out with your parents and Faith for the week. That would be fun, too, right?" His smile came through the phone. "And I might even drive over to Flagstaff to take you out to dinner. I'm due for a trip to the city."

Ainsley thought about her options. Before she could answer him, her call waiting beeped. She held the phone out from her ear to see who was on the line. Dustin's name flashed on the screen. "You're so sweet," she said. "But I should probably just force myself to get on the plane. I hate to back out now that I'm here." The line beeped again. "My other line is beeping though, and I need to catch it."

"That's fine. I'll be in touch soon."

She quickly disconnected and clicked over. "Dustin?"

"Hey, you." He was quiet for a second. "I wasn't sure what time your flight leaves, so I was kinda taking a chance on you being midair."

"I've still got another hour before I board." Her voice cracked.

"Are you okay? You don't sound so good."

She knew he wouldn't understand. It would be just like trying to explain her phobia of the canyon. But she decided to tell him anyway. "I'm having a hard time convincing myself to get on the plane." She bit her lip. "If something were to happen to me. . ."

She paused. "Well, I just don't want to take the chance of leaving Faith behind. I'm all she has left." Her eyes filled with unexpected tears, and she braced herself for him to poke fun.

There was silence on the other end. Finally he sighed. "I wanted to have this conversation with you face-to-face. But I guess over the phone will do. At least maybe you'll have a few days to think about it."

"What are you talking about?" she asked, puzzled.

"I'm talking about you. Now, you're probably going to get mad at me about this, and that's fine. You've been mad at me before." He paused. "Remember when I told that waiter at the Bright Angel that you had a huge crush on him? And he wouldn't stop calling you for the whole summer?" He chuckled.

She smiled in spite of herself. "Don't think you can change the subject by dragging me down memory lane. But yes, I do remember that. His name was Dewayne, and I think he actually offered to show me his 'really cool' bug collection. You thought you were just hilarious with that little prank." She shook her head at the memory. "But please continue. Make me mad. After all, I have some time to kill." She couldn't keep the animation out of her voice. Talking to Dustin always made her feel lighter somehow. Even when they were talking about serious subjects, he had a way of bringing out her lighter side. It had been that way since they first met.

"I know you're scared of the canyon," he said quietly. "And of the airplane. And probably of any number of other things I haven't picked up on yet."

She was silent. "And?"

"And ever since you told me you might have to transfer to another park, I've been thinking a lot about your fears. You just said you don't want to take the chance of leaving Faith behind because you're all she has left. But I think maybe you need to consider why you named her that in the first place." He was quiet for a moment, letting his words sink in. "Where has your faith gone, Ainsley?"

He was pulling this on her now? As she was about to get on a plane? A possibly crashing, aneurysm-causing, life-ending plane? "Oh, I don't know. Maybe my faith left me about the same time my husband was killed in a fire." She seethed. "And furthermore, what do you even know about anything? You have no idea what all I've been through these past years."

"No. I don't. But it wasn't for lack of trying, and you know it." He sighed. "I thought we were past that, anyway." His voice grew soft. "I want to remind you of something. God has His own plan for you. And whether or not you get on an airplane to go have a much-needed vacation doesn't change that plan. There's a verse I really like in Matthew that says, '*Who of you by worrying can add a single hour to his life?*' Remember that one?"

Once upon a time, that had been a memory verse in vacation Bible school. Had she strayed so far that she'd forgotten? "Of course I remember it," she snapped. Only the knowledge that he was trying to be nice and help her overcome her fears kept her from lashing out at him.

"All I'm asking is that you let go of the fears that are binding you. It must be hard to breathe, carrying that kind of load. And I'll bet you still aren't sleeping."

She wrinkled her nose. He did know her well, even after all these years. She was lucky to get three hours straight. "Maybe," she conceded.

"Here's what I'm going to do," Dustin said. "When I hang up, I'm going to pray that God gives you courage. To face the plane. To face the canyon. To face whatever else it is in your life that's holding you back."

It was hard to be mad at someone who was going to pray for her. Ainsley shifted in the uncomfortable seat. "Jake offered to come pick me up. He said I didn't have to go on this trip if I didn't want to." She heard the taunting tone to her voice but didn't care. Dustin would have her jumping out of an airplane again if she let him. But Jake wanted to keep her safe. There was something to be said for that.

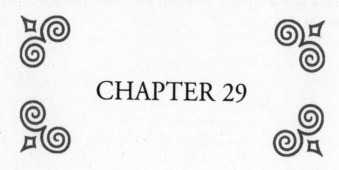

CHAPTER 29

When I think about the future, I'm excited. I can't tell you what a wonderful feeling that is. For so long, I didn't even consider anything past the moment I was in. But lately, I've started thinking about things I want to do, places I want to go. And you're a big part of that. I want to take you to Disney World. I want to see your face the first time you see the ocean. Of course, before those things can happen, I'm going to have to conquer some of my fears.

Was she for real? Dustin had known a lot of women in his time, but none who had ever gotten under his skin as much as Ainsley did. With Lindsey, he could sort of swipe her away like an irritating gnat. But Ainsley took hold of him and left him replaying her words hours, days, years after she said them. And now, to let him know Jake was trying to play the role of hero. It just ticked him off. So much that he almost wanted to tell her about his upcoming date with Lindsey. Except that he was embarrassed about that, falling into his old ways.

"I'm sure that Sir Jake does want to come pick you up. Probably carry you off on his white horse to some remote castle." He was being childish. And that made him feel even worse. Couldn't she see what was going on? "At lunch the other day, it was like he didn't think you could even handle driving yourself to your sister's house."

"He was only trying to protect me."

Dustin snorted. "Protect you from living your life." He paused. "And you made it to Rachel's just fine, didn't you?"

She was quiet for a moment. "Yes. I did. I was a little stressed once we got into traffic in Flagstaff, but it went fine." She sighed. "I don't want to argue with you. And you're right. I do want to go on this trip."

He regretted being so harsh. But as far as he was concerned, nothing he'd said was off base. "I think once you're there, you'll be glad you got on the plane. A beach vacation with your two best friends. No responsibilities. Good food and lots of laughs. That sounds pretty great to me."

"It isn't a bad way to spend a few days. If someone would just knock me out and wake me up once I get there, I'd be happier, though."

He laughed. "There are things you can take for that, you know. Antianxiety medication or whatever. But if I remember correctly, you probably don't want to go that route."

"You do know me well, don't you?" She chuckled. "My dad's been aching to prescribe me something to help me sleep, but I keep declining. I'm sure he'd be all about antianxiety meds if he knew what I'm going through."

Dustin shifted in the seat of his patrol car. "Actually, I did a little research. I found some techniques for you to try the next time you're doing a ranger program near the rim." He wasn't going to admit to her that his interest in antianxiety remedies developed the day he found out her nerves were what caused Jake to be present at her ranger program. "I printed them all out for you, if you're interested."

"Why don't you bring them over when I get back?" She sighed. "In the meantime, let's figure out how I'm going to get on this plane. We're about to start boarding."

"I guess suggesting you sleep on the flight isn't a possibility, huh?" He grinned.

"Funny."

"Okay. How about this—you know I'm praying for your safety. If I know your parents and siblings, they are, too. Maybe once you get on the plane, you can just think of all the people who are saying prayers for you."

"I can do that."

He heard an announcement in the background. "Good. Now, go get on that plane. I hope you have fun this week."

"I will." She paused. "Thanks, Dustin," she said softly. "You're the best."

"Aw, shucks." He chuckled. "You aren't so bad yourself."

He clicked off the phone and tossed it on the seat next to him. Before he pulled the car out of the parking lot he'd stopped in, he said a quick prayer for her safety. And for her happiness. Because even though he'd decided to leave behind any delusions he'd had of the two of them being more than friends, he wanted her to have the best life she could have. Even if it meant he had to stand by and watch her fall for someone else.

◎◎

Jake sat in his camper, cell phone in hand. Ainsley had sounded awful on the phone. He halfway hoped she'd call him back to say she'd decided to forego her trip. He looked at the phone for another moment. She'd probably boarded the plane by now.

He hadn't gotten the chance to tell her that he was considering taking a little trip of his own this week. Dwight had called a couple of days ago to see how things were going. And to see when he was returning to the police force. Honestly, Jake didn't know. He was happy leading hikes. But at the same time, he wasn't quite ready to turn his badge in yet. After talking to Dwight, he'd been thinking that maybe he should go to Phoenix for a few days and see if he could sort things out.

Jake flipped open the cell phone and hit a number. "Hey, sis," he said once she picked up. "Just wanted to see what you have going on this week."

"Changing some diapers. Wiping some noses. Trying to keep the cat alive." Marie chuckled. "You know, the usual."

He grinned. "How would you feel about a visitor later in the week?"

"Please don't tell me you finally called Super Nanny on me. I'm really in control here, regardless of how it looks from the outside."

"I did, but she says your house is a lost cause." He chuckled. "Actually, I'm thinking about coming home for a few days."

She squealed. "We'd love to see you. Have you told Mom yet? Please don't get her hopes up until it's a done deal."

"I haven't told her." Jake hadn't talked to his mother too much these past several weeks. He knew if he was speaking to her on a regular basis, she'd probably manage to convince him to move back to Phoenix immediately. And he wasn't ready to make that decision.

"Good. I swear, that woman is about to come up there for a visit. And you know how much she hates the crowds at the Grand Canyon in the summertime."

His mother hated crowds, period. She did most of her Christmas shopping in the summer or online. So if she was considering coming for a visit, it must mean she really wanted to see him. "Tell you what. Let's consider this my decision." He grinned. "I'll get there in a couple of days. I just have to tell my boss, and then I'll be on my way."

"That sounds great. We'll be happy to have you stay here, although Mom's probably going to want you there instead."

Jake hadn't thought of that. He really wanted to go back to his own apartment. But the couple subletting it probably wouldn't take too kindly to him showing up. "I'll stay with Mom. I know she gets lonely there by herself."

"Okay. I'm going to tell the kids when we hang up. So there's no backing out. Otherwise, Uncle Jake will no longer be on their favorites list. Instead, you'll be on the bad list with broccoli and prunes."

He chuckled. "I don't want to get dropped off their list, so you can bank on seeing me soon."

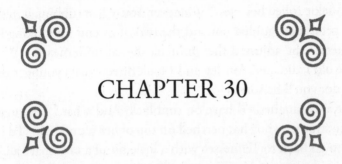

CHAPTER 30

Since I'm your mother, I probably shouldn't confess this to you. But I'm going to. I'm trying to be totally honest about my feelings in this journal. Even the feelings I'm ashamed of. So here goes: After your dad died, I didn't want to have anything to do with God. Nothing. I didn't want to go to church. I didn't want to see a Bible. I certainly didn't want to pray. Why would I want to talk to Someone who'd taken away Brad? I was so angry.

Ainsley sank onto a lounge chair and inhaled. "I could get used to this." After enjoying a leisurely breakfast, she'd been more than happy with Kristy's suggestion they spend some time at the beach. The warmth of the sun on her skin threatened to lull her to sleep. And considering her sleep patterns of late, sleep would be a welcome respite.

"Do you need more sunblock?" Vickie asked. "My thirty-something skin is a little more sensitive than it used to be." She held up a bottle of 45 SPF and shook it.

Ainsley motioned toward Kristy. "Try telling her that."

Kristy flopped over onto her stomach. "It's all about vitamin D. There've been studies done about it." She grinned. "I'm just trying to make sure I don't have a deficiency."

Vickie rolled her eyes. "Whatever. You're just rubbing it in that you get a nice, golden tan and the two of us end up looking like lobsters." She adjusted the umbrella she sat underneath. "When we're old ladies and Ainsley and I look fifteen years younger than you do, you'll be sorry."

Kristy laughed. "I have on sunblock. And a hat." She tugged at the straw cowboy hat perched on top of her blond hair. "I'd just like to go back to Tennessee with a little bit of a tan, that's all."

Ainsley stepped in. "I agree. With both of you." She grinned. "If you tanned like she does, you'd be out there, too," she said to Vickie. "And you." She turned to Kristy. "Just be careful. Sunburns are no fun." Now that she'd restored peace, she leaned against the chair and closed her eyes. If she didn't know better, she'd swear the salty ocean air had magical healing powers. She hadn't felt this relaxed in a long time.

"I can't tell y'all how nice it is to get away." Kristy gazed out at the ocean. "I haven't been out of Tennessee since my honeymoon."

Ainsley and Vickie exchanged a glance. "How's married life, anyway?" Vickie asked. "Any advice you have for me?"

Kristy laughed. "It's great. When I say 'get away' I don't mean from Ace, so don't worry." She grinned. "I meant from work. From real life. You know?"

Vickie nodded. "I definitely needed this break. Between working and planning a wedding, I'm exhausted."

Ainsley felt their gazes upon her. "You both know I needed to get away." She shook her head. "I don't know whether I'm coming or going most of the time." She took her sunglasses off so she could see them better. "Although, I almost didn't come on this trip."

"What do you mean?" Vickie wrinkled her smooth forehead.

"If it was because of Faith, you know you could've brought her with you. We would've loved to have seen her."

"I know. I mean, I do miss her, and leaving her was hard." She sighed. "I'm just going through a tough time right now. I'm scared of things. Irrationally scared."

"What do you mean?" Vickie asked gently.

"At first, it was just a fear of the canyon itself. You know, I imagine all the ways the people I love could fall into it." She sighed. "But then I almost couldn't get on the plane to come down here. All I could think of was that if my plane crashed, Faith wouldn't have any parents left." Tears filled her eyes. "I know I'm a weirdo."

Kristy closed the magazine she'd been reading and sat up. "I know I'm in no way qualified to talk to you about grief," she said. "But when we were in college, I took a counseling class that covered it." She raised her sunglasses to the top of her head. "The main point the teacher made was that everyone handles it differently. There is no wrong way to deal with it."

Vickie nodded in agreement. "She's right. I don't think you're weird at all. Of course you're worried about things. But I think you're doing an amazing job handling everything that's been thrown at you these past couple of years."

Ainsley sniffed. "You don't think I'm crazy for being so scared of random stuff? I mean, there was a time when I could jump out of a plane without batting an eye. And now. . .now I practically have a panic attack just sitting in traffic." She shook her head. "Jake says it's only natural that I see danger now more than I used to. Not only because of Brad's accident, but also because of Faith."

Vickie and Kristy exchanged a look.

"What?" Ainsley demanded. "I saw that."

Vickie bit her lip. "It's just that we don't know a lot about what's really been going on with you since you moved back to the Grand Canyon." She looked expectantly at Ainsley. "Are you dating again?"

◎◎

Julie turned up the volume on the car radio. The booming bass of the Black Eyed Peas filled the space around her. "Oh, driving, how I've missed you," she said out loud. The red Toyota Pathfinder had been an early graduation gift, and leaving it behind for the summer might be the most unfair thing Julie had ever heard of.

She tapped her fingers on the steering wheel with the beat of the music. Claire had mentioned catching a movie later, but in the meantime, Julie just wanted to drive around.

A truck behind her honked. One glance in the rearview, and her heart pounded. Heath. A second later, her cell phone buzzed.

"I got off work early today," he said. "I was going to call you later, but this works out even better."

She grinned. "Are you stalking me?"

Heath laughed. "Nope. Just on my way home."

He paused. "You wanna come over for a little while?"

Practically as soon as she'd walked in the door of her childhood home, her parents had warned against her seeing Heath. But at least this way, it wasn't a planned meeting. Stopping by his place for a few minutes wouldn't hurt anything. It wasn't like she was going to be in the same town as him for a week and not see him. Surely her parents weren't that dense.

"See you there." She disconnected the phone and tossed it onto the seat beside her. The conversations she'd had with Heath lately had been strained. It seemed like each time they spoke, they weren't on the same page about anything. She couldn't help but compare that to the feeling she had spending time with Colt. Which might make her the worst girlfriend in the state of Arizona. Maybe the whole country.

Ten minutes later, she pulled into a spot outside of his apartment building. Heath waited for her on the sidewalk in front of the stairs. "Hey, cutie," he said, grinning.

He enveloped her into a tight hug, and she inhaled. His scent was as intoxicating as ever, almost like a drug. She'd seen an Oprah show once about people who were addicted to other people. Maybe that was the problem here. "Hi," she whispered. "Miss me?"

He planted a kiss on her cheek, and the rough stubble from his five o'clock shadow scraped against her face. "You have no idea." He grabbed her hand and led her up the stairs to his apartment.

"Wow." Julie looked around. "I don't think I've ever seen your apartment this clean before."

Heath grinned. "Would you believe me if I said I'd turned over a new leaf?"

Not really. But maybe she should give him the benefit of the doubt. She sat down on the faded blue couch that had been in the apartment when he'd moved in.

Heath opened the refrigerator and pulled out a beer. It looked like some things definitely hadn't changed. "You want anything?" he asked. "I have a Gatorade. The red kind."

She shook her head. "No. I'm good." She glanced at the can in his hand. "Do you really have to drink that now?"

He opened the can and took a swig. "Apparently I do. Try not to be such a prude, okay?"

Julie bit her lip. "What all have you been up to this summer?"

"I've been up to nothing this summer." He shrugged. "Working and hanging out." He sat down next to her. "Same old stuff."

Julie sighed. Getting Heath to communicate could be difficult sometimes. "So nothing interesting has been happening this summer?" Claire had seen him with Miranda twice now. Of course both times they'd been in a group. But still. Julie couldn't shake her suspicion, no matter how much she wanted to trust him.

"Nah." He put his feet on the coffee table. "Just missing you is all." He cocked his head toward her and grinned.

She hated herself a little for the fluttery feeling in her stomach. What did a guy like him who could sweep any girl off her feet with just a glance see in her? Surely he must really care about her. If he wanted to be with a girl like Miranda, wouldn't he just break things off? "Don't you want to know how my summer has gone so far?" It would've been nice if he didn't need prompting. She thought briefly of Colt, who always wanted to know what she had to say and what she thought, but pushed him from her mind.

"I know how your summer has been." He reached over and pulled her to him. "Miserable. Babysitting a brat. Hanging out with your aunt. No car. No me." He ticked them off on his hand. "Sounds like a disaster."

She frowned. "It really hasn't been bad at all."

Heath leaned down and kissed her lightly on the lips. "Are you saying you haven't missed me?"

Julie shook her head. "No." She smiled. "I'm just saying that the rest of the summer is turning out to be pretty fun. I guess if you were there, it would be perfect."

"About that." He met her gaze. "I've got some vacation time coming up soon. I was thinking about coming for a visit."

She was shocked. Maybe he really did miss her. "I'd like that." She leaned over for another kiss, but her phone began to ring. "I need to get it," she said. "It's Mama."

Heath drew his brows together. "Can't it wait?"

Julie shook her head. "I should go." She'd seen how much Ainsley worried about Faith. It made her more aware of how her own parents must worry about her. And even though a part of her wanted to turn the phone off and spend the next hour snuggled up with Heath, she knew it would be a bad decision.

Heath followed her to the door. "Two months ago you

would've just turned off your phone," he grumbled.

"Don't be silly." She planted a quick kiss on his cheek. But as she hurried down the stairs, she considered his accusation.

"Seriously, Jules? You're just going to leave?" Heath followed her down the stairs.

"My mom will worry." Julie stopped when she reached her SUV and turned to face him.

"Worry you're with me, you mean." Heath took one last swig of his beer and crushed the can in his hands. "You have got to be kidding me. We haven't seen one another in more than a month."

She sighed. "I know. And I'm so sorry. I'll make it up to you." She and her parents had agreed that she could go out to dinner with Heath later in the week. "I'll see you Thursday night for dinner."

He glared. "If you think I'm going to do the whole knock on your door, make small talk with your parents thing, you're wrong." He threw the crushed can on the ground. "I know they think I'm not good enough for their precious little girl."

Julie bit her lip. She knew when he got like this, his temper only escalated. There was no reasoning with him. "That's fine. I don't expect you to come make small talk with them." In fact, she'd just as soon keep her daddy and Heath far apart. "How about I meet you here?"

He regarded her for a long moment. Finally, he reached out and roughly pulled her toward him. "Fine. Go home to your mommy like a good little girl." He bent down and kissed her on the lips. He knew she hated for him to kiss her with beer on his breath. But he did it anyway. "I'll see you Thursday. Don't be late." He let go of her, and she scrambled into her vehicle.

Julie pulled out into traffic, not bothering to look to see if Heath still stood outside his apartment. He ran hot and cold. Sometimes she felt as if she were constantly walking on eggshells around him. She turned her radio up, determined to enjoy the drive. By Thursday, Heath would probably be over it. And if not, at least she'd be headed back to the canyon soon. Back to the canyon. And back to Colt.

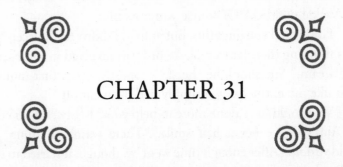

CHAPTER 31

As much as I hated to leave you, taking a vacation with Vickie and Kristy was a good decision. I love the way the three of us help each other. I can always count on them for the truth—even if I'm not going to like it. And I try and do the same for them. When you've been friends as long as we have, there's a certain amount of honesty and trust that is inherent. I know they'll call me out if I'm in denial about something, and I appreciate it. Sometimes I think they serve as a mirror for me—they help me to see how I really feel about certain things.

Ainsley pulled her legs underneath her and stared out at the ocean for a long minute. Finally, she looked over at her waiting friends. "Can I tell you something?"

"Yes," Vickie and Kristy murmured, almost in unison.

She sighed. "I can say this without feeling like I'm about to be judged, right?"

Vickie widened her brown eyes. "Yes. Please tell us what's going on."

"You know I miss Brad." Ainsley tucked a wayward strand of hair behind her ear. "Every day, I miss him. But I accept that he isn't coming back."

Vickie nodded. "Of course you miss him."

"I didn't tell you guys this, but at first, I didn't really accept it. I kept thinking there was a mistake or I was involved in some really bad dream." She shook her head. "Honestly, those first months, I felt like my entire oxygen supply had been cut off."

"We should have done more to help you," Kristy said quietly.

Ainsley gave her a half smile. "There wasn't anything you could've done. After enough time went by, though, it started to sink in. Really sink in." She swallowed. "And now, it's been more than two years. Since I've seen him or touched him or heard his voice." She bit the inside of her cheek. "At first, being back at the canyon was so hard, because I felt like memories were haunting me."

"And now?" Vickie asked.

"Now I realize that I can either live in the past or look toward the future. And I choose the future."

Kristy adjusted her hat. "I think you're very brave."

Ainsley laughed. "You wouldn't think that if you'd seen my knees quaking when I tried to present a ranger program at the rim the other day."

"Work notwithstanding," Kristy said. "If I were in your shoes, I'm pretty sure I'd still be in your parents' basement."

"I'm glad you're starting to look to the future." Vickie smiled. "But what exactly does that mean?"

Ainsley shrugged. "I'm not saying I'm ready to run off and marry someone else tomorrow or anything." She grinned. "But I'm open to the possibilities. I will always miss Brad. And I'll always love him." She glanced down at her bare ring finger. "But I want to love again. I want to be loved again."

"I have no doubt that you'll find someone who makes you happy," Kristy said.

Much to Ainsley's chagrin, she felt a blush creeping up her face. She took a breath and hoped her friends would mistake it for the early stages of sunburn. She glanced at them from the corner of her eye. No such luck.

"So, tell us more about Jake." Vickie adjusted her wide-brimmed hat.

Ainsley leaned against the chair. How could she explain her relationship with Jake? "He's really nice." She bit her lip. "He always wants to help me with whatever problem I'm having. He used to be a cop, so he has that whole hero thing going on."

"Used to be a cop?" Kristy glanced over at her. "What does he do now?"

Ainsley explained the situation. "I think he really understands what I have been through. He always wants to keep me safe. It's like he doesn't want me to be afraid of anything."

"Well, those are great qualities to have," Vickie said with a smile. "But how do you feel about him? That's the question."

"That's kind of the problem." Ainsley took a breath. "He's really cute, and he's pretty easy to talk to. But it's been so long since I've been in this position. I'm not really sure what to think."

"Maybe you don't need to know what to think," Kristy said. "I mean, you're just getting to know him, so maybe you should just enjoy yourself."

Vickie nodded. "That's true. Maybe it's too early to decide. Why don't you just enjoy yourself and see where it goes?"

Were her friends right? Maybe there was no need to define relationships yet. If things were meant to happen with Jake, they'd have to unfold naturally. She'd been guilty in the past of overanalyzing. But this time, she'd just be patient.

◎◎

Dustin rapped on Lindsey's door and waited. He glanced down at his jeans and faded red polo. Lindsey always liked it when he wore red. Said it was a power color. He didn't feel very powerful tonight, though. Just knowing who he was having dinner with and why made him feel very weak. If he were honest with himself, he knew even Lindsey couldn't distract him from his growing feelings for Ainsley. No one could.

The door swung open, and Lindsey stood, grinning. With her blue eyes and blond hair that came just to her shoulders, she looked almost angelic. "You're late."

Angelic until she opened her mouth. "Sorry. Work took a little longer than I expected it to."

She stepped outside. Her turquoise dress matched her eyes. It also left little to the imagination.

Dustin kept his eyes on her face. How many times had he warned the teen boys about not putting themselves into tempting situations? And here he was, going out to dinner with a beautiful woman wearing a low-cut dress. He hoped they didn't run into anyone he knew.

"Well," she purred. "Aren't you at least going to compliment me?" She did a little twirl on the front porch.

"You look great." And that was the thing. She did look great. But looks could be deceiving. "But don't you think that dress is a little. . .much for a midweek dinner?"

She tilted her head and blinked. "I don't know what you mean. I just like to look my best."

He sighed. "Where do you want to go?" He motioned toward his Jeep Cherokee. "I drove over just in case you want to go to Tusayan."

Lindsey grinned. "I think I'm in the mood for the Arizona Room. Is that okay with you? The chef there trained under me. I want to see if he's any good or if it was a waste of my time."

The Arizona Room had always seemed more intimate than any of the other restaurants in the park. It was smaller in size than the El Tovar and dimly lit. "Fine." He glanced at her three-inch heels. "Do you want to drive over there?"

"What do you think?" She flashed him a smile and lifted one shapely leg. "I'm sure not walking in these heels."

He motioned toward the Jeep. "Let's go, then." He held the passenger door open for her and helped her climb in, careful to avert his eyes. There should really be a rule against dresses with so little fabric.

Dustin drove over to the parking lot nearest the Arizona Room. The restaurant was situated between the Bright Angel Lodge and the El Tovar Hotel, right on the canyon's rim. He pulled into an empty spot. "You hungry?" he asked.

"Starving." Lindsey grinned and tossed her hair.

It irritated him that she didn't make a move to exit the Jeep. He walked around to the passenger side and opened the door.

She held her hand out for him to help her out of the vehicle.

He gingerly grasped her hand, not surprised when she clung to him on their way to the restaurant.

"This dinner is way overdue," she said. "I was beginning to think I'd never hear from you again."

Dustin held the door open for her, and they entered the restaurant. He shifted uncomfortably at the stares Lindsey got from the other patrons. Her low-cut dress and high heels were a far cry from the average tourist in the restaurant. He offered up silent thanks when the host led them straight to a table. He didn't want to wait in the small space any longer than he had to.

Once they were seated, Lindsey grinned. "So, to what do I owe this little outing?"

He shrugged. "I just thought it would be nice to get together, that's all."

The waiter set a basket of rolls and two glasses of water in front of them. "Are you ready to order, or should I come back?" he asked, his eyes straying to Lindsey's neckline.

Dustin rolled his eyes and wished he could put one of Faith's bibs on her to cover her up. "We're ready." He ordered the salmon, his favorite dish on the menu.

"Let me have the pork medallions with orange glaze." Lindsey handed her menu to the waiter. "And make sure Lamar knows he's cooking it for Lindsey Jane." She smiled prettily at the young man. "I want it to be perfect. Don't forget."

"Oh, I won't. I'll tell Lamar right away." The waiter gawked at Lindsey for another second before heading back to the kitchen.

"Good grief," Dustin said as the young man walked off. "I thought his eyes were going to pop out of his head."

She gave him a tinkling little laugh. "Oh? I didn't even notice."

"I'll bet you didn't." Dustin pulled a steaming roll from the basket and slathered it with butter. He took a bite and felt her eyes on him. He swallowed and met her gaze. "What?"

"Why did you ask me to have dinner?" Her blue eyes pierced his.

"Company." He shrugged.

Lindsey sat up straight. "I don't buy it. You clearly don't want to be here. You've all but cringed every time I get near you." She glared across the table. "So what's the deal?"

He frowned. He couldn't tell her that he'd only called because he was trying to move on from Ainsley. "There isn't a deal."

She slapped her hand on the table. "Dustin Cooper. I have known you for a long time, remember? I thought something was odd when you called me in the first place but figured I'd go along to see what happened." She scowled. "Let me guess. . .things didn't work out with Ainsley so you're looking to make yourself feel better." She raised her perfectly arched eyebrows.

"Keep your voice down," he said quietly. "You attract enough attention as it is."

"Get over yourself and answer my question. Does your asking me to dinner have anything to do with Ainsley?"

He raked his hands through his hair. "Fine. Yes. Are you

happy? I realized that there was no way Ainsley and I can ever be anything more than friends. It made me sad. So I called you."

"And does sitting here with me make you feel better?"

He shook his head. "No. It makes me feel like a jerk. To her and to you."

Lindsey was quiet. "You aren't a jerk. You're just a dumb guy who never had the nerve to tell the girl he likes how he feels, and now you're paying the price." She leaned forward in her seat. "If you were a jerk, I'd pour this ice water on your head and stomp out." She grinned. "But I'm not going to do that."

He managed a smile. "Thanks." He had to admit he'd eyed the full water glass when she first started raising her voice. Had this been a few years ago, he'd be soaked by now.

"So tell me the story. We've been through this once before, so you may as well lay it all on me again."

Dustin tensed his jaw, debating whether Lindsey was the person he wanted to confide in. "There's no story. Not really."

She rolled her eyes. "Do you remember all those years ago when you introduced Ainsley to Brad? And how you felt once you figured out they were seeing each other?"

He nodded. He'd never once imagined anything would come out of an innocent introduction. Back then, he'd figured that someday he would be the one who would end up dating Ainsley. "Yes."

"I remember how bummed you were. I also remember how you refused to tell her that you had feelings for her." Lindsey tore a roll into little pieces and dropped them on her plate. "You just pushed them aside and ignored them until they finally went away."

"It wasn't that big a deal." He shifted uncomfortably. If he'd had an inkling Lindsey would use this little dinner date to psychoanalyze him, he never would've asked her to come. "It wasn't like I was in love with her or anything."

"Maybe not. But you definitely thought something was there. You were so torn up that I think you dated every girl in the state of Arizona in an effort to get over her." She twisted her mouth into a grin. "And I know you moved on, but are you going to risk letting that happen again?" She narrowed her eyes. "And seriously. It kills me to be giving you good advice where Ainsley is concerned. I don't see what all the fuss is about."

He opened his mouth to speak, but she raised a hand to cut him off. "No. Don't defend her to me again. Even though I'm not particularly fond of her, I do want you to be happy." She shook her head. "And this time, if she does end up falling for someone else, I'm not going to be around to pick up the pieces."

Dustin furrowed his brow. "What do you mean?"

"I'm moving at the end of the summer. As much as I like this place, it's time for me to move on. I'm going to be the new head chef at a restaurant opening this fall in Phoenix." She grinned. "So you'd better listen to my advice while you have me here."

He couldn't imagine the park without Lindsey in it. "I'm happy for you, Linds. I know you've felt stifled here for the past couple of years."

"I'm excited. I should've left years ago, but sometimes change is hard even for the adventurous." She raised an eyebrow at him. "But we can talk about me later." She patted the table. "Right now, we need to figure out what to do about you. What is holding you back from pursuing her?"

He sighed. "On the one hand, I'm worried that she'll laugh in my face at the thought of the two of us as more than friends. And on the other hand, I wonder what Brad would say if he knew."

"You wanna know what I think?" She grinned. "And I know you do, because I'm probably the most brilliant person you know."

He chuckled. "Please, enlighten me."

"Brad would probably want Ainsley and Faith to have someone in their life that they love. Now, do you think he would rather that be some random guy he's never met, or the guy who was like a brother to him?"

"I hadn't thought of it that way."

"And let me tell you, it was one thing for you to be friends and hang out with Ainsley and Brad. But if she moves on to some new guy, do you really think you're still going to be part of the picture? I think not."

She was right. If Ainsley ended up with Jake, there was no way Jake would be comfortable having Dustin around. At least that was the vibe he'd gotten the other day at lunch. "So what are you saying?"

"That you need to think seriously about telling her how you feel." She met his gaze. "And if you aren't prepared to do that, you need to leave her alone."

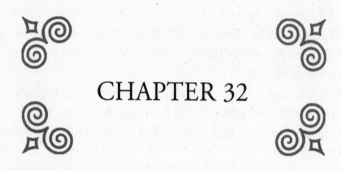

CHAPTER 32

I guess I'm still struggling to find a balance. I wonder sometimes if that's even possible. I'm pulled in a million different directions on any given day. I want to be good at my job. I want to be a good mother. I want to be a good friend. I want to stay close to my family and be a good daughter, sister, and aunt. I want to be a student of God's Word. I want to just be me for a little while and go to a yoga class or a spa. And I don't know how to reconcile all these pieces of myself.

This is one of the best vacations ever," Kristy declared over dinner. They'd walked along the beach to a seafood restaurant with outdoor seating. "I mean, I could get used to this view." She waved her hand toward the brilliant blue ocean.

"I agree." Ainsley grinned. "I haven't been this relaxed in ages. Maybe ever."

Vickie took a sip of tea. "And it isn't just the beach. I wish we lived closer to each other. I miss you guys."

"Stop. We can't get all emotional." Ainsley grinned. "Otherwise you'll start crying and ruin dinner."

Kristy chuckled. "Speaking of emotional, I realize I'm not exactly known for being the most emotional person." That was an understatement. Kristy rarely cried and had always had a hard time expressing her emotions. She smoothed her blond hair. "But I have a little announcement to make." She paused dramatically. "Ace and I are expecting a baby." She gave them a beaming smile.

Vickie squealed. "I'm so excited for you."

"I've been wanting to ask you all day," Ainsley admitted. Ever since their conversation about being ready for motherhood, she'd been suspicious. "I've never seen you eat as much random stuff as I've seen you ingest since we got here." She laughed. "I remember that part of pregnancy—when I craved so many different things."

Kristy laughed. "That's where I am. It's like the flavor of everything is enhanced." She beamed. "I really wanted to wait until just the right moment to tell my news." She gestured at the setting sun. "And I figure this was the perfect time."

"How far along are you?" Vickie asked.

"Just a few weeks. I'm not telling anyone else yet. Just you guys and my mother." She grinned at Ainsley. "I'd taken an at-home test just before I talked to you on the phone."

Ainsley chuckled. "I've been dying to ask you ever since then but know from experience how annoying that can be."

"We wanted to get confirmation from the doctor before I told anyone."

"I don't blame you." Ainsley grinned. "And I'd offer you my maternity clothes, but I'm not sure how they'd fit." Vickie and Kristy had always been able to share clothes, but Ainsley was much taller. When they were in college, they'd envied her long legs, and she'd envied that they'd had two closets full of clothes to choose from.

"Okay, enough about me." Kristy grinned mischievously. "Vickie, how is the bonding going with your future stepdaughter?"

Vickie nodded. "Actually, it's going pretty well. Katherine is really wonderful. And helping her go through the grief of losing her mother has had a huge impact on me." Vickie's fiancé, Thatcher, had been married right out of high school, and his daughter, Katherine, was born when he was only eighteen. Thatcher and his wife divorced when Katherine was two. At first, it had been difficult for Vickie to adjust to Thatcher having a grown daughter, but now she seemed to take it in stride.

"How so?" Ainsley asked.

"You know I haven't had the best relationship with my mother. But watching Katherine deal with something so difficult has made me much more tolerant." She gave them a tiny smile. "Thatcher and I want to have kids of our own someday, too. And we finally have a date set for the wedding. I have the cutest save-the-date cards to show you back at the condo."

"How fun." Ainsley grew silent. She loved catching up with her friends, but for some reason, it made her a little sad. She'd known the excitement of planning a wedding to a man she loved and remembered the thrill of finding out she was expecting. Listening to them tell about what was going on in their lives caused her to wonder if she would ever have one of those kinds of moments again.

"You aren't off the hook." Kristy met her gaze from across the table. "Tell us more about what's going on with you."

"There's nothing more to tell." She shrugged. "Just working and being a mommy. Faith's walking really well now and starting to talk."

Vickie and Kristy exchanged a glance.

"So. . .what about Dustin?" Kristy asked.

Ainsley furrowed her brow. "What do you mean? He's fine."

Kristy rolled her eyes. "Are you seeing much of him?" She jerked back from the table. "Ow." She wrinkled her nose at Vickie. "Hello. Don't kick the pregnant girl."

"Sorry." Vickie giggled. "Subtlety has never been your specialty, has it?"

Ainsley looked from one friend to the other. "What exactly are you guys getting at?"

"We just think. . ." Vickie paused. "We remember that you used to be really close to him."

"And we kind of thought that something might be happening with you two," Kristy explained. "But then you started talking about this Jake guy, so we're just trying to figure it out."

"You thought something might be happening between me and Dustin?" Ainsley shook her head. "We're friends. I mean, we spend time together and all. He's crazy about Faith." She grinned. "And the feeling is likewise." She glanced at the girls. "But that's it. We don't date or anything."

"Why?"

Ainsley shook her head. "We just aren't like that. I've never really considered him that way."

"Never?" Kristy asked. "Because I seem to remember that when you first met him, you thought he was awfully cute."

"That was almost ten years ago. I was practically a child." She grinned. It was true, though. She'd had a little crush on him when they first met, even though they were total opposites. But she'd gotten over it quickly as they'd settled into a friendship. "And I could say the same thing about you. I seem to remember you coming for a visit and spending the whole time flirting with him."

Kristy giggled. "I couldn't understand how you had such a good-looking friend yet were single." She shook her head. "And I guess it was soon after that when you met Brad."

Ainsley nodded. "I think you're right." She grinned. "Okay, fine. So I can appreciate that he's cute."

235

"If you had to choose between him and Jake, who do you choose?" Vickie asked.

Ainsley made a face. "I don't like this game." She sighed. "They're very different. I don't know Jake that well, so we're still getting to know one another. The only thing that bothers me there is that he never includes Faith and Julie. He asks me out to dinner and lunch, but it's always just the two of us." She shrugged. "Dustin, on the other hand, is one of my oldest friends. I like that he knew me before I was a wife or a mother. I feel like he knows the real me, if that makes sense. And he always wants to hang out with me and Faith together. He seems to really care about her."

Kristy and Vickie exchanged a glance.

"Which one do you enjoy spending time with more?" Kristy took a sip of water.

"That's hard to say. I enjoy both of them, but for different reasons. Jake never wants me to be upset about anything. He actually offered to have someone come and pick me up from the airport because he knew I didn't want to get on the plane."

"Hmm," Vickie said. "How about Dustin?"

Ainsley rolled her eyes. "He pushes me to get out of my comfort zone. He says he knows I'm still fearless, but I've just hidden that part of myself. The other night, he told me I was one of the bravest people he knows—he just wishes I could see it."

Kristy bit her lip. "Interesting."

"What?"

"Just that it looks like you have two wonderful men who you enjoy spending time with." Kristy grinned. "I seem to remember a couple of months ago when you said you doubted you'd ever go out on a date again."

"It's been a pleasant surprise," Ainsley admitted. "It's weird, but fun." Maybe she was finally adjusting to being single again. She'd spent six years with Brad. After his death, she'd been certain she'd never be interested in another man again. But she finally felt free to move on.

"I think you're doing great," Vickie said, smiling. "And I agree with Dustin. I think you're very brave."

Ainsley chuckled. "I don't know about that. But you know, one thing that helps is that I know Brad would want me to move on." She tucked a wayward strand of hair behind her ear. "We had a conversation about it once, right after we were married." She gave them a tiny smile. "I don't know if that's normal for all married couples, but since he had a dangerous job it seemed okay. One night after he'd been away at a training session for a few days, he told me that if anything ever happened to him, he wanted me to promise that I'd move on and be happy." She laughed. "I jokingly told him that if anything ever happened to me, he'd better not even look at another woman or I'd haunt him."

Kristy laughed. "I'll bet that went over well."

"Of course, I ended up telling him that I felt the same way. I don't think either of us ever thought it would actually happen, but I do know he was serious about it. He would want me to find happiness, whatever it may be." She sighed. "And knowing that makes things a little bit easier now."

Vickie nodded. "He would definitely want you to be happy." She reached over and covered Ainsley's hand with her own. "We all do. I can't tell you how good it is to see the light in your eyes again."

"That's exactly how I feel. Like I've come out of the darkness and into the light." She grinned. "Or maybe like I've come out of my parents' basement and am back in the real world."

"Same thing." Kristy chuckled.

❧

Jake slowed his truck down in front of the tiny house. The peeling paint and high grass said it all. No one lived there any longer. He pulled over and put the truck in Park.

The memory of Gina sobbing in the front yard, begging him to help her, flooded his mind. If only he'd reacted differently. Faster. Smarter. Something.

He sighed and rubbed his jaw. He hadn't shaved in a couple of days, and his face felt like sandpaper.

A bald man walked his dog past Jake's truck and shot him a curious look.

Jake waved and hoped he looked like an upstanding citizen, despite his stubble and unkempt hair. No need to alarm the neighbors. They were probably still shaken up by the grisly events of that fateful night.

He put the truck in Drive and pulled it onto the deserted road. With a flick of the radio knob, a country song filled the cab of the truck. The twangy voice wailed about lost loves and unfulfilled dreams. Jake could identify. If his new career as a hiking guide didn't pan out, perhaps there was a place for him in Nashville among the down-on-their-luck songwriters.

The cell phone buzzed from the console, and Jake turned the radio down.

"Heard you were back in town." Dwight's gravelly voice gave away his pack-a-day habit. "You back for good, or is this just a pit stop?"

"I guess it's just a pit stop. I'm here to visit my family and all. But I'm headed back up to the canyon in a day or two."

Dwight growled. "When can we expect you back? Chief's put me with a rookie who thinks he's ten feet tall and bulletproof."

Jake cringed. He hadn't considered how his absence would impact Dwight. "Sorry, man. I'm still trying to get my head on straight." He cleared his throat. "I told the chief that I'd give him an answer by the end of the month."

"Look, McGuire. I know you're beating yourself up for what happened with that young couple. But you can't save the world. I think you might need to take a look at all the good you've done.

You've helped put away a lot of bad guys." Dwight's tone might be gruff, but Jake knew he meant well.

"Thanks." Jake ended the call and placed the phone back in the console.

He drove aimlessly around the city. Past his old hangouts, his old high school. Eventually he found himself parked outside of the police station.

What did he really want to do? Leave his career behind and make a new life for himself? Or return to the force and try harder to make good decisions?

Thirty minutes later, Jake pulled his truck into his sister's driveway. He parked next to her minivan and hopped out of the truck. Before he could even ring the doorbell, the door flung open.

"They're finally sleeping," Marie whispered. "And so help me, if you wake them, I'm going to leave you alone with them for the afternoon, and I'm going to a spa." She grinned broadly and pulled him into a tight hug. "It's so good to see you."

"You, too." He followed her into the sunny kitchen and plopped on a barstool.

Marie set a plate of chocolate chip cookies and a glass of milk in front of him. "I'm trying to entice you into moving back home." She sat down across from him and broke off part of a cookie. "So? What's the deal?" She munched on a bite of cookie and eyed him expectantly.

"Time to catch my breath, please?" He bit into a still-warm cookie and chewed it thoughtfully. "These are good."

She widened her eyes. "Well, yeah. They were made with love." She grinned. "And with Jenny standing on a stool next to me, licking the bowl." His three-year-old niece could always be counted on to help do the important jobs in the kitchen, like lick the bowl or beaters.

He smiled. "I can't wait to see her. And Thomas." He doted

on the kids like they were his own.

"They feel the same way." She motioned toward an overflowing dining table. "There's an assortment of artwork over there for you." She took a sip of milk. "You've had time to catch your breath. I want to know what's going on inside that head of yours."

Jake and Marie were only a year apart and, once they'd passed a rocky adolescence, had become close friends. He'd always been able to talk to his sister about anything, and she'd understand and offer advice. Usually good advice, although he rarely admitted it to her. "I'm still trying to decide how to answer that age-old question—what do I want to do with the rest of my life." He sighed.

"Okay. Let's break it down." Her matter-of-fact way of handling things instantly made him feel better. "Do you enjoy what you're doing now?"

He shrugged. "I enjoy hiking. But the more I do it, the more I don't know if I'm cut out to be a guide. I get frustrated easily with the hikers, especially the novices. They never want to listen to advice, and in the end, that always makes the hike tougher." He shook his head. "It's like they read a guide book about hiking the canyon and think they know it all."

She chuckled. "Patience has never been your strongest point, has it?"

He shook his head. "I'm getting better at it, though."

"But you don't think being a hiking guide is your life's calling?"

"I think at this point I can safely say no. Especially considering I find more and more reasons to tell them I'm not available to lead a hike." The past few weeks, he was more likely to be found exploring on his own or hanging out near the main visitor center, hoping to run into Ainsley, than leading a group hike.

"Okay. What about going back to the police force? Do you think that's where your heart is?"

He raked his fingers through his hair. "Yes and no." He grinned.

"Well, that's as clear as mud. Can you explain that a little bit?"

Jake sighed. "Maybe I'm tired of my heart being with my job. This summer has taught me that there's more to life, you know?"

Marie widened her eyes. "Really? You, Mr. Sixty-Hour Week? You think there might be life outside of work?"

"Don't get all excited." He wrinkled his nose at her. "I've been living in a tiny camper, all alone. I've had lots of time to evaluate my life."

"And what do you see?"

He shrugged. "A man who has spent years putting work ahead of everything else. A man who when asked what his hobbies are can only say golf, even though I only play once in a blue moon. A man who is alone. Completely alone."

Marie chewed thoughtfully on a cookie. "So you're saying that you're ready to have a personal life?"

Jake groaned. "I shouldn't be talking to you about this."

"I've been trying to set you up with a girl from church for the longest time. So this little turn of events makes me happy." She glanced at him. "What's that look?"

"Nothing." He was quiet for a moment. "Maybe I've met someone." He met her surprised gaze.

"And do you think it has potential? Is that why you're on the fence about coming back to Phoenix?"

He shook his head. "That's just it. I'm not sure it could ever go anywhere. It's complicated. She's been through a lot, and right now, I'm just trying to be a good friend to her."

Marie grinned. "That's awfully gentlemanly of you."

His face grew hot. "Regardless of what might happen with her, she's at least shown me that I want to have someone in my life. I want to settle down and have a family." He shook his head.

"Watching that young couple die right in front of me has really made me take stock. I guess what I'm saying is that even if I return to the police force, I'm going to be making some changes in my life."

She reached over and patted his hand. "Change is good. Hard to do sometimes, but good. It sounds like you've gotten some good perspective on things."

"I used to think being a cop was the best thing about me. But this summer, I don't have that title, and I still feel like I have something to offer."

Marie shook her head. "You've always had a lot to offer. But maybe you didn't realize it until you took a step back. Being a policeman is honorable and brave and heroic. But you know what? Even if you weren't a cop, you'd still be those things."

Maybe his sister was right. Jake wasn't sure. But he did know that the guilt that had eaten away at him at the beginning of the summer was beginning to subside. He'd blamed himself for the situation with Gina and Tommy for so long. But no one on the force blamed him. Dwight didn't blame him. His family still thought he was honorable.

All Jake needed to do now was forgive himself and put it behind him completely.

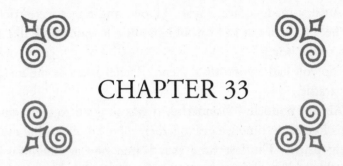

CHAPTER 33

*Your daddy and I went to San Diego on our honeymoon.
It was the most amazing trip. The whole time, all I could
think was that he was mine forever. And when that forever
was cut short, I thought my own life was over. But these
past months have shown me that I am much more resilient
than I thought I was. Maybe I sold myself short, thinking
I'd never be whole again. I still miss your daddy, and always
will. But you have helped me see that life goes on.*

I'm totally jealous of your tan." Julie popped her gum from
the backseat. They were on their way back to Cottonwood after
picking Ainsley up from the airport.

Ainsley turned around and grinned at her niece. "Don't make
fun of me, but it's actually fake."

"No way," Julie exclaimed.

"Yep. Yesterday, Vickie and I were so disgusted we still had
pasty white skin that we went over to Walgreens and bought some
kind of spray-on tan." She grinned. "It stunk to high heaven, but
we look every bit as tan as Kristy."

Rachel glanced over at Ainsley. "Not too bad. I probably wouldn't have known if you hadn't told." She chuckled. "Unless I happened to look at your elbow."

Ainsley made a face. "Yeah. Elbows and knees were tricky." She held an arm out in front of her. "But at least I look like I've been to the beach."

"So you had a good time then?" Rachel asked as she merged with traffic.

Ainsley nodded. "Wonderful. It was so good to see them. It seems like every time we get together, there are major life events taking place." The last time they'd seen one another was for Kristy's wedding. Before that, it was for Ainsley's baby shower. "It was nice to just be together without any kind of schedule."

"No schedule sounds lovely to me." Rachel shook her head. "But I guess my life is about to lose its schedule with Julie starting college." She glanced in the rearview mirror at her daughter. "I'm not going to know what to do with myself without having all her activities to attend." She sighed.

"Oh, Mama. You'll be fine." Julie giggled from the backseat. "At least you won't have to wait up nights anymore, worrying about where I am."

Rachel snorted. "I'm pretty sure I'll still be keeping tabs on you, even though you're at school. That's why we have text messaging on our phones." She grinned. "So you can text me when you get to the dorm after a night out."

"I feel certain Julie will be in at a reasonable hour every night so she can study." Ainsley turned to look at her niece. "Right?"

Julie shrugged. "It's not like I'm gonna go crazy or anything, but it will be nice to have a little freedom."

Ainsley glanced over at her sister. Rachel's worry lines were evident on her forehead. Ainsley wondered how many of those lines were caused by Heath. "Did you see Heath while you were home?" She pulled the shade and flipped the mirror open so she could see Julie's face.

"Um. Yeah." Julie stared out the window. "He's kinda mad at me right now."

So there was trouble in paradise. Rachel and Dave must be elated. But as any good parents of a teenager, they likely weren't expressing their relief out loud. She glanced over at Rachel. Her face was a mask of disinterest. "What's he mad about?" Ainsley asked. She knew Julie likely hadn't filled her mother in on the tiff, so she figured getting Julie to talk about it would be good for Rachel to hear.

"He said I was acting distant. Like I wasn't happy enough to see him or something."

Rachel sputtered but didn't say anything.

"What did he expect you to do, throw a parade?" Ainsley grinned. She caught Rachel's smirk out of the corner of her eye.

Julie sighed. "I don't know. I never do anything right."

Ainsley decided to let that statement go and hit her from another angle. "Have you talked to Colt this week? I wonder how things are going at the park."

"A couple of times. He just wanted to fill me in on stuff. They had a devo over at Dustin's house one night. And the Brewsters are looking for someone to dog-sit Max for a couple of nights. I told him I might want to do it if that's okay with you. It would only be at night. During the day, he can stay out in their fenced yard."

Ainsley nodded. "That's fine with me if your mom doesn't care."

Rachel drew her brows together. "Would you feel comfortable staying at a stranger's house overnight?"

"Yeah. It isn't a big deal. Colt would probably come over and stay until bedtime. And then Max would be there to bark at any strange noises or anything. Besides, it's right next door to Dustin's, so if I needed something, he could be right over."

Rachel glanced over at Ainsley. "How is Dustin?"

"Fine. He's started hosting devotionals for the teens, either at his house or out at the amphitheater." She sighed. "I think that's been really good for him." Talking about Dustin made her realize how much she'd missed him. She'd been tempted to call him several times from the beach, but something held her back. Perhaps Kristy and Vickie's questions had gotten to her.

"I imagine so. Any time you're teaching from God's Word, it seems like you learn more than your students." Rachel grinned. "At least that's been my experience, and I only teach first graders at church."

Ainsley nodded, suddenly eager to change the subject from Dustin. "You know, Rach, once Julie is off at college, you should come spend some time with me and Faith." One of the things she missed about living in her parents' basement was frequent visits from Rachel.

"I'll have to do that. I went to see Faith while Mom and Dad were keeping her. She's grown so much."

"I know. It's hard to believe how fast she's growing up. I feel like if I blink, she'll be off to college, too."

Rachel frowned. "That's not too much of an overstatement, actually." She was quiet for a moment. "But you did better this week than I expected you to. I told Julie I halfway expected you to call me from the airport and tell me you'd changed your mind."

Her sister wasn't far from the truth. "Being away from her was difficult. That's the longest we've ever spent apart and the only time I've been away from her overnight. But Mom said she was just fine, and I talked to Sandra several times while Faith was staying with them, and she said she was okay. I think she cried a little while she was with them, which makes me feel bad."

"They haven't spent nearly as much time with her as Mom and Dad have. I'm sure they understood."

"I know. It makes me feel a little guilty, though, that they don't know her as well as my family does." She sighed. "I should've done a better job of making sure they had time with her."

"Sis, I think you're being way too hard on yourself. The past couple of years haven't been easy for you." Rachel reached over and patted her leg. "Besides, Faith isn't even two yet. If you want to make sure she spends time with Brad's parents, now's the time to start."

Ainsley nodded. "I guess you're right."

"I'm the big sister," Rachel teased. "I'm always right."

"Whatever." Ainsley chuckled. She leaned her head against the seat, already anticipating the reunion she was going to have with her daughter. Only a couple of hours to go, and Faith would be in her arms.

⊙⁀⊚

Dustin stood in the middle of Pioneer Cemetery. The historic cemetery on park grounds honored the men and women who'd devoted their lives to the Grand Canyon. He'd visited often over the years, always taking special care to read each stone. He felt it was the least he could do to remember fellow canyon residents.

Many of the stones bore the names of couples who'd met at the canyon. There must be something about the beauty of the Grand Canyon that inspired love. Dustin walked by one such grave. The man had worked at the canyon, installing the transcontinental phone line. The woman had worked as a Harvey Girl. According to the inscription, they met and fell in love while working at the canyon.

He passed the graves of many other Harvey Girls. The Fred Harvey Company had been instrumental in making the Grand Canyon a premier tourist destination. With the help of the Harvey Girls, who served as hostesses and waitresses, the service had been first-rate. Dustin hadn't visited the Harvey Girl Museum at the Bright Angel Lodge in a year or so, but each time he did, he marveled at the rich history of the park.

The Kolb brothers had also been laid to rest in the cemetery. Their photography studio had clung to the edge of the canyon since 1904. Emery Kolb worked there as a photographer until his death in the 1970s. Kolb Studio was one of Dustin's favorite spots on the park. He stood for a moment at Emery's grave, considering the changes the man must've seen during the many decades he'd lived and worked at the canyon.

Dustin continued his journey around the cemetery, finally coming to the small marker that was the reason for today's visit: BRADLEY STEVEN DAVIS, DEVOTED HUSBAND, SON, AND FATHER-TO-BE.

Dustin kneeled down in front of his old friend's memorial. Brad had been buried in his family's plot, near Flagstaff. A memorial had been placed at the park's cemetery by some of the locals.

"Hey, man." Dustin glanced around to make sure the cemetery was deserted. He'd come here often over the past couple of years but didn't make it a practice to talk to the air very often. Only in times of great distress, times he'd give anything to have his friend available to go out for pizza and talk. "We're missing you here." He sighed. "Ainsley's back, but you probably know that." Did Brad know that? Dustin didn't really know what the rules were. But he sort of had a feeling Brad knew. "And your daughter, Faith, is amazing. She looks just like her mama except for her eyes. They're like looking right at you."

He mustered up the courage for his visit. "Listen. I'm here to tell you something that I'm hoping you're okay with." He sighed. "I've fallen for her." No need to say who *her* was. Dustin was sure Brad already knew. "I didn't plan on it. When I found out she was coming back, I really thought it would just be nice to have my friend back. But the more time I spend with her. . .well, the more I realize that I definitely have feelings. And not just for her. Faith has me wrapped around her little finger. Don't worry, though. I'm going to tell her stories about her daddy as soon as she'll sit still long enough." He chuckled.

"Anyway, I guess I'm here to get your permission. I know it seems weird. Believe me though, when I say I'd rather just have you back where you belong." He blinked against his tears. "But since that isn't possible, I want you to know that if Ainsley ever returns my feelings, I'll do everything I can to make her happy. Faith, too. And none of us will ever forget you." Dustin said a silent prayer and rose to his feet.

With one last glance at Brad's memorial, Dustin walked slowly out of the cemetery. He felt more at peace with his decision to continue to see Ainsley. He didn't know if or when he'd tell her how he felt, but he did know that he wouldn't feel guilty about it any longer.

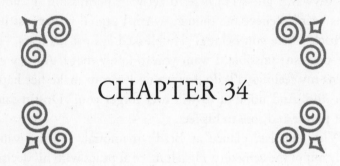

CHAPTER 34

I need to do a better job recording the moments of your life. I keep thinking I'm going to find the time to make scrapbooks and that kind of thing but never do. If I keep this up, someday when you're older, you're going to think I neglected you. I assure you that isn't so. When you were first born, the thought of taking family pictures made me really sad. I felt like, because it would just be you and me, it wasn't really a family. But I'm learning that sometimes even though a family doesn't look exactly like you thought it would—it's still just as special.

No way." Ainsley laughed as the music started. "It can't be." When Dustin had called earlier to see if she wanted him to stop by with dinner, she hadn't imagined the night would end up with them sitting in the living room, listening to old songs, and laughing.

Dustin grinned. "Oh, yes. Here it is. Your favorite monster ballads of the '80s and early '90s." Along with dinner, he'd brought an old CD of hers that had somehow ended up in his collection.

The living room filled with the sounds of Ainsley's youth.

Faith stopped what she was doing and stood up. She bounced with the music and clapped her hands.

"I see she has her mother's taste in music." Dustin laughed as the little girl scooted around the living room.

"Dance, dance," Ainsley said to Faith. She glanced over at Dustin. "We have living room dance parties every now and then. Can you tell?"

He laughed. "She's hilarious." He reached over and turned the music down.

Faith frowned at him. "Dance," she said.

"I'm sorry, tiny dancer. It's too loud." He grinned. "But maybe we can read a story?" He pulled out a book from the nearest shelf. "Baby's Firsts," he read from the cover. He opened it. "Baby's first picture."

"That's the ultrasound picture," Ainsley explained.

Dustin flipped through the rest of the book. "The rest of the book is blank." He looked up at Ainsley, puzzled.

She shrugged. "I guess it fell by the wayside."

"Too bad. I would've liked to see a record of your firsts," he said to Faith.

Ainsley looked at her watch. "She needs to go to bed soon."

"One story?" he asked. "Come on, I'm trying to be her favorite Uncle Dustin. I bring her puppies, let her dance to '80s music, and read her stories past her bedtime." He raised his eyebrows.

"Fine." Ainsley stood. "You know what? Actually that could really help me out. Do you think you could read her a story and maybe rock her a little bit while I jump in the shower?" As soon as she asked the question, she wondered if she'd lost her mind. So many things could go wrong. Dustin could look away for a second, and Faith could eat a button or a penny. She might fall and bump her head, and he'd never notice. But the lure of a few quiet moments to shower and wash her hair was too much.

"Do you mean you're trusting me to babysit your child?" He grinned. "Man, I've just leveled up."

She rolled her eyes, glad he couldn't read her mind. "Yes, I guess I'm trusting you with my child. But a little selfishly." She smiled. "Finding time for a shower is tricky. I hate taking one while she's asleep because I'm afraid she'll wake up and I won't hear her." She sighed. "I don't know what I'm going to do when Julie's gone. Just having her away for the night is hard." When the Brewsters had asked Julie to dog-sit for them while they were out of town, she'd jumped at the chance to play with Max.

Dustin picked Faith up and grabbed Bo Bo from the couch. "We'll be fine." He turned to Faith. "Let's go read a story," he said.

Faith yawned and nodded.

"I can't get over how she's taken to you," Ainsley said. "It's amazing."

He grinned. "I go way back with her parents. She must sense it." He motioned down the hallway. "Go take your shower." He grinned mischievously. "I didn't want to say anything before, but I kind of thought you looked a little worse for wear."

She wrinkled her nose at him. "If someone would've given me more than fifteen minutes' notice that they were stopping by, maybe I'd have been more prepared for company." Her mouth turned upward in a smile. "Besides, for your information, we did a little exercising this afternoon. That's why I look 'worse for the wear.'"

"Did you start running again?"

Ainsley sighed. "No. But I did yoga in the backyard. I tried to teach Faith some positions, but she was more interested in playing in the dirt."

"Can't blame her for that."

Ainsley hurried through her shower, thankful she used two-in-one shampoo and conditioner. A mom had to cut corners wherever she could, even if it only saved a couple of minutes. In her bedroom, she slipped on a pair of yoga pants and a T-shirt left over from her college days. Worry niggled at her. Did the house seem oddly quiet?

She tried to push the thoughts away and concentrate on untangling her long hair. The baby monitor. Of course. She crossed the room to her nightstand and flipped it on. Now if anything happened to Faith, she'd hear it. Her daughter was probably already sleeping.

Ainsley picked up the comb just as Dustin's muffled voice filled the room. "I used to be your daddy's best friend," he said.

She eyed the monitor in horror. He had no idea she could hear him. She knew she should turn it off. But instead, she sat down on the bed and listened.

"We were only a little bit older than you are when we met." He paused. "He was such a good man. I looked up to him so much. Someday I'll tell you all about growing up with him."

Ainsley's breath caught in her throat. The raw emotion in his voice shocked her.

"And your mama is some kind of wonderful. She knew me before she knew your daddy. I always knew she was special."

Faith murmured.

Ainsley knew that sound. Faith tried to keep herself awake as long as possible during her nightly story.

Dustin continued. "These past two years have been the hardest ones I've ever had. At first, I was so mad." Dustin paused. "I was mad at everyone. But then I realized your daddy wouldn't want me to be mad. He'd want me to live the best kind of life I could live."

Ainsley wiped away the hot tears from her eyes. She fought the urge to go to Faith's room and give him a hug.

"So I am. I found God, right out here in the canyon, just like your daddy said I would if I'd just look. It's taken me a lot of praying, and believe me, I still mess up. But the important thing is that I'm trying."

Faith jabbered in response.

"And I think your daddy would be proud of the man I've become." Dustin sighed. "Although I'm not sure your mama is. I've tried to show her I'm not the same old guy she used to know, but I don't think she believes it."

Ainsley couldn't take it anymore. She wiped her eyes and set the monitor back on the nightstand.

She paused at the door of Faith's room.

Faith was sound asleep in Dustin's arms.

Ainsley wasn't sure if she'd ever seen a more perfect sight. "She okay?" she whispered.

He looked up from the rocking chair. "Yep." He stood up and walked over to the crib. "How do I lay her down?"

"Just on her back is fine." Ainsley leaned over and kissed Faith's smooth forehead.

Dustin laid the child in the crib and put Bo Bo next to her.

Ainsley turned off the lamp, and they stepped out into the hallway. "Thanks," she said softly.

"Are you kidding? That was awesome. I've never gotten a baby to go to sleep before."

"You're a natural." She motioned toward the living room. "Come on before she wakes up."

Dustin grinned at her. "Glad to see you clean." He chuckled. "You want to go outside and look at the stars?"

"Yes. Just let me grab the monitor." She froze. She didn't want him to know she'd heard him talking. She glanced over at him, but he didn't seem fazed.

"Okay. Front or back?"

"Back. You can see better out there because there isn't a streetlight." She went and grabbed the monitor, and they stepped out into the backyard.

They sat in silence for a moment.

"Are you okay?" Dustin asked, glancing over at her. "You seem sad."

She wasn't sad. She was confused. For the first time, she felt on edge being so near him. She thought of Vickie and Kristy asking her why she'd never considered Dustin as more than a friend. Was it possible that she had feelings for him? After hearing the vulnerability in his voice over the baby monitor and the sincere way he talked about wanting to be a better man, she saw him in a different light. She'd been too hard on him all this time. Even when he'd tried to show her how much he'd grown as a person, she was blind to it. Until now.

◎◉

Dustin watched Ainsley from the corner of his eye.

"I'm fine." She gave him a tiny smile.

He was struck for the millionth time how much he loved spending time with her. And with Faith. The little girl had him wrapped completely around her finger. And he'd never been happier. But with that happiness came a strong sense of guilt. He knew Ainsley wasn't his to love. But he was falling for her anyway. Maybe he should just tell her. But the thought of losing her forever was too much for him to handle. Better to keep her as just a friend than take the chance on not having her in his life at all. After all, what kind of man fell in love with his best friend's widow? It sounded like one of those Lifetime movies he'd always avoided like the plague. "I'm glad you had fun on your trip. But I'm even gladder that you're back."

"Really?" She slid a little closer to him and bumped her shoulder against his. "Did you miss me?"

He met her gaze. "Actually, yes. A lot." He leaned closer to her. "Did you miss me, too?" he whispered against her ear.

She shivered. "If I say no, would you believe me?"

He tipped her chin toward him. "Not a chance." He winked. "Besides, I know you better than about anybody, so I'd be able to spot that lie a mile away."

She sighed. "You do know me pretty well. And I thought I knew you pretty well, too."

"Thought you did?" He drew his brows together. "What does that mean?"

Ainsley reached over and took his hand. "I can see how much you've grown up. How much you've changed. At first I just thought it was one thing, like your house. But as the summer has gone on, I can see that you've really got it together." She smiled. "Much more than I do. Who would've thought that nearly ten years after we first met, I'd be the one with a life in shambles and you'd be Mr. Got It Together?"

He looked down at their intertwined hands, enjoying the feeling of her soft skin against his. "Your life isn't in shambles. In fact, I happen to think you're on a pretty good track." He let go of her hand and stood up. "Come here," he said, pulling her into a standing position. He'd been after her to let go of her fears. Maybe it was time to let go of his.

"What?" Even though she looked unsure, she stood to face him.

He pulled her into a tight hug. She molded to his body perfectly.

Ainsley rested her head against his chest. "Okay, fine. I missed you."

"More than you expected to?" He couldn't hide the hopeful tone in his voice.

She pulled back, laughing. "You're relentless. Yes. More than I expected to."

"Good," he said softly. "That makes it easier to do this." He leaned down and kissed her softly on the lips. At first, she stiffened, but after a couple of seconds, he felt her relax into the kiss. It was perfect.

She pulled back, smiling. "What was that?" she asked with a shaky voice.

"Do I really need to explain it?" His mouth twisted into a grin. "Because I can walk you through it again, step by step." He hoped his attempt at humor would keep her from noticing his trembling body. Another couple seconds of kissing, and his knees would've given out.

Ainsley chuckled. "Not what I meant, and you know it." She motioned at the patio. "Can we sit down? I'm a little. . ."

"Me, too." He laughed. "I've always wondered what happened when people crossed that line."

"Line?" she asked once they were seated on the patio step.

"You know. The line between friends and more."

She nodded. "Right." She met his gaze. "I guess now we know."

He put his arm around her. "Just for the record, I didn't plan on doing that. In fact, I've been telling myself I'd never give in to those feelings." But now that he'd crossed the line, he had to admit, he'd never felt better.

She swallowed. "What changed?"

"I don't want to waste any more time, you know?"

CHAPTER 35

Every now and then, something will come along in your life that will totally take your breath away. Sometimes it's a sight. A lot of people who visit the Grand Canyon feel that way. Sometimes it's an experience. When I went skydiving, it happened to me. But sometimes it's another person. I don't think it happens very often. And when it does, you should definitely take notice.

Ainsley's lips still tingled from Dustin's kiss. But at least her heart rate was back to normal. Mostly. "I understand that concept completely."

"I figured you would."

She considered things for a moment. "So you weren't going to give in to your feelings?" She glanced over at him. "Can I ask you how long you've wanted to cross the friend line?"

He sighed. "A few weeks. The night I cooked dinner and borrowed the puppy was the first time I considered telling you, though." He grinned. "My heart was beating so loud that night I figured you could hear it."

She laughed. "If it makes you feel any better, I was clueless. I guess when you leaned over and unclipped my hair, things got a little. . .a little weird for a second. But then it was back to normal."

"Well, it wasn't back to normal for me. I really beat myself up about it, too. I know this"—he pointed to himself, then to her—"is complicated. And I felt really guilty for even thinking about you in any way except for as my friend."

Ainsley pondered his words. She'd always imagined that whenever the day came that she kissed someone new, she'd feel guilty, too. But she didn't. Kissing Dustin felt natural. The thought of spending time with him as more than a friend didn't scare her. And considering the fact that everything else in the world seemed to terrify her, that must be a good sign.

Dustin rubbed his jaw. "There's something I need to tell you. I have a feeling you might hear it through the grapevine, so I want it out in the open."

She wrinkled her nose. "What?"

"After dinner that night, I got so freaked out about things, I called Lindsey and asked her out." He cringed. "It was stupid. As soon as I did it, I knew it was a mistake."

"What happened?"

He sighed. "She called me out almost immediately. Said she could tell I didn't want to be there with her. She suspected I was only trying to stay away from you. She was pretty mad about it at first but ended up being okay." He grinned. "But I know you two have never been friends, so I wouldn't put it past her to mention it to you the next time she sees you."

Ainsley was surprised Lindsey hadn't been waiting at the house when she got back from the beach. Or left a message. Or put it on a billboard just outside of the park. "You know Lindsey has always disliked me." She met his gaze. "She actually used to hit on Brad every chance she got, at least up until we got engaged."

He hung his head. "I know."

Ainsley shot him a glance. "You do? Did Brad tell you?"

"No." His mouth formed a straight line. "I sort of put her up to it." His voice was so low, she barely made out the words.

"What?" Ainsley stood to face him. "I don't understand. Why would you do something like that?"

He held his hand out to her. "Sit back down. Let me explain."

"I'd rather stand, thanks." Her heart rate may have slowed down after the kiss, but now it was elevating at a quick pace.

Dustin rose from his spot on the patio step. He put his hands on the sides of her arms. "You have to understand. I didn't want you to get hurt. There you were, this wonderful woman who was so trusting. I'd known Brad my whole life. And he was a great guy, but he always was kind of a flirt."

She snorted. "If he was, it was only because he learned it from you."

"I'm not saying anything about him that you don't already know. He always had a girlfriend. All through high school, all through college." He shrugged. "I know it was stupid, but I wanted to test him. To make sure he was really crazy about you." He swallowed. "I figured if Lindsey came on to him and he ignored her, it must be the real deal. And that's exactly what happened."

Ainsley fumed. "You set him up to cheat on me. Were you jealous? Oh, what am I saying? Of course you were. You were jealous of him your entire life." Her hands trembled. "You wanted his parents. You wanted his accomplishments. And later, you wanted to make sure he wasn't happy."

He drew back like he'd been slapped.

She'd gone too far, but she didn't care. He deserved it.

"You have it all wrong. Yes, I admired him. I looked up to him." He shook his head. "But I would never have done anything to hurt him. Or you." He took a step toward her. "You have to believe me. It was really for my own peace of mind. I just needed to know he loved you—really loved you, that's all."

She glared at him.

"Honestly. The truth was that when you and I first met, I always thought that someday you and I would get together." He hung his head. "In my mind, you were my 'someday girl' who was perfect for me. Except that I wasn't ready for a relationship or anything, so I was happy just being your friend." He sighed. "But then you met Brad, and that all changed. I was honestly happy for you guys. I wanted you both to be happy. But I also wanted to make sure you didn't get hurt. Lindsey knew the whole story and offered to hit on him to make sure he was genuinely in love with you."

Ainsley tried to process all that he'd said. "Of course she did. Lindsey would've liked nothing more than to wrangle him away from me. And you let her try." She scowled.

"Please don't be mad. I was only trying to look out for you. And then when she mentioned putting Brad to a test, it sounded like a good idea." His eyes pleaded with her to forgive him.

"You need to go." She paced in front of him. "Now." She stopped and met his eyes. "I can't deal with this right now." She motioned between them. "With *any* of this." Not the history, not the kiss. Especially not the kiss.

Dustin nodded. "I'm sorry." He turned on his heel and walked back into the house.

Ainsley sank down onto the patio step, clutching the baby monitor like a lifeline.

CHAPTER 36

*People will disappoint you. It's a fact of life. But it's up to
you how you handle it. You can either let it ruin your day,
or you can accept it and move on. I wish I could tell you
I've always handled disappointment well, but I haven't.
I'm learning, though.*

Julie paced the length of the living room, trying to figure out
what to do. Sometimes, she wished she was still ten years old
so her parents could make decisions for her—although she was
pretty sure she knew what they'd tell her to say in this situation.

She picked up the phone and dialed Colt's number.

"Hey," he said.

She could tell he was grinning, see his smile in her mind.
"What are you up to?"

"Just got home from work. I'm about to play some basketball
with my brother." He paused. "How about you?"

"Um. . ." She paused, wondering if calling him had been a
bad idea. "I just found out that Heath is on his way here."

"Here? To the park?" Colt asked.

"Yeah. He's staying at Maswik Lodge." Saying it out loud to Colt brought it home for her. Heath would be here soon. Close enough that she could walk to his lodge.

"Hmm. So I don't get it. I thought you'd be happy to have him here for a visit."

She sighed. "We didn't exactly get along great when I was home. And I had no idea he was coming. He mentioned it once, but I never thought he'd actually do it." She sank onto the couch and propped her bare feet on the coffee table. "I wish he'd called first."

Colt didn't say anything for a moment. "Did you try and talk him out of it?" he finally asked.

"No. I mean, it's his vacation, and he can do whatever he wants to." Plus she knew if she urged him not to come to the park, it would be a huge fight. And she was so tired of arguing.

"Will you get to see him much? I mean, considering you'll have Faith and all."

Julie flipped aimlessly through an old photo album Faith had pulled from the shelf earlier. "I tried to explain things to him, but of course, he wouldn't listen."

"Do I need to come beat him up for you?" Colt asked.

She chuckled. He sounded sincere, but the thought of Colt in a fight made her laugh. Not that he wasn't strong enough, because he definitely had plenty of muscles. But he was way too nice. "Thanks for offering."

"I'm serious." His grin came through the line. "You just name the day. I'll round up a posse and run him out of town." He laughed. "He'll never know what hit him."

She shook her head. "I'll keep that in mind."

"Actually, I mean it." Colt's voice grew somber. "You call me if you need me."

Julie was touched by his sincerity. "Thanks," she said softly.

The trouble was that she didn't know if she wanted Heath there or not. On one hand, she was excited at the prospect of seeing him. Of showing him around. Of kissing him and holding his hand. But on the other hand, she knew none of that thrilled her the way it used to. And she was pretty sure Colt was the reason.

◎‿◎

"Are you okay?" Jake asked Ainsley. They sat out in the courtyard of the main visitor center. She'd seemed thrilled when he'd called and offered to bring her lunch, but now that they were together, she was awfully quiet.

"I'm fine." She managed a tiny smile. "I have a lot on my mind is all."

He nodded. That was something he certainly understood. "Do you want to talk about it?"

She drew her brows together. "It's complicated. But let's just say that a friend of mine did something a long time ago that makes me feel betrayed." She grinned. "Sorry to be so vague, but I really don't want to get into it too much."

"That's fine." He glanced over at her. "But if it's something that happened a long time ago, maybe you shouldn't hang on to it. Sometimes you just have to let stuff go." Even in his own life, he was beginning to learn the upside to letting go of the past. He'd never forget what happened to Gina and Tommy. But maybe he could learn from the experience and move on.

"You're probably right." She sighed.

"Trust me." He grinned.

She bit into the hamburger he'd brought her. "Man, this is delicious," she said.

"That's part of the beauty of having lived in a tiny camper for the duration of the summer. I know all the best food around." Jake felt like he was going stir crazy in the small space. "Because I refuse to make anything in the mini kitchenette except for peanut butter and jelly."

"So you aren't one of those cook-over-the-campfire kind of guys?"

Cooking out at a campfire sounded like fun. But not for one. "Nah. Just seems like a lot of trouble to go to for just me."

"Have you come any closer to deciding what you're going to do at the end of the summer?" Ainsley lifted the water bottle to her mouth and took a dainty sip.

"Actually, while you were on your fabulous beach vacation, I went to Phoenix for a few days." He'd toyed with the idea of calling her to see about picking her up from the airport but had ultimately decided against it. Picking someone up from the airport was very much a boyfriend thing to do. And although Jake liked her, he wasn't under any delusions. She seemed to enjoy his company but kept him at a safe distance. As someone who'd spent his lifetime keeping a wall between himself and others, he was able to recognize the signs.

"How did that go?"

"I got to see my family, which was a lot of fun. My niece and nephew have grown so much since I've been away." He grinned. "And of course, it was nice to see my mom and sister."

"How about your work? Did you talk to them?"

"I talked to Dwight on the phone. He's itching to have me come back. It sounds like his new partner is driving him crazy." He sighed. "I definitely miss home."

"That's how I felt about being away from here. I wasn't sure if I missed it just because it had been the only home I'd known with Brad, or because it was where I belonged."

"And now? What's the verdict?"

She cocked her head to the side. "I think I belong here. I love the sense of community. And the memory of Brad isn't haunting like I was afraid it would be. It's more like a happy memory." She smiled. "So if I can just get back into the groove of doing ranger programs along the rim, I'm here to stay."

Annalisa Daughety

"I'm glad one of us has things figured out." He knew which way he was leaning. Although, one glance at the beautiful woman beside him, and he knew she could sway him the other way. All she'd have to do was give him a signal that she might be interested in him, and he'd be happy to live in the tiny camper for a while longer.

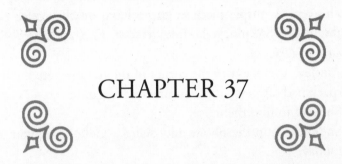

CHAPTER 37

Your dad used to say that I was the kind of person he'd want around in the midst of a crisis. I've had a couple of ranger programs where there've been emergencies. Once, a man had a heart attack, and another time, a little girl got stung by a bee and had a severe allergic reaction. Both times, I handled the situation calmly, and thankfully, both visitors were eventually okay. These days, though, I second-guess myself more than I used to. I think I've become so used to relying on other people I've forgotten how to handle things for myself.

Ainsley knew something was wrong the moment she stepped inside the house. Every day, Faith and Julie met her at the door. Faith loved to be scooped up and twirled around.

But today, they were nowhere to be found.

Ainsley rushed through the house into the backyard, hoping to see them playing in the dirt.

The yard was empty.

Her heart seemed to drop into her stomach. She pulled her cell phone from her pocket and dialed Julie's number. One ring, and it went straight to voice mail.

There must be an explanation. They'd gone with Colt or Dustin for ice cream. That must be it. She fought to keep her breath even. A purple piece of paper lying on the coffee table caught her eye. She plucked it from its spot. *Faith and I are hiking. Be back by dark.*

Ainsley's eyes went to the corner of the room where the baby backpack had sat most of the summer. It was gone.

She had to find them.

She picked up the phone and dialed. "Colt? Have you seen Julie today?"

"Not today," he said. "Why? What's up?"

Ainsley cleared her throat. "She and Faith aren't here. Julie left a note saying they'd gone hiking, so I just thought maybe you were with them." What was Julie thinking?

"Maybe they're with her boyfriend. I think he got here last night."

Ainsley's heart pounded. "Heath? Is here? Are you sure?"

"Yeah. Julie said he had some vacation time coming. I don't think she was all that happy about him visiting, to tell you the truth. But she'd never come out and say it."

Her niece and daughter were with someone who couldn't be trusted. Ainsley sank onto the couch. "Colt, any chance you'll help look for them?"

"Of course. What do you want me to do?"

"Just come to the house. I'm going to call Dustin."

He agreed and hung up.

She hadn't spoken to Dustin since the night of their argument. The night of their kiss. She wasn't sure which one she'd dwelt on more these past couple of weeks.

The phone rang twice before he picked up. "Hey there." He sounded surprised to hear from her. "I've been hoping to talk to you."

"I wish it were under different circumstances." She quickly explained the situation. "Can you come over? I want to find them before it gets dark."

"Don't worry. I'll be right there."

Who was he kidding? It might be one thing to tell her not to worry about a plane ride or a ranger program. But her baby was somewhere with a man who had a short fuse. And Julie, even though she'd matured this summer, still had a blind side when it came to Heath.

She had one more phone call to make. "Jake? I need your help."

As soon as he learned of the situation, he assured her he was on his way. "I'll take care of everything. Don't you worry."

Ainsley flipped the phone over and over in her hand. She needed to call Rachel. She hated to give her sister the news. She closed her eyes, hoping Julie and Faith would come walking through the door in the next minute. She thought about what Dustin had said to her before she flew to Florida: *"God has a plan."*

Please, Lord. Bring them back safely.

She punched the numbers on the phone. It couldn't be put off any longer.

"Hey, sis," Rachel said. "I'm so glad to hear from you."

"You're not going to be for long." Ainsley blinked back tears. "Julie and Faith were gone when I got home from work today. I found a note from Julie saying they'd gone for a hike."

"She didn't ask you first? That's weird," Rachel said.

"I called Colt to see if he knew where they went. Actually, I was kind of hoping he was with them." She sighed. "He told me that they were probably with Heath. Apparently Heath got here yesterday."

The silence on the other end was deafening. "Heath is there?" Rachel whispered. "The last I heard, he was mad at her. Remember your discussion in the car with her? When she visited during her vacation, he complained that she was acting distant."

"I know. I thought for sure it was the beginning of the end for their relationship. Honestly, I'm not sure she knew he was coming here." Ainsley pushed a lock of hair from her face. "Rach, do you think he's. . .unbalanced or anything?" She hated to voice her fears, even to her sister.

"I don't know if I'd call him that. He has a temper. But I don't think he'd do anything to purposely hurt either of them."

Ainsley's mind drifted to Jake's story about the young couple. Sometimes love made people do crazy things. And losing love might push Heath over the edge. "There's someone at the door. I have a few people coming to help me look for them."

"Keep me posted," Rachel said. "I'll be praying. And if I don't hear something from you in a couple of hours, I'm driving up."

"Just pray. I'll call you soon." Ainsley crossed to the front door and flung it open. All three guys stood on the porch. "That was good timing."

They came inside, and suddenly her living room felt very small.

"Colt, do you have any idea where they might have gone?" Dustin asked.

Colt shook his head. "No. I talked to her yesterday, and she told me he was staying at Maswik Lodge. She seemed surprised he was here." He adjusted his baseball cap. "I thought they were kinda on the outs, but I guess not." He frowned.

"Do you have a picture of Heath?" Dustin asked. "So we'll know what he looks like."

Ainsley locked eyes with Colt, his brown eyes full of worry. "I'm not sure. There's a bulletin board in her bedroom. Maybe there's a picture of him there." She rushed down the hallway. Sure enough, there was a picture on the bulletin board of Julie hugged up to a tall guy. He looked a little older than Julie, so she figured it must be Heath.

She handed the picture to Dustin.

Jake and Colt crowded around him to look.

"Okay. Now we need a plan." Jake paced in front of the couch. "Colt, how about you walk along the rim trail. I know Julie's familiar with it, so maybe she's just showing him around."

Colt nodded. "Yeah. We hiked out to Hermit's Rest one day not too long ago. She could've taken him out there for sunset or something."

Jake nodded. "And Dustin. Why don't you hike down Bright Angel? They surely wouldn't go too far with a toddler. Maybe to the three-mile rest house."

Dustin glowered at Jake. "And what are you going to do?"

"I thought maybe I'd head to the main visitor center area and then possibly go a little ways down the South Kaibab Trail." Jake stopped pacing and faced Dustin. "Does that sound okay to you?"

"Fine," he said sullenly. "What about you?" He turned to Ainsley. "Where are you going to look?"

Jake stepped in. "Why don't you stay here?" He motioned to the phone she still held in her hand. "That way, you'll be here if they call. Or if they come back."

"You've got to be kidding me!" Dustin exploded. "You expect her to just stay here and wait?" He turned to Ainsley, and his blue eyes bored into hers. "She'd never agree to that. Right?"

She felt the tears spring into her eyes. "I think it's a good idea."

"You know the canyon better than anyone." Dustin raked his fingers through his blond hair. "Even after two years of not hiking it. You still know those trails like the back of your hand."

"There's no need to put her through that, man. She'll be better off here." Jake smiled at Ainsley and patted her on the back. "Don't worry about a thing. We'll find them."

Dustin shook his head. "Unbelievable." He locked eyes with Ainsley.

She looked away and refused to respond. "Be careful. Call me when you find them."

The three of them set off, but not before Dustin cast one more incredulous look in her direction. She sank onto the couch, phone in hand. *Julie, where in the world are you?* She leaned her head back against the couch. Dustin's words haunted her. Her daughter was out there somewhere, and although Julie would do her best to keep her safe, there were no guarantees.

Her eyes landed on the old photo album Faith had dragged out the other day. It was sticking halfway out from beneath the coffee table. She picked the album up and flipped through it. She came to a shot of herself, standing next to the Bright Angel Trailhead sign. She traced her fingers over the old photograph, knowing the person on the other side of the camera had been Brad.

She stood up and on shaky legs went to the closet. She pulled out her old backpack, the one she and Brad had taken on so many hiking trips. She packed it full of water bottles, a first-aid kit, and a handful of snacks. She pulled her old hiking boots out of the closet and quickly laced them up.

Dustin was right.

He'd told her once that the fearless girl she used to be was still inside her. But it wasn't about being fearless anymore. It was about taking charge. It was her daughter. Her niece. The people she loved. It was about having faith in herself to handle the situation. And about having faith in God to see her through to the other side.

She scribbled a quick note for Julie and left it on the coffee table. *If you get here and I'm not home, please stay put and call me ASAP. ILY.*

Ainsley flung her backpack over her shoulder and raced out

the door. The fading daylight alarmed her. *Lord, keep them safe. And give me strength.*

Julie held a sippy cup of water up for Faith. "Get a drink, sweetheart."

Faith grinned from her perch on the rock ledge at the one-and-a-half-mile rest house. She took a long drink of water. "Ahhh," she said, wiping her mouth with the back of her hand. Her wide smile showed another tooth beginning to peek out on the bottom.

With one hand firmly around Faith's waist, Julie glanced worriedly at her watch. They should've started back ages ago. A mile and a half hadn't seemed too far on their way down, but she knew going up it would be difficult. She pulled her cell phone from her pocket. Still no service. Ainsley was going to kill her.

"What was I thinking?" she asked Faith. "I should've just told him no and let him come on the hike alone."

When Heath had shown up at Ainsley's earlier in the day, things had gone well, at least for a little while. She'd made lunch for them, and he'd been so cute, playing with Faith.

He'd kissed and hugged her, and things seemed almost normal between them. Julie had even gotten up the courage to present him with one of the drawings she'd done of the canyon. She'd signed it at the bottom and everything. But instead of treating it like a prized possession, Heath had folded it into a little square and put it in his pocket. The gesture made Julie's heart sink. It was like he didn't even care how much trouble she'd gone to.

And then while Faith napped, they'd had a huge argument. "I took vacation time and drove all the way up here. I'm paying for a room you won't even visit me in. The least you can do is go with me on a hike."

Julie had looked at enough pictures of the Bright Angel Trail to know that she could handle the hike. She'd been exercising, and as luck would have it, the week was unusually cool. It was still hot outside, but not the miserable heat they'd seen in early July. "I can't keep Faith out for too long," she'd said.

Heath acted like he was on board with that plan, but once they actually got going, he had no concern for getting back before Ainsley got home from work. At least she'd thought to leave a note, otherwise her aunt would think they'd been kidnapped.

"Aren't you two done yet?" Heath asked, his irritation obvious. "Let's go. I want to see what's around the next bend." He put an arm around Julie's waist.

She jerked away from him. "We need to hike out now." The memory of him folding up her artwork like it was trash still made her cringe. And there was no way she'd be visiting him in the lodge later tonight, like he'd asked her to do. He only cared about one thing—himself.

"Can't you chill out? I'm on vacation." He nodded toward Faith. "Is it my fault that you had to bring the munchkin?"

Julie glared at him. "No. But it's your fault that we're this far down into the canyon. I asked you to turn around ages ago." Julie lifted Faith and bounced the little girl on her hip.

Faith laughed. "Again."

Julie continued bouncing and glared at Heath. "I'm responsible for her. And it's time to get her back home so she can eat dinner and go to bed. Not to mention the fact that my phone doesn't have a signal so I can't call my aunt and tell her where we are."

"You don't have to be a jerk about it." He frowned. "You've been acting distant all day. I came to this stupid place to see you, and I don't even feel like you're happy to see me."

Julie shook her head. For the first time, she saw Heath clearly. "You know what? I don't need to listen to this." She eyed the baby backpack. Heath had worn it on the way down. Was she strong enough to carry Faith up the steep trail to the top?

"Maybe I don't need to listen to you, either." He scowled.

"I'm done playing around. You're either in this or you aren't." He raised one eyebrow. "Make your choice."

She frowned. Surely he wouldn't just leave her a mile and a half down in the Grand Canyon with a toddler. Would he? She swallowed. "So what. . .I'm supposed to either go on with you farther into the canyon or we're through?"

He gave her a slow grin. Once not too long ago, that lazy smile would've melted her heart. But today, it only repulsed her. She thought about the things people had said to her about finding a guy who would treat her with respect and kindness. Heath was neither of those things. She'd tried for long enough to make him into something he wasn't. "That pretty much sums it up."

She nodded. "Faith and I are going home. I don't care what you do."

Rage filled his face, twisting his features. "Are you kidding me?" He shook his head in disgust. "I've wasted so much time on you." He sneered at her. "Have a nice life."

"You, too," she said softly, watching him stomp off. And she meant it. She hoped that someday he became the person she'd caught glimpses of every now and then. But regardless, he wouldn't be her problem any longer.

"Faith, are you ready to go home?" She bounced the little girl on her hip. "You've been a good girl today." She stepped down on one of the rocky steps that led up to the rest house, and her foot slid on a loose rock. She struggled to keep upright as her ankle gave way and twisted. Pain seared through her right leg. "Ow." She lifted her leg, nearly losing her balance again. Julie sank onto the step, pulling Faith into her lap. "Julie just needs to let her foot rest for a minute, okay?" After a moment, she stood Faith on the step. "Hold my hand," she directed.

Faith clung to her hand, watching with interest.

Julie slowly stood with her weight shifted to her left leg. She gingerly shifted it to the right. "Ow." Tears filled her eyes. She forced herself to step up one more step, still holding Faith's hand. Okay. She could do this. "Come here, Faith." She helped the little girl step up until they were on the same step. She bent down and lifted Faith into her arms. The extra weight was too much for her ankle to bear. "I can't hold you and walk." She sighed. "Let's go back underneath the rest house." The little stone rest house would provide shelter from sun and rain, but that was about it. At least it would give her a place to sit with Faith until help came along. Colt had mentioned that rangers patrolled the trails regularly, so surely someone would come along soon.

"Faith, let's sit down and lean against the wall." She tugged on the little girl's hand.

They sat down next to the baby backpack. "Do you want a snack?"

"Yesh." Faith nodded.

Julie fished around in the pouch for the ziplock bag of Goldfish crackers. They were Faith's favorite. "Here are some Goldfish." She handed a small handful of crackers to Faith. While the child was occupied by eating, Julie pulled her cell phone out, hoping to see at least half a bar of service. No such luck. "I think we're stuck here for a little bit, sweet girl."

Faith grinned, showing the remnants of an orange goldfish.

Please, Lord. Get us out of this mess.

Julie sighed and clutched Faith's hand. Lesson learned. She never should've come in the first place. She'd known better but had wanted to keep Heath happy. But that came at the expense of Faith's safety and Ainsley's worry. She glanced at her watch. Her aunt must be frantic. Tears began to leak down Julie's face, but she wiped them away before Faith could see them. She knew the smart little girl would be able to tell if she was upset.

"Do you want me to tell you the story of Super Faith?" Julie asked. She'd been making up stories all summer, and the ones that got the best response always starred a girl named Faith.

She nodded.

Julie grinned through her tears. She reached into the backpack and pulled out Bo Bo.

Faith clutched the stuffed dog and happily popped another cracker in her mouth.

At least one of them was content. "Once upon a time, there was a little girl named Faith who went on a hiking trip," Julie began, hoping against hope that the story would have a happy ending.

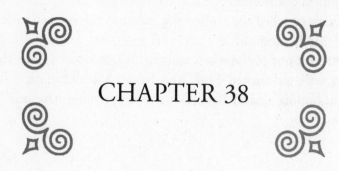

CHAPTER 38

Sometimes things happen that you can't control. Good things. Bad things. It doesn't matter. And if you turn out anything like me, you aren't going to deal with that very well. But I'm here to tell you: God has plans for you that are better than anything you could ever dream up on your own. So it's okay when life doesn't go exactly as you have planned. I read somewhere that the best way to make God laugh is to tell Him your plans. And you know what? I think that might be true.

Ainsley caught up with Dustin just before the Bright Angel Trailhead.

He stood, talking to a couple of hikers who'd just ascended the trail.

Even though she knew it was rude, she interrupted. There was no time for niceties. "I'm hiking down so you don't have to." She adjusted her pack. "If you want to go back to the house and wait, that would be good."

He reached out and caught her arm. "Thanks, you've been very helpful," he said to the hikers.

"Let go. There's not much daylight left." She pulled away from his grasp.

"That couple thinks they saw them hiking down. They described the red pack with Faith in it, and the girl they saw matched Julie's description."

"Was Heath with them?"

He nodded. "Sounds like it. They described a tall man in his early twenties. He was the one carrying Faith."

Ainsley felt as if her heart had been pierced. She nodded. "Okay. I'm hiking down."

He reached out and stroked her face with the back of his hand. "I'm sorry. About everything."

She pulled back. "Not now. Right now, I just want to focus on getting Faith and Julie out safely."

"I'm glad you decided to search. Are you okay?"

She gave him a wry smile. "Not the least bit shaky. Every other day, each step I took near the canyon made me cringe. But now, knowing Faith is down there. . .I think I could bungee jump off the side if I thought it would get me to her quicker."

They started down the trail. "You don't have to come."

He sighed. "I want to in case Heath gives you any trouble."

"Thanks."

They continued down the trail, pausing every now and then to let other hikers pass. Each time they had to stop, Ainsley could practically feel daylight ticking away. But trail etiquette said hikers going down should yield to hikers coming up out of the canyon, mainly because those hiking uphill were exerting more energy than those walking down.

"Wow." Ainsley glanced around as they passed through the first tunnel. It was manmade but spectacular nonetheless. She was pretty sure it had been made using dynamite back when they were first creating the trail.

"You'd forgotten how beautiful, huh?" Dustin said from behind her.

She nodded. "Not only that, but I'd forgotten how much I love this place."

"So no fear?"

She glanced back at him. "There's fear. But I'm not paralyzed by it." She waved her hand toward the edge of the path. It dropped off into nothingness. "I'm doing this with purpose, though. You know?"

"You'd do anything to keep them safe. I understand."

She nodded. "Plus, I thought a lot about what you said when I was at the airport. You know, about where my faith had gone. I thought a lot about that at the beach. And then today, after you guys left, it hit me again." She bit her lip. "I can either spend the rest of my life worrying about every little thing and seeing danger around every corner, or I can put my trust in God. I don't want to use Brad's death as an excuse for me not to live. And sometimes, life is scary. But when I look at it with the perspective of I'm going to go through the scary times leaning on the Lord, I think I can do it."

" 'I can do everything through Christ, who gives me strength.' " Dustin grinned. "That was the topic of the devotional I led last week. I admit I was thinking of you when I put it together."

She stepped to the side of the trail closest to the canyon wall and stopped to catch her breath. "I wish I could've heard it." She took a long swig of water.

He grinned. "Me, too."

They stood in silence for a moment.

"Okay. Let's keep going." She motioned toward the trail. "I just needed to rest for a second."

Dustin nodded. "Lead the way."

Forty-five minutes later, Ainsley spotted the top of the one-and-a-half-mile rest house. Every bend they'd come around, she'd been certain Faith and Julie would be there. And each time, she'd been disappointed. So she wasn't sure she should even let herself hope that maybe they'd be there.

"You want me to go check it out?" Dustin asked.

She nodded. "I'll check the bathroom. You check the rest house."

"Just holler if you see them." He caught her arm. "We're going to find them. Those hikers at the top were pretty certain about the descriptions. And if we make it all the way to the three-mile rest house before we find them, there'll probably be a ranger there who can help us. You know that." He sighed. "There's at least a phone there." He motioned at his backpack. "And I have my park radio. If we don't find them soon, I'm going to radio Colt's dad. He can touch base with Colt on the rim and swing by your house if we need him to."

Ainsley was quiet for a minute. "If they aren't here, I want you to radio him for help. It's almost dark." She fought against the waves of fear rising to the surface. This was no time to panic. She headed up the rough stairs that led to the rustic bathroom. Just as she got to the top, she heard a loud whistle.

Ainsley turned on her heel and took the steps two at a time. She slid twice but caught herself before she fell. By the time she made it to the stone shelter, she had to gasp for breath. "Dustin? What is it?" she called.

She saw them before they saw her. Relief poured over her like rain. Faith, sound asleep in Julie's arms, looked like an angel. Dustin knelt beside them, inspecting Julie's ankle.

"Thank goodness." Ainsley couldn't get to them soon enough. She hustled up the step and skidded to a stop. She dropped her backpack and knelt beside them.

"I hurt my ankle," Julie said, her face streaked with tears. "I think I can walk on it, but I couldn't walk and carry Faith, too."

Ainsley reached down and took Faith from Julie's arms. Her daughter barely stirred. "Sweet baby." Ainsley stood and buried her face in Faith, struggling to keep her emotions in check. Using her foot, she slid her backpack toward Dustin. "There's a first-aid kit in there with an ankle wrap."

"Thanks." He watched her for a long moment. "There isn't too much swelling. I think it's just a very minor sprain."

"Ouch," Julie groaned. "It really hurts."

"You're lucky that's the only thing that happened," Ainsley exploded. "What were you thinking, hiking this trail? And with Faith?" Ainsley shook her head. "Do you know how many people are looking for you? How worried everyone is?" Her voice got louder with each sentence. "There are a million things that could've gone wrong. This is a dangerous place for people who aren't prepared. Clearly you aren't as responsible as I gave you credit for."

Tears streamed down Julie's face. "I'm so sorry."

"Sometimes sorry isn't enough. Not when your safety is at stake. And the safety of my child."

Dustin rose and took Ainsley by the elbow. "Come here." He led her to the corner of the rest house. "Cut her some slack, okay?" His voice was soft. "She's been through a lot today, too. And they're both okay."

Ainsley jerked her chin away from him.

"I know you're upset. And I know you're emotional. But you don't want to say things you'll regret later. I'm not excusing her. It was a dumb thing to do." He met her gaze. "But we've all done dumb stuff, especially when we were seventeen."

She sighed. He was right. She could see remorse all over Julie's face. "Okay, fine." Maybe she should at least listen to Julie's side of the story. She owed her niece that much.

Dustin quickly wrapped Julie's ankle. "Is it too tight?"

She shook her head. "No," she said, wiping her nose. "It feels better." She put on her hiking boot and carefully stood.

"Why don't you walk on it a little and see if you think it will hold up to hike out?" Ainsley suggested.

Julie nodded and began to walk the length of the rest house.

"Here, can you take her for a second?" Ainsley asked Dustin.

He pulled Faith from her arms. The little girl stirred but didn't wake.

Ainsley made her way over to Julie. "I'm so glad you're okay." She pulled her niece into her arms.

Julie collapsed against her, sobbing. "I really didn't mean to come this far." She wiped her eyes. "Heath had Faith in the baby backpack, and he started off down the trail." Her lower lip trembled. "I tried to get him to stop, but he wouldn't. Then we had a huge fight because I wanted to turn around and hike out."

"Where is he now?"

Julie motioned toward the trail. "He went on. He wanted to go a little bit farther down into the canyon." She let out a tiny sob. "Everyone was right about him. And I was so stupid. I never want to see him again."

"Good riddance, huh?" She smoothed Julie's hair.

Her niece gave her a weak smile. "Yeah."

"Okay. How about we get out of here?" she asked.

Dustin nodded. "That sounds good." He looked down at Faith. "Although someone sure is stirring a lot. I think she's about to wake up."

Faith's eyes fluttered. "Ma–ma," she said when she spotted Ainsley.

Ainsley held out her arms, and the little girl jumped into them. "Hi, sweet baby. Are you ready to go home?"

Faith grinned and put her hands on either side of Ainsley's face. "Go."

Dustin picked up the baby backpack and slung one strap over his shoulder.

"No. Wait." Ainsley caught the strap with her hand. "I'm going to carry her." She motioned at Julie. "You can help Julie if she needs it."

He narrowed his eyes. "Are you sure? Hiking out is going to be hard enough as it is."

She raised an eyebrow. "I'm going to carry my daughter." She couldn't put into words how important it was for her to complete the task. Somehow, she knew if she could successfully hike out with Faith on her back, she would be able to face anything.

Dustin held his hands up in surrender. "Okay."

They got Faith situated and started the long climb to the top.

Ainsley barely felt the burning in her muscles. For the first time in a long time, she felt like she could handle things again. *Thank You, Lord, for keeping them safe. And for showing me that I can face scary situations and come out of them okay.*

"I guess you can check hiking down into the canyon off your list," Dustin said to Julie.

She smiled. "I never imagined it would be quite like this. Faith and I sang songs and told stories and ate a lot of Goldfish while we waited on you guys to find us."

"What were you going to do if we never came?" Ainsley asked.

"I knew a ranger would've come along eventually. Colt told me about the special rangers whose whole job is just to hike the trails to see if people need help." She sighed. "I knew we were better off to just stay put. We had a place to sit, and Faith could walk around under the shelter."

Julie had handled the situation the best way she possibly could. "You did a great job of staying calm. I know it must've been scary."

"Yeah. I was mainly worried about you. I knew how upset you'd be. Faith was really good, though. I'd brought snacks and

284

water and stuff, so we were okay."

"I'm glad."

They hiked in silence for a minute. The last bits of light illuminated the path, but in a few minutes, it would be dark. "Check your phone. As soon as you have service, we need to call everyone and let them know you guys are okay." Ainsley sidestepped a large rock.

"Easy," Dustin said from behind her. "Let's just take our time hiking out. I know it will be dark soon, but there's a full moon tonight. We'll be able to see just fine."

In every aspect of the day's events, Ainsley could see God's fingerprints: an unusually cool day, Julie thinking to take snacks and drinks, and now a full moon to guide them out.

CHAPTER 39

I don't think I've ever been more scared than when I found out you were in the canyon with Julie and Heath. I don't blame Julie. After I heard her story, I think she never intended to hike that far. Do I wish she'd called me? Of course. But I also understand that she felt like she could handle the situation. And I have to admit she had things under control when we got to you. I was proud of her and of you, too. She kept her cool, and apparently you were a little trouper.

J ulie couldn't remember a hot shower ever feeling better. Her entire body ached, but her ankle had finally stopped swelling.

She hobbled into her bedroom and threw on a pair of running shorts and an old Diamondbacks shirt. Twisting her hair up into a loose bun, she took a deep breath. She had to face the music.

Ainsley sat in the kitchen, sipping a cup of hot tea. She looked up as Julie entered the room. "Feel better?"

Julie sank into the chair next to her aunt. "Definitely."

"Prop your ankle up. That will help with the swelling." Ainsley stood. "And you need to keep ice on it." She pulled a bag of frozen peas out of the freezer and wrapped them in a dish towel. "Here." She gently placed the bag on Julie's ankle.

"Thanks." She grimaced at the icy sting.

Ainsley sat down and resumed sipping her tea.

"I'm really sorry." Julie chewed on the inside of her lip. "I never should've taken Faith anywhere without asking you."

Ainsley sighed. "You know, it isn't even that you took her somewhere. You could've taken her for ice cream or to see Max or whatever." She reached over and patted Julie on the arm. "You taking her somewhere isn't the issue. I trust her with you each day and expect you to make good decisions." She tucked a loose strand of red hair behind her ear. "Part of the problem is that you didn't tell me Heath was here."

"I'm sorry." Julie hung her head. She'd been worried about her parents finding out and jumping to the conclusion that she'd invited him. "I honestly didn't know he was coming until he was already on his way."

"That's what Colt said." Ainsley smiled at her niece. "By the way, Colt is sitting out on the front porch, waiting on you to get through with your shower. I tried to get him to come inside, but he said he'd rather sit out there."

Colt was here? He must think the worst of her. Probably wanted to tell her that he couldn't be friends with someone as irresponsible as her. "Oh." Julie picked at some loose skin around her fingernail.

"You realize that if you'd have told me Heath was visiting here I would've made other arrangements for Faith today." Ainsley sighed.

"Um. I was kind of glad she was with me," Julie admitted. "I just wish we hadn't been gone for so long. I mean I honestly didn't plan on going into the canyon at all with her. We were just going to walk along the rim trail." Her eyes filled with tears. "But Heath had the baby backpack on, and he started down the Bright Angel Trail. He said we'd just go down a few steps, just so he could see what it was like." A single tear fell down her freshly scrubbed face. "Before I knew it, we'd gone too far."

"Julie, I'm not going to fuss at you." Ainsley looked closely at her. "I see the look on your face. It's obvious how bad you feel. Let's just be thankful that everything turned out okay—and hope you learned a lesson from it." She waved her arm in the direction of the front porch. "Now go see Colt. He was really worried."

"Thanks." Julie stood, clutching her ice pack. She hobbled to the front door, the fluttery feeling in her stomach growing with each step.

"Hey there."

Colt looked up from his perch on the top step. He stood as she closed the door behind her. "You okay?" he asked.

She lifted the ice pack. "Ainsley thinks I should keep my ankle iced. And I'm a little tired from all the excitement." Tired didn't seem to touch how she felt. More like emotionally exhausted, but she didn't want him to think she was a drama queen. She sat down on the top step and straightened her leg out in front of her.

Colt sat down next to her, close enough that their shoulders touched. He looked tired, too.

"Ainsley told me you hiked the rim trail looking for us." She glanced over at him. "Thanks. I know you'd worked all day. That was a long way to hike for nothing."

He shook his head. "It wasn't for nothing. I hoped I'd find you, actually." He grinned. "I kind of wanted to see this boyfriend of yours."

She bit her lip. "He isn't my boyfriend anymore."

"Sorry."

Julie shook her head. "Don't be. I've never felt so stupid." Tears pooled in her eyes, and she angrily wiped at them. "And I'm *not* crying over him. I'm just upset over my stupidity." She glanced over at Colt. "I should've listened to everyone around me. All those people. My parents, my friends. You." She gnawed on her lip. "Why did I think I knew better?"

Colt bumped his shoulder against hers. "Don't be so hard on yourself. You wanted to believe the best in him. Sure, he turned out not to deserve it. But it isn't an awful trait to have." He smiled at her. "You just need to be more selective next time with who you believe in."

She nodded. "No doubt." She was quiet for a moment. At the beginning of the summer, she'd been pretty sure Colt was interested in her. She couldn't help but wonder if those feelings were still there. "I have to tell you something." She turned toward him. "Things weren't going well for me and Heath for pretty much the whole summer. I told you that, when I was home for vacation, he accused me of being distant."

"Yeah." Colt cocked his head. "Why was that?"

"I think you know why. It was because of you." She met his gaze but quickly looked away. "You showed me how it felt to be treated with respect."

He nodded slightly. "You deserve it."

Julie watched him from the corner of her eye. "So I was kinda afraid you might be here to tell me that you don't want to be friends with me anymore."

Colt narrowed his eyes. "Of course I do. Just because you make dumb decisions when it comes to guys doesn't mean I'm gonna desert you." He grinned. "Besides, someone needs to keep you out of trouble when we get to college."

"I'm glad. About the friends part, I mean. Not that you're going to be monitoring me while we're at school." She grinned. "Although, we'll probably get there, and you'll find a girlfriend immediately and ditch me." She held her breath, hoping he'd tell her there wasn't a chance of that happening.

Colt raised an eyebrow. "And how would you like it if I found a girlfriend?"

She bit her bottom lip. "I don't think I'd like it," she said softly. "At all."

"To tell you the truth, I was kinda hoping maybe you and I could go out sometime. On a real date." He looked at her intently. "Maybe once we're at school?"

Her mouth turned upward in a smile. "You'll never know until you ask." She hoped she didn't sound too eager.

He leaned over and pulled her into a side hug. "Maybe I will." He motioned toward the house. "You should get inside and get that ankle propped up." He stood and held out his hand.

She placed her hand in his and let him pull her upright. "Good night."

"Night."

She watched him walk away. She'd been through nearly every emotion possible today. Sadness when Heath had callously folded up her artwork. Anger when he'd insisted on hiking down the Bright Angel Trail even though she didn't want to. Remorse when she'd thought of how scared her aunt would be to find them missing. Fear when she'd realized she and Faith were alone in the canyon. Relief when Ainsley and Dustin had found them. And now. . .happiness. Happiness at the thought of a future with Colt.

Jake tapped lightly on Ainsley's door. He hoped she wasn't getting ready for bed or anything. It wasn't that late, but it had been such a long day. Even so, he wanted to talk to her.

The porch light came on, and she slowly opened the door. "Come in," she said, holding the door open for him.

He stepped inside. Faith and Julie were nowhere to be seen.

As if she had read his mind, Ainsley motioned toward the

hallway, where the bedrooms were. "The girls are in bed. Faith was out like a light as soon as she ate." She took a seat on the couch. "And Julie's exhausted. Her ankle is still a little swollen, but I think it's going to be fine."

He sat down next to her. "I'm glad they're both okay. I was worried."

She smiled. "I can't thank you enough for your help. It meant a lot."

Jake nodded. "It was my pleasure. I wish I could've done more." The whole time he was out looking for Julie and Faith, all he could think of was how it would feel to find them and be able to deliver the news to Ainsley. But he was thankful everything had worked out. "I think I need to apologize to you."

Her hazel eyes grew wide. "Apologize? What for?"

He sighed. "I haven't given you enough credit this summer. Ever since I found you that day, crying on the park bench, I've been quick to try and fix things for you."

She shook her head. "It's fine. I kind of liked knowing you wanted to rescue me."

"That's just it. You don't need to be rescued. I started to realize it when you got on the plane even though you sounded so terrified. You're much stronger than you give yourself credit for being." He sighed. "And today, I had no business trying to keep you from looking for your daughter."

"It's fine." She reached over and gave his hand a squeeze. "Really."

"I think it was my own stuff that made me behave that way. I felt so helpless in the situation in Phoenix, you know? I guess I got here and felt like even though I couldn't save Gina, maybe I could be useful to you." He shrugged.

"That's understandable. But I'm learning that I'm stronger than I realized. I think I have a tendency to second-guess myself. Maybe I've always been that way, I don't know. But I got so used to depending on Brad, and then I stayed at my parents' house for such a long time, and they handled everything." Her lips turned upward in a smile. "I think being the one in charge of everything was just an adjustment. I'm sure you picked up on that fear. You were only trying to help."

He nodded. "I'm glad you see it that way." She had every right to think he was some kind of Neanderthal the way he'd treated her. He reached over and touched her hair. She wore it long and loose. "I've never seen your hair down before. You look like a Botticelli painting."

She blushed. "Thanks."

He cleared his throat. "Anyway, I wanted to stop by and tell you that I'm leaving."

Ainsley's hazel eyes widened. "Leaving? Does this mean you're. . . ?"

He nodded. "Going back to Phoenix. Back to the police force."

"I sort of thought you were leaning that way."

"Tonight gave me the final push I needed to make the decision. For the first time in a long time, I felt like I had a purpose." He gave her a slow grin. "Leading hikes is fun, but it's more of a hobby than something I can really sink my teeth into."

"I'm sorry you're leaving. But glad you're happy with your decision."

He met her gaze. "I want you to know that if I thought it would matter if I stayed here and fought for you, I would."

She wrinkled her forehead. "What do you mean?"

"I mean that if I thought you'd choose me, I'd consider staying." He gave her a half smile. "But I see you with Dustin. I know you two are just friends. But you light up around him." He shook his head. "I can't compete with that."

Ainsley widened her eyes but didn't say anything.

Jake reached over and took her hand. "But at least you've

shown me that there are women out there worth fighting for." He grinned. "My track record hasn't been that great, so I guess these past few years I've thrown myself into my work. Meeting you and spending time with you has made me realize that I want to share my life with someone." He squeezed her hand. "So thanks for that."

She raked her fingers through her hair. "I wish you the best." She smiled.

"And you've always got a friend in Phoenix. If you find yourself there in the future, please call." He meant it. He felt no ill will toward her. Sure, it would've been nice if they'd had a real spark—because she was certainly the kind of woman he could see himself with. But now that he'd made his decision, he couldn't wait to return to Phoenix.

"Will do. And the same goes for you. Next time you come for a visit, I hope you'll let me know."

He nodded. "I hope to make hiking and camping more of a regular activity. I'm determined not to fall into my same old habits when I return to work." He glanced at her. "So you think you're staying here?"

She nodded. "After today, I know I can do whatever ranger program I'm assigned. No matter what the location." She grinned. "So I'm here for the long haul."

CHAPTER 40

How do you know when you're ready to move on? I asked Dr. Sinclair that question during one of my first visits and didn't get a straight answer. Since then, I think I've figured it out. When something bad happens to you, you go through a time where it's too painful to even consider how happiness feels. People always say time heals all wounds, and at this point, I can attest to that. It isn't that I miss your dad any less. It's just that I can't allow missing him to continue to consume my life. I think figuring that out means it's time to move on.

Dustin waited on Ainsley's porch for what seemed like forever. The porch light was on. The living room light was on. So he was certain she must still be up. He lifted his hand to knock again, but the door opened before he made contact.

Jake McGuire stood on the other side of the door. "Hey, man. Come on in." He motioned toward the hallway. "She just went to check on Julie's ankle."

Dustin hesitated in the doorway. Coming over had been a big

mistake. "Listen, I was just gonna let her know that Heath made it back safely." He jerked his head in the direction of the park lodges. "He's at the lodge and plans to leave in the morning." He couldn't keep the slow grin from his face. "I had a little chat with him." Dustin had been waiting at Maswik Lodge for Heath when he returned from his hike.

"I guess that went over well, huh?" Jake stepped back from the door so Dustin could come inside.

Dustin stayed rooted to the spot in the doorway. "He's a punk kid. You know the type." He shook his head. "I think Julie learned her lesson, though."

Jake nodded. "Some lessons are tougher than others."

"That they are." He took a step back. "I'm going to get out of your hair. Give her the message though, okay?"

"What message?" Ainsley asked, coming into the living room. Her hair, long and loose, caught his attention. Even exhausted and in dirty hiking clothes, she was beautiful.

Dustin quickly explained why he'd stopped by the house. "But I'll be going now. I didn't mean to interrupt anything."

"No, wait," Jake piped up. "I was just leaving. You stay." He turned to Ainsley. "I'll be around for the next few days. I'll stop by the visitor center before I leave."

She reached up and hugged him.

Watching the embrace, Dustin felt as if someone had punched him in the stomach. He'd been prepared for her to fall for someone else. But that didn't mean he had to like it.

Jake pulled away from Ainsley, grinning. He nodded at Dustin as he passed by. "Good night," he said, pulling the door shut behind him.

Dustin turned to face Ainsley. "Sorry. I didn't mean to run him off."

"You didn't. He was already about to leave when Julie asked me for more ice." She nodded toward Julie's room. "He was just waiting to tell me good-bye." She leveled her gaze at Dustin. "He's leaving the park. For good."

Dustin widened his eyes in surprise. "Oh?"

She nodded. "Yeah. He's returning to the police force. He was already leaning toward going back, but I think the adrenaline of tonight made him realize how much he missed it." She motioned toward the couch. "You want to have a seat?"

He grinned. "Actually, how about if we go out on the patio? It's a nice night out. Full moon and everything."

She nodded. "Let me grab the monitor, and I'll meet you out there."

The full moon illuminated the backyard. Faith's little plastic slide practically glowed in the moonlight. Dustin sat down on the top step, looking up at the sky. The memory of the last time he and Ainsley were in this spot flashed through his mind. The warmth of her lips. The softness of her skin. And the blaze of anger that erased it all.

"Penny for your thoughts." She came and sat down next to him.

He shook his head. "I'm not sure they're even worth that."

She chuckled. "I think they're worth a lot more than that." She paused. "Maybe double."

Dustin smirked. "Funny."

"Thanks for your help tonight. I couldn't have done it without you."

"Sure you could've."

They sat in silence for a moment.

Dustin turned toward her. "Listen. I want to apologize. I'm sorry I upset you the other night." He'd gone over and over it in his mind. On the one hand, he wished he'd never told her about his part in Lindsey coming on to Brad. But on the other, he was glad it was out in the open. He didn't want to have any secrets from her.

"I probably overreacted about it. That was so far in the past. Before Brad and I were even engaged." She sighed. "I think the whole night was just an overwhelming night for me. You know?" She looked at him with wide eyes.

He nodded. "You might not believe this, but it was an overwhelming night for me, too."

"How so?"

He grinned. "Kissing you for the first time. You have no idea how much courage it took for me to do that."

She chuckled. "You seemed like an old pro at it. I was the one who could barely stand afterward. I was so nervous I think my knees were knocking together."

"I thought I heard something, but I didn't want to say anything."

Ainsley cut her eyes at him.

He burst out laughing. "I'm totally kidding, kid." He pulled her into his arms.

She rested her head against his chest and sighed.

"So are we going to give this a shot?" he asked, smoothing her hair.

She was silent.

Uh-oh. He thought it had been going well. She'd forgiven him. The vibe was still between them. He pulled her away from him so he could see her face. "Hey," he said softly. "What's going on in that head of yours?"

She sighed. "I hate to do this."

He cringed. "That doesn't sound good." But he'd known this might happen. When he'd crossed the line and kissed her, he'd done it knowing she might not return his feelings.

"I need you to give me some time." Her hazel eyes were pleading. "Just a little time to get things sorted out." She pointed at her head. "In here." She placed her hand over her heart. "And in here."

Some time. Okay. That didn't sound so bad. "Of course. We don't even have to discuss it again until you're ready. You can have all the time you need."

She bit her lip. "Actually, I kind of think I need some time where I don't see you. Is that okay? I don't want to hurt you or anything." She took a breath. "But I think it would be best."

Talk about getting punched in the stomach. Dustin tried to shake it off. "If that's what you need, that's fine." He pulled her toward him and kissed her on the forehead. "You know where I am." He jerked his head toward the front of the house. "I'm out. You go get some sleep, okay?"

She nodded. "We'll talk soon."

Her words echoed in his head as he walked home. Would they talk soon? Only time would tell. In the meantime, all he could do was wait.

⊙🌀

Julie put the last of her things in her suitcase.

"Need some help?" Ainsley asked, walking into the room.

Julie shook her head. "No. I've got it." She looked at her aunt. "Are you sure you don't mind me leaving early? I've still got a few weeks before college starts." Julie had planned to return to the Grand Canyon after freshman orientation weekend, but Ainsley had suggested she take the last few weeks before college and spend them with her parents.

"I'm sure. And I know your mom and dad are thrilled." She smiled. "Besides, I know it will be nice for you to be in your own bedroom for a little while." She picked up a stray stuffed animal from the floor and held it up. "Without any of Faith's toys invading your space."

Julie grinned. "I don't mind. I'm going to miss her so much. And you."

"We're going to miss you, too. I'm just hoping Faith starts

speaking in complete sentences soon so I'll have someone to talk to."

"She's almost there. I think she said a three-word sentence yesterday."

Ainsley smiled. "Thanks largely to you. I know you've been reading to her a lot. You're going to make a wonderful teacher." She sat down on the bed. "I'm sorry you never got the chance to shadow Colt's mom."

A blush crept up Julie's face. "Actually, I think I'll come shadow her a day or two during fall break." She met her aunt's inquisitive gaze. "So I might need to stay with you a couple of nights."

"Am I to gather that there might be something going on between you and Colt?" Ainsley raised her eyebrows.

"We're just friends." Julie shrugged. "But with potential." It was pretty cool, actually. She and Colt had gotten to know one another slowly. He'd turned into one of her best friends. And now that there was the possibility they might turn into more someday, it made her nearly giddy with happiness.

Ainsley chuckled. "He's a great guy. I think there could be lots of potential there. But I think it's smart for you to take it slowly, especially after dealing with Heath."

"Yeah. We kinda talked about it. I mean, we're going to be at the same school and all, so we'll get to spend a lot of time together. There's no reason to jump into anything." She grinned. And it's nice knowing that he shares my beliefs about stuff. You know?"

"I think it's wonderful."

"Ma–ma," Faith called from down the hallway.

"Sounds like someone is up from her nap." Ainsley stood. "What time are you leaving?"

"He's supposed to call when he's on the way." She and Colt were riding together to Flagstaff. Her parents would come pick her up on Sunday after orientation.

"Okay. You probably won't have time for dinner, but I'll go put some snacks together for you to have in the car."

Julie sank onto the bare mattress and looked around the room. It looked more like an office now than a bedroom. She'd taken her bulletin board down with all the pictures of her and her friends. The cards her mom and Claire had sent her over the summer were in her suitcase. And all the drawings she'd done over the summer had been carefully packed away.

It was funny to think about how she'd fought against coming to the Grand Canyon for the summer. It had ended up being a wonderful experience. She'd gotten closer to her aunt and to Faith. She'd enjoyed getting to know Dustin. And there was no way she'd trade meeting Colt for anything. All in all, it had been the summer of a lifetime.

She hauled her suitcase into the living room and set it beside the door. "Hey, little miss," she said to Faith. "Whatcha doin'?"

Faith grinned and banged her hands on the coffee table.

Ainsley walked down the hallway to grab the rest of her things. She slung her old duffel bag over her shoulder and picked up her backpack from the bed. Colt should be here any minute. She put the bags with her suitcase and sat down on the couch.

"Here are some snacks," Ainsley said. "Nothing fancy. Just peanut butter crackers and some baby carrots."

"One last healthy snack before we go, huh?" Julie laughed. She took the ziplock bags from her aunt. "Seriously, thanks."

"Is he on his way?"

Julie stood. "I'll call him to see." She picked her purse up from the coffee table and dug through for her phone. "That's weird."

"What?" Ainsley asked.

"My phone is gone. I put it in my purse while I was packing so it wouldn't accidentally get put inside another bag."

"Let me call it, and we'll see if we hear it." Ainsley punched a number on her phone.

They leaned forward to listen.

The faintest ringing sounded down the hallway.

Ainsley and Julie exchanged a glance.

"Follow that ring." Julie grinned.

As they got closer to Faith's room, the ringing grew louder. They stopped in the doorway of the room.

The only visible part of Faith was her behind. She was partially inside the bottom cabinet that held her toys and books.

"What in the world?" Julie asked.

Ainsley went to Faith and pulled her out of the cabinet. "Looks like I missed one when I baby proofed."

Julie knelt at the cabinet and began to pull things from it. A dish towel. The spare keys. Her book. Ainsley's brush. And finally, her cell phone.

They looked at Faith, who grinned back at them.

"Looks like you have a little thief on your hands." Julie laughed.

Ainsley kissed Faith on the cheek. "Not a thief. Maybe she's going to be a collector of some sort."

The phone in Julie's hand buzzed. She glanced down at the incoming text. "He's almost here." She grinned. "Faith, you little stinker." She tickled the little girl's belly.

Faith giggled and squealed.

Twenty minutes later, Julie and Colt pulled out of the residential section of the park.

Julie wiped her eyes. Saying good-bye had been much harder than she'd expected.

"Mind if we make a little pit stop?" Colt asked.

She shrugged. "Fine by me."

"It includes a shuttle ride."

Julie glanced over at him. "Where to?"

"Maybe it's a surprise." He pulled the car into the parking lot near the Backcountry Information Center. "Come on."

She got out of the car and followed him to the road. "Where are we headed?"

"To the Red Route transfer point." He reached over and grabbed her hand. "Just chill and trust me." He grinned. "Can you do that?"

Julie couldn't keep the laugh from escaping her mouth. "Yes."

They ran toward the bus and made it on just in time. The doors closed behind them.

"Now you can relax," Colt said. "I'll let you know when we're there."

She had a perma grin on her face. She loved to be surprised.

The bus stopped at several locations. Each time, Colt shook his head. "Just wait."

"Hermit's Rest," the automated announcement said.

Colt stood. "Here we are." He grabbed her hand and helped her down the steps.

Hand in hand, they walked past the rock arch that she'd posed underneath when they'd hiked the trail. He led her to the overlook, and they stood in silence.

Julie glanced down at their intertwined hands. "So. . . ," she said.

He dropped her hand and turned her toward him. "I know I told you I was going to ask you on a real date when we get to college." He grinned. "So I'm asking you now. As soon as we're settled into our dorms, I want to take you out to dinner. Maybe a movie."

"Dinner and a movie sounds great."

He chuckled. "I know that's pretty generic. That's why I brought you here today. Because I wanted one part of our date to be really memorable."

She wrinkled her forehead. "What do you mean?"

He leaned down and kissed her gently on the lips. His hand cupped her face. "That's what I mean," he whispered. "Even though dinner and a movie might be generic, I wanted our first kiss to be memorable." He grinned and waved his hand toward the canyon. "It doesn't get more memorable than this."

She agreed. Although the thing that made it memorable had nothing to do with the canyon and everything to do with the guy next to her.

CHAPTER 41

These past weeks, I've really learned a lot about myself and what I'm capable of. I think it all started when you and Julie were down in the canyon. Hiking out of the canyon with you on my back made me proud of myself. But there's a lot more I want to accomplish. Dreams and goals are important things to have in your life.

Ainsley's heart pounded. It had been more than four weeks since she'd last seen Dustin. Had she kept him waiting for too long? She knocked tentatively on the door and waited.

He opened the door, and his whole face lit up when he saw her. He'd gotten a haircut since she'd seen him last. His blond hair was a little shorter and spikier than before. But his eyes were the same old blue. "Hey, you." He gave her a slow grin. "I was beginning to think I may never see you again."

She hung her head. "Sometimes things take a little longer than you expect." She followed him inside the house, full of apprehension.

"Have a seat." Dustin waved her to the couch.

She slowly took a seat, clutching the gift she'd brought him to her chest.

"So, what have you been up to?" he asked once he'd sat down beside her.

She held the book out to him. "You can see for yourself."

He narrowed his eyes. "Faith's Book of Firsts?"

"Just open it." Her heart pounded inside her chest. She knew what she was asking of him was huge. More than most guys could handle.

Dustin turned to the first page. "There's the first photo, but I've already seen that one." He flipped to the next page. "So it isn't blank any longer?"

She shook her head. "Just look."

He traced his fingers over the words as he read them aloud. "Faith's First Ranger Program. She looks happy." He glanced at her. "And so do you."

Ainsley looked at the picture. "I did a ranger walk and talk along the rim. Julie and Faith came to show their support." She smiled at the memory. "Faith kept calling out to me the whole time. Thankfully, the other visitors thought she was cute." She pointed at the picture. "This was afterward. I set my hat on top of her head, and she started laughing. Which is why Julie and I are cracking up in the picture, too. You know how funny her little laugh is."

Dustin gave her a sideways look. "So you're back to doing ranger programs no matter where the assignment might be?"

She nodded. "I sure am. And I haven't had a single panic attack."

"Awesome." He flipped the page and grinned. "Check it out. Faith's First Canyon Sunset."

"We hiked to Hopi Point. We had a picnic and then watched the sunset." She laughed. "Well, I watched the sunset, and she watched the people next to us. They had a dog she befriended." She laughed again.

"You both look beautiful." He turned to the next page. "Faith's First Day at Day Care."

Ainsley pointed at Faith. "Can you believe she loves it? I had a hard time dropping her off, but look at that face. She loves being around other kids."

"Julie came over to tell me good-bye." He glanced at her. "Does that mean Faith's in day care daily?"

She nodded. "I thought Julie needed to spend some time with her parents before she left for college. Plus I knew it was time for me to learn to handle things on my own. That meant taking Faith to day care and getting out and doing things with her. Just hiking out to Hopi with her was a big step for me. But we did it, and we had a great time."

He smiled. "I'm so glad. You really are a wonderful mother. I'm thankful you're finally letting go of some of those things that were holding you back and really embracing the things you love."

"And you're going to love this next page." She reached over and flipped the page for him.

"No way. Faith's First Puppy." He widened his eyes. "I can't believe you got one for her."

"We adopted him from the pound. He stays outside during the day but comes in with us at night. I like having him there as a guard dog. And Faith likes having him there to play with."

"Does he have a name?"

She laughed. "Love. His name is Love."

"As in. . .love the puppy?" He laughed.

"You got it. As soon as Faith got her hands on him, she started saying, 'Love,' so I figured, why not? It'll be a great story for her when she gets older."

He nodded. "They must make quite a pair."

"You should see them together. He seems to live up to his name already, because you can tell how much he loves her. He sleeps right in her doorway, curled up in a little ball."

Dustin stared into her eyes. "Will I ever get to see them together?"

She gave him a half smile. "Turn the page."

He flipped the page. "Faith's First Fishing Trip." He glanced at her. "There's no picture."

She nodded her head at the book. "Keep going."

Dustin turned another page. "Faith's First Train Ride." He narrowed his eyes at her.

"You know. The Grand Canyon Express that runs from here to Williams."

He threw his hands up. "I know. But there's not a picture on that one, either."

She couldn't contain her grin. "It's because they haven't happened yet. I was hoping you might like to help us fill in the blank pages." She was asking him to be part of their lives. Hers and her Faith's. She knew he understood the magnitude of that, especially when she caught the moisture in his blue eyes.

Dustin's face broke into a huge grin. "I'd love to help the two of you make some memories."

"We'd like that, too. Both of us." Watching Faith bond with Dustin over the summer had been amazing. She knew that no matter what, Dustin should be part of Faith's life.

He shut the book and turned toward her. "I can't tell you how happy it makes me. I've been on pins and needles these past few weeks." He shook his head. "To tell you the truth, I was afraid I'd blown things with you."

"There were things I felt I needed to do on my own. Once Julie left, the easy thing for me to do would've been to find someone to lean on. And I know you would've been right there to help out." She smiled. "But I needed to handle things myself for a little while. And figure out how I felt about things."

"You mean how you feel about me?"

She nodded. "That's exactly what I mean."

Dustin's heart pounded. "And?" He steeled himself to hear her say she only wanted to be friends. It would be okay. He would be her friend and Faith's pseudo-uncle. It might not be what he wanted, but he'd do whatever she thought was best.

She reached over and grabbed his hand. "I have a confession. I overheard you talking to Faith the night you rocked her to sleep. It was that night that I realized how much I care about you." She squeezed his hand. "And my feelings are definitely more than just friendly. But there's something I want you to know."

He grinned. This sounded promising. "What's that?"

"I'm honestly ready to move on. I don't want you to think that the only reason I'm spending time with you is because of your ties to Brad." She shook her head. "That isn't it. This is about you and me. Not my memories." She swallowed.

Dustin pulled her to him and kissed her on the forehead. "Thanks for saying that. And I want you to know that I don't expect you to forget about Brad. I'm not going to forget about him. I want Faith to know all about him." He smiled. "He helped me become the man I am today. I owe him a lot."

Ainsley's eyes filled with tears. "It means a lot to hear you say that. That you have a heart big enough for me, Faith, and Brad is amazing."

He tipped her chin up. "In case you haven't realized it, I'm crazy about you."

"It's a good thing. Because I'm pretty crazy about you, too."

Dustin pulled her to him and gently kissed her lips.

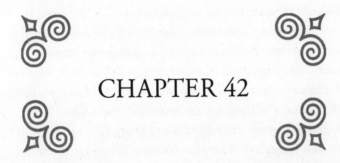

CHAPTER 42

When I look back over the summer, I can't help but see the reasons we were all brought together in that most majestic of spots. Some say calling the canyon grand doesn't do it justice, and I agree. The wounds we carried, along with the fears, hopes, and dreams, bound us together in unexpected ways, and I think we were all healed a bit just by being near one of God's most beautiful masterpieces.

Julie learned a tough lesson about true love and came away stronger, more prepared for the next chapter in her life. She will never forget what transpired in the canyon. Some might say her eighteenth birthday was the day she passed the threshold into adulthood, but I say it happened on a random July day in the midst of a crisis when she left her childhood behind.

Jake was the first one to bring me out of my shell. In some ways, I think meeting him helped me get used to the idea of moving on. But he would've been happy to keep me in my cocoon of isolation forever just to protect me from future hurts. And that's no way to live.

For him, the summer was one of self-realization and

forgiveness. The decision to go back to the police force in Phoenix suited him. His time at the canyon taught him that there's more to life than work, and I'd like to think I helped him come to that realization.

Dustin might be the biggest surprise I've ever had. How could someone I'd known so well—and shared so much with—turn out to be so different than I thought he was? I've always stuck to the belief that people can't change. But in his case, I was wrong. He believed in me when I didn't believe in myself. He pushed me to meet my fears head-on and helped me to see that God would always see me through.

And me. I guess I've changed the most. I'm alive again. Alive. Where there used to be numbness, there is now great feeling. But with that comes fear. And pain. And happiness. And laughter. And such a deep appreciation for this crazy thing called life.

Ainsley wrote the last sentence with a flourish, appreciating the fact that it was also the last page. It was as if God had known exactly how many words she'd need to tell her story and He'd given her the perfect amount of space. She closed the blue journal with a snap and slipped it into a box. The next person to read it would be Faith. At this thought, Ainsley smiled and put the box in the top of her closet.

ᘓᘔ

"Ms. Davis, I must say I'm pleased with your progress." Dr. Sinclair peered at her through his wire-rimmed glasses.

Ainsley smiled. "Me, too. I feel more like myself than I have in such a long time."

"How about your insomnia? Have your sleep patterns

improved?" He drew his brows together.

She shrugged. "I don't know that I'm ever going to be the kind of person who sleeps perfectly every night. But these past few weeks, I have noticed that when I do sleep, it's much more restful." She wasn't sure if it was having a guard dog or getting more exercise or just being more at peace. But for whatever reason, she felt better.

"That's wonderful." He stood. "Our time is up. And I know you don't have any more appointments scheduled, but if you ever feel like you need to come in and talk, feel free to do so." He walked her to the door. "It's been a pleasure working with you."

As Ainsley stepped out into the bright sunshine, her phone rang. She glanced at the screen and answered with a grin. "Hey there."

"Just thought I'd check in to see how you're doing," Kristy said. "I saw that I'd missed a call from you."

"Yeah, I thought I'd better check on the mommy-to-be." She grinned. "Plus, I just wanted to talk."

"How are things at the Grand Canyon?"

Ainsley sat down on a bench and turned her face toward the sun. "I'm actually in Flagstaff today. Faith's spending the weekend with Brad's parents." She planned to do a better job of making sure Faith knew Brad's side of the family.

"So are you just hanging out with your folks?"

"Julie is moving into the dorm tomorrow. So we're having a joint birthday and good luck party for her at Mom and Dad's." She adjusted her sunglasses. "Dustin is driving over from the canyon with Julie's friend Colt."

"So I take it that conversation went well?" Ainsley had filled her friends in on the situation with Dustin, but she hadn't gotten the chance to tell them about their talk.

Ainsley grinned. "It went very well. We're spending a lot of time together. Most of the time, we just hang out with Faith. But

I've left her with Edie a few times, and we've gone out just the two of us. We're taking it slowly, but I've fallen hard for him." She giggled. "And the feeling is shared." She knew she'd never forget the love she'd had for Brad. One look at Faith, and she remembered. But she also knew that the feelings she had for Dustin were growing stronger every day.

"That sounds promising."

"It just feels right, you know?" Ainsley laughed. "Listen to me. I sound like a sixteen-year-old with a crush."

"I think it's wonderful. It's nice to hear you so happy."

Ainsley smiled. "I never expected to be in this place. It just goes to show you that you never know what God might have in store."

EPILOGUE

Nine months later

The roar of the airplane was louder than she remembered.

"You can do this." Dustin grabbed her hands. "Are you excited?"

She took a deep breath. "Excited. Nervous. Crazy." She laughed. "Happy."

He leaned down and kissed her firmly on the mouth.

Their display of affection caused catcalls and whistles from the other passengers in the small plane.

"You're first," the instructor said to Dustin. "We're nearly ready."

Dustin gave Ainsley's hand a squeeze. "Remember, I'll be waiting for you. And so will your whole family." He grinned. "Mrs. Whittaker and Edie are even here to show their support."

She laughed. "I know. Julie's streaming it live online so Vickie and Kristy can watch. I guess me conquering my fears is cause for celebration."

He looked at her with a twinkle in his eye. "I think *you* are cause for celebration. I love you."

"I love you, too." The first time they'd said *I love you*, six months ago, Ainsley had been overwhelmed with emotion. God had blessed her with not one, but two great loves, and she thanked Him for both of them every day.

With one last kiss, Dustin went to stand by the instructor he'd be tandem skydiving with.

"Ainsley? You ready?" Richard, her instructor, grinned. "We're going to go soon after Dustin and Tad."

She nodded. Was she ready? Over the past several months, she'd slowly gotten her life together. Adjusting to being a single mom without the help of her parents or of Julie had been a huge undertaking. But Faith was blossoming in her day care, and she loved playing with the other kids. Ainsley successfully delivered ranger talks at every location on the park. She'd even started hiking again.

So when Dustin had asked her if she was ready to jump out of a plane again, she'd agreed almost immediately. They'd decided to do it on the first anniversary of the day she moved out of her parents' basement.

She watched as Dustin, strapped to Tad, went out the door of the plane. She said a silent prayer for his safety and for her own.

"Okay. We're on deck." Richard gave her a wink. "One more jumper, and then it's our turn. You remember what to do."

They'd gone over and over it. How to fall, what would happen, how to hold her arms and body. Then when Richard gave the command, Ainsley would pull the parachute. "I remember."

"Showtime," Richard said.

She barely had time to think. One minute she was inside the plane, and the next, she felt as if she were floating. It might look fast to an outsider, but in the moment, it felt like she was drifting in space. The silence struck her, just as it had the last time. So quiet it was almost eerie. The air hit her skin, and it seemed as if her face would never be the same.

Richard gave the command for the parachute, and Ainsley pulled.

The chute caught the wind and jerked her into a sitting position. She looked down, watching as the ground got closer. Her whole world waited below. In some ways, this had been the final leap of faith to reclaim her life.

"Remember how to land," Richard said in her ear. "Be careful not to hurt your ankles. Better to land on your behind than that." He laughed.

"Right," she called out. They were, of course, yelling in order to be heard.

He pulled the string on the parachute so they spun around.

She squealed with delight. It felt wonderful to be doing this. And knowing that she'd be reunited with Faith and Dustin once she returned to Earth made it even better.

"I need you to pay close attention to the ground," Richard said. "When I point, I want you to look."

She nodded. She didn't remember this from last time.

"Now," Richard said, pointing.

She would've seen the sign even without him pointing it out. MARRY ME, AINSLEY in huge bold letters. A tiny figure standing next to it. An even tinier figure next to that one.

The sound that left her throat was half laugh, half scream.

The ground got closer and closer, and in seconds, she felt solid earth beneath her. Richard helped untangle her from him, and she began to run.

Dustin met her halfway and swept her up in his arms, twirling her around. Before she could say anything, he set her on her feet and dropped to one knee, a ring box in his hand.

He didn't even get to say any words because she knelt down and covered his mouth with hers. The tears streamed down both of their faces, and she wasn't sure which tears were hers and which were his.

"Yes," she whispered. "Yes."

Suddenly, they were surrounded by all the people they loved. Ainsley glanced down at Faith dancing with excitement amid the laughter and tears and shouts of congratulations.

She scooped Faith into her arms and gave her a kiss.

Dustin reached over and put his arms around both of them. "I love you both," he whispered. "And I'm honored to be part of your lives."

"We love you, too." Ainsley said.

"Look here and smile," Julie called, holding up a camera.

The three of them smiled at the camera.

"I think that can be the first page in a new memory book," Ainsley said. "Our first family picture."

Dustin grinned. "Sounds perfect."

Ainsley took in the scene around her. What a difference a year could make. Not too long ago, she'd thought her journey was over. But these past few months had made her realize it was only just beginning.

She set Faith on the ground and watched Dustin pick her up and swing her around.

Faith collapsed in gales of giggles.

Dustin looked over and caught her eye. "Love you," he mouthed.

She glanced down at the ring on her finger. *Thank You, Lord, for showing me that it's possible to live and love again, even after tragedy.*

ANNALISA DAUGHETY, an Arkansas native, won first place in the Contemporary Romance category at the 2008 ACFW Genesis Awards. After graduating from Freed-Hardeman University, she worked as a park ranger for the National Park Service. She now resides in Memphis, Tennessee. Read more at www.annalisadaughety.com.

Dear Reader,

Thank you for journeying to Grand Canyon National Park with me. I hope you enjoyed a glimpse inside the park, but even more, I hope you found a character you could identify with in some way. I know how valuable your time is, and I am honored you took time out of your schedule to read *Love Is Grand*. If you haven't already, I hope you'll check out the other books in the Walk in the Park series. National parks are such treasures, and using them as settings has been so much fun. I'd love to hear from you! Visit my website at www.annalisadaughety.com or drop me an e-mail at annalisa@annalisadaughety.com. I'm also on Facebook and Twitter and would love to connect with you there.

Blessings,
Annalisa Daughety

Other Books by

ANNALISA DAUGHETY

LOVE IS
A BATTLEFIELD

AND

LOVE IS
MONUMENTAL